SHERLOCK HOLMES
The Spirit Box

ALSO AVAILABLE FROM TITAN BOOKS

Sherlock Holmes: The Will of the Dead
George Mann

Sherlock Holmes: The Stuff of Nightmares
James Lovegrove

Sherlock Holmes: Gods of War
James Lovegrove

Sherlock Holmes: The Breath of God
Guy Adams

Sherlock Homes: The Army of Dr Moreau
Guy Adams

COMING SOON FROM TITAN BOOKS

Sherlock Holmes: The Thinking Engine (August 2015)
James Lovegrove

SHERLOCK HOLMES

The Spirit Box

GEORGE MANN

TITAN BOOKS

Sherlock Holmes: The Spirit Box
Print edition ISBN: 9781781160022
E-book edition ISBN: 9781781160091

Published by Titan Books
A division of Titan Publishing Group Ltd
144 Southwark Street, London SE1 0UP

First edition: August 2014
10 9 8 7 6 5 4 3 2 1

A CIP catalogue record for this title is available from the British Library.

Printed and bound in the USA.

What did you think of this book?
We love to hear from our readers. Please email us at:
readerfeedback@titanemail.com, or write to us at the above address.

To receive advance information, news, competitions, and exclusive offers
online, please sign up for the Titan newsletter on our website.
www.titanbooks.com

For Miranda Jewess and her marvellous red pen

SHERLOCK HOLMES
The Spirit Box

CHAPTER ONE

FROM THE NOTEBOOKS OF JOHN H. WATSON, MD

War had come to London.

It was late in the summer of 1915, and at night we looked to the leaden skies in fear of enemy zeppelins. When they came, they unleashed terrible firestorms across the rooftops of the city – a stark reminder of the conflict that was ravaging the continent.

The newspapers were full of death and destruction, and repair crews toiled to clear the wreckage of burned-out civic buildings and homes. There were those whose charred remains had to be extracted from what was left of their beds.

As a young man, surrounded by the maimed and the dying in the parched killing fields of Afghanistan, I had thanked God that my loved ones back in London would be spared such scenes. It changes a man, to bear witness to such things, to see the savagery with which one human being can end the life of another, or to hold the hand of a wounded comrade as he slips away into oblivion. It hardens one's soul.

For years I thought that I had left such things behind in that hot, troubled land, but during that fateful, war-torn summer I found myself wondering more than once if those nightmares had somehow followed me here, to London, finally catching up with me after all this time.

Nothing brought this home to me more than the death of my nephew, Joseph Watson, the sole child of my late brother and the last of the Watson line. That dear boy was now lying somewhere in a field in France, another forgotten face, another entry in the tally chart of the dead, cut down by the chatter of machine-gun fire as he'd gone over the top. The thought of it haunted me as I rattled uselessly around my small house in Ealing, wishing there was more that I could do.

I was old, and somewhat curmudgeonly, and had refused to evacuate myself to the country. This was not, I fear, the stoic resolve of an old soldier, but more a stubbornness born of an unwillingness to allow the devilish Kaiser Wilhelm to unseat me from my home. I was not above allowing myself a small measure of hypocrisy, however; I had sent my wife to stay with her sister in the Lincolnshire countryside, in the hope of sparing her the worst of the danger. We do what we must for those we love.

Consequently, with little else to fill my time, I'd offered my services to my old regiment, and although they had dutifully expressed their gratitude, I knew that there was little a man of my advancing years might do directly to aid the efforts of our men abroad. They had suggested I might accept an advisory position, but it soon became clear that even my medical expertise had been superseded by advancements of which I'd not had the time or inclination to remain appraised.

I was feeling morose, and I was not alone. With the coming of the German bombs a terrible malaise seemed to have struck London. For the first time since the war had begun, people were losing hope. The war was wearing us all down, slowly and deliberately eroding the spirit of the nation. Thoughts of victory seemed further from people's minds than ever before, and I feared the country was condemning an entire generation of brave young men to a miserable, prolonged death in the muddy trenches of the continent. It seemed endless. I had no doubt that it was necessary – noble, even, to make such a concerted stand for freedom – but nevertheless, endless.

For a week I had been unable to shake the black mood that had settled over me, ever since receiving the telegram containing news of Joseph's death. Mrs. Watson had been in the country for close to a month, and I was deeply in need of companionship. I'd attempted to concentrate on my writing – I was engaged in the early stages of writing a novel – but even this had offered little solace. I'd never been a man to dwell on his misfortunes, but those lonely weeks, along with a growing sense of attrition at the hands of the German bombers, were beginning to take their toll.

It was just at this lowest of ebbs that my fortunes took a sudden, unexpected shift for the better, and I was to find myself once again reacquainted with my old, dear friend, Mr. Sherlock Holmes.

It began, rather inauspiciously, with a rap at the door. I had just settled down to a meagre lunch of tea and buttered crumpets – a far cry from the once magnificent repasts of Mrs. Hudson – when the unexpected caller made their presence apparent. Sighing, I abandoned my plate on the hearth and, stretching to ease my stiff back, made haste to the door.

A young man – hardly more than a boy – was standing on the doorstep, apparently admiring the flowerbeds beneath the bay window. He looked up when he heard the door open, and smiled warmly. He was dressed in a smart black suit, with a starched collar and tie, and was wearing a peaked cap jauntily on his head.

"Dr. Watson?" he said, in a broad cockney accent.

I raised an expectant eyebrow. "You have me at a disadvantage, sir," I replied.

The man laughed. "My name is Carter. I'm here on behalf of Mr. Mycroft Holmes." He paused for a moment to allow the name to sink in. "He requests your immediate assistance with a somewhat… *delicate* matter."

"Mycroft Holmes," I muttered, a little taken aback. It had been some years since I'd had the pleasure. I couldn't begin to imagine what use I might be to a man like Mycroft, but I understood enough about his methods to know that it had to be important if he'd sent a man to fetch me from my home. "Immediate, you say?"

"I fear so, Dr. Watson," said Carter, with a quick glance at his watch. "If you're willing, we have an important appointment to keep."

"Yes, yes," I replied, all thoughts of my abandoned crumpets gone. I admit that I felt the stirrings of an old vitality at the thought of this new, unexpected intrigue, and besides, any opportunity to get out of the house and actually *do* something seemed most appealing. "Just hold on a moment while I fetch my coat."

Carter had parked his motorcar just a few yards from the bottom of the garden path: a sleek, black beast of a vehicle, which gleamed in the watery afternoon sunlight. The automobile was open-topped, but the canopy was raised to ward off the threatened shift in the weather; the sky was bruised and smeared with the grey thumbprints of rain clouds. I turned my collar up, and – with some trepidation – stepped up onto the running board and clambered into the back seat.

I was still adjusting to such mechanical modes of transport, and to be truthful, I had yet to feel entirely secure hurtling along the roads at speed. It was not that I yearned for the simpler days of hansom cabs and horse-drawn carriages – I had never been fearful of progress – rather that I simply couldn't help but wonder what effect such rapid velocities might have upon the human form. Or, perhaps more truthfully, I feared what a sudden impact at such speeds might do to my fragile old bones.

Mycroft's summons had somewhat lifted my spirits, however, and so I banished such considerations and decided to throw myself wholeheartedly into this new endeavour, whatever it might prove to be.

I watched as Carter finished cranking the engine, and – checking his watch again and grimacing as he took note of the time – hopped up into the driver's seat and released the parking brake. We shot away down the road, rocking me back in my seat. I grabbed for the armrest.

I'd meant to ask the young man precisely where we were headed, but I'd missed my chance, all hope of conversation now drowned out by the bass rumbling of the engine. I eased myself back on the leather seat and tried to relax, making the most of the fleeting, stuttering view, and attempting to ignore the unwholesome effluvia of the city.

It was some time before we crossed into the city proper, and as the familiar landmarks shot by, I was struck by a sudden realisation: we were heading in the wrong direction.

I leaned forward in my seat, tapping Carter on the shoulder. He glanced back to see what was wrong. "Is everything quite well, Dr. Watson?" he called, raising his voice in order to be heard.

"Yes, well enough," I replied, "only – where are you taking me? This isn't Whitehall."

"I'm sorry Dr. Watson, but you'll have to speak up. I can't hear you over the noise of the engine."

I sighed. "I said – this isn't *Whitehall*," I repeated.

"No," confirmed Carter, nodding. He returned his attention to his driving. Exasperated, I shook my head. Did the man take me for an old, addled fool?

Presently we turned down Belgrave Street, narrowly avoiding a collision with a horse and carriage coming in the opposite direction. The startled animal reared up, threatening to bolt, and the driver, perched upon his dickey-box, bellowed an outrageous curse and waved his fist in our direction. Laughing, Carter swerved out of the way, sending me sprawling across the back seat.

"Apologies, Dr. Watson!" he called, before parping his horn to warn a gaggle of nearby pedestrians to clear the way, and finally drawing the motorcar to a stop outside the entrance to Victoria Station.

Carter shut off the engine and jumped down from the driver's seat. He opened the passenger door for me. "Here we are, Dr. Watson. And just in the nick of time, too," he added, with genuine relief. He sounded a little breathless.

"I'm confounded if I know what we're doing here," I muttered as I climbed out of the vehicle. "I hope you're not expecting me to take a train. You said we were on our way to see Mycroft Holmes."

Carter gave another infuriating smile.

"Look," I said, trying to keep the accusation from my voice, "I'm not particularly fond of surprises. Are we here to meet Mr. Holmes or not?" I was aware that I was growing a little cantankerous, but I was simply looking to the man to give me a straight answer.

"We are," said Carter. "He'll be arriving in just a moment. We're to meet him from his train. If you'll come this way?"

"Very well," I replied, following him through the main station doors.

Inside, the place was bustling, and I wrinkled my nose at the thick, familiar scents of oil and steam. Engines wheezed at two of the platforms, billowing clouds of smoke, which mingled in the still air, forming fleeting clouds amongst the steel rafters. They dispersed as I watched, rolling away across the underside of the glass roof and out into the pale afternoon beyond. The noise of chatter was close to deafening.

A crowd appeared to be concentrating around platform three, and Carter pointed it out, indicating that we should join it.

A train had just arrived, pulled by a recent model of electric engine, and the throng appeared to be predominantly comprised of people who had come to the station to greet their friends and loved ones.

"What train is this?" I demanded.

"The two o'clock arrival from Brighton," said Carter, with a knowing grin.

"Brighton?" I echoed. "Then…" I trailed off. The very thought of it seemed too much. "Oh, it can't be?"

I searched the platform, trying to discern the faces of the disembarking passengers: two clergymen with overcoats and hats; a portly fellow with a neat moustache; a young man with a harelip; an elderly woman with a scarf around her head; a group of three soldiers, each of them looking dour and forlorn. All of life was here. All except…

I saw him then, emerging from one of the first-class carriages, carrying a small leather case.

It had been some time, but that familiar, aquiline profile was unmistakable – the jutting, inquisitive chin, the hawk-like nose, the thinning black hair swept back from his forehead, now speckled with strands of grey. His face was lined, but he wore his age well. He looked lean and fit, and I found myself wondering if he'd finally given up on those dreadful chemicals he'd insisted on administering to himself for so many years.

He turned and looked in our direction, and I saw his eyes twinkle in recognition. His thin lips curled into a smile.

"Holmes!" I exclaimed, rushing forward to clasp his hand. "Sherlock Holmes!"

"As enthusiastic a welcome as I could ever hope for," said

Holmes. "I see the war is treating you badly, Watson. You've lost five pounds."

"The war is treating us *all* badly, Holmes. And it's four. No more than that."

"Five, I think, Watson, but let us not quibble. It's good to see you."

"It's been too long," I said. "London misses you."

Holmes laughed, that familiar, exuberant, derisive laugh. "Really, Watson. I think it is only Scotland Yard that misses me. The criminals, I am sure, are quite satisfied with the arrangement."

"And how are your bees?" I asked. I had not known what to make of Holmes's declaration, all those many years ago, of his intention to relocate to the Sussex countryside to study the lifecycle of bees. At first I'd wondered if it had all been an elaborate joke, its punchline somehow lost on me, but it had soon become apparent that he was perfectly serious. He'd vacated our old lodgings at Baker Street, packed up his books, files and other ephemera, and moved himself wholesale to the country.

For a while afterwards I expected him to return to London with his tail between his legs, having found life in Sussex too sedentary, too downright *boring*, but it seemed his newfound interest in apiculture was enough to occupy his considerable mind. I'd visited him once in the interim, and found him quietly content amongst his hives.

"Fascinating," replied Holmes. "I'm compiling a second volume of my observations. Human beings could learn a great deal from those magnificent creatures, Watson. Their social structures are defined and organised with admirable logic."

I grinned. "I'm pleased to discover you haven't changed at all, Holmes. All that country air must be doing you the world of good."

"Ever the doctor, Watson," he replied.

I suddenly realised that in my haste I had not yet established the reason for his visit. Surely he would not have journeyed into the heart of a war zone simply to make a social call? Although, I reflected, nothing at all would surprise me about Sherlock Holmes.

I glanced back at Carter, who was politely watching us from the far end of the platform, allowing two old friends a moment of privacy to reacquaint themselves with one another. "The driver – he said it was Mycroft?" I began, the confusion evident in my voice. "I mean, when he came to collect me, he indicated it was Mycroft who organised all of this?"

"Ah, yes. Of course – it's not yet been explained," said Holmes. "Well, no fear, Watson. All will become clear in time."

"Now look here," I said, "I'll not stand for any of your cryptic pronouncements. Not this time."

Holmes put his hand on my shoulder, fixing me with his cool, penetrating gaze. His tone was suddenly serious, direct. "We have a case, Watson, of a most timely and sensitive nature."

"A case!" I exclaimed. "I thought you'd *retired*?"

"As you so eloquently described, Watson, the war is treating us *all* badly." He clapped a hand on my shoulder. "Come. I shall explain further during the journey."

He started off toward Carter, leaving me momentarily alone on the platform.

"You'll be lucky," I muttered, hurrying to catch up. "The damn thing makes an infernal racket."

CHAPTER TWO

"So, are you going to tell me why you're here?"

I was once again ensconced in the back of the automobile, bouncing along the King's Road and feeling decidedly green around the gills. Beside me, Holmes appeared to be faring little better.

"I received a telephone call from my brother yesterday morning, just after breakfast," he said, resting his head against the seat back and closing his eyes. I wondered if he were trying to imagine he were somewhere else, instead of flying along the road at an unconscionable speed inside a metal box. I certainly was. "He outlined for me his desperate concern regarding the situation in London, the effect the Kaiser's bombing raids are having upon the morale of the people, even their support for the war."

"Well, he's not wrong," said I. "I've felt it myself. The thought of Londoners dying in those dreadful blasts, the burr of the zeppelins drifting overhead – it sometimes feels as if the end times are upon us."

"You always have had a penchant for melodrama, Watson," said Holmes, with a chuckle.

"Melodrama!" I returned, with some consternation. "Holmes, the country's at war! The enemy fly uncontested above the streets of the capital, dropping incendiary weapons upon the rooftops of our people. I hardly think it is melodrama of which I speak."

Holmes remained silent, allowing my brief flare of anger to burn itself out. I knew he wasn't chastised by my outburst, but in turn he knew me well enough to at least pretend that he was.

"I see the war has affected you deeply, Watson," he said, after a minute or two.

"I rather suppose it has," I agreed, my moustache bristling with something akin to embarrassment. I decided to steer the conversation back to the subject at hand. "Surely, though, that's not the reason for Mycroft's call? I mean, as celebrated a figure as you are, he cannot expect you to single-handedly boost the morale of the nation."

"Quite," said Holmes, with the hint of a smile. "No, I rather think there are those more suited to such pursuits. Mycroft's request was far more specific, and better tailored to my particular field of expertise."

I nearly suggested "obtuseness", but the irony would have been lost on Holmes. "Go on," I prompted.

"It seems, Watson, that the present atmosphere in London has given rise to a proliferation of suicides. There are three particular cases of which Mycroft has requested I apprise myself: a British Army officer, Captain John Cummins, who strenuously urged surrender before feeding himself to a tiger at London Zoo; a famed suffragette, Mary Temple, who wrote to *The Times* to renounce militant activism the day before throwing herself beneath an Underground train; and Herbert Grange, a Member of Parliament who worked at the War Office and is said to have given a pro-German speech to the House before hurling himself into the Thames."

"Yes, I'm aware of all three incidents," I said. "There's been extensive discussion of them in the press. Does Mycroft believe there to be a connection between these unfortunate deaths?"

"That remains to be seen, Watson, although brother Mycroft rarely deals in absolutes. I suspect there is more to this matter than at first appears," replied Holmes, as cryptic as ever. "What is abundantly clear to me is that three apparent suicides of high-profile individuals are not going to assist Mycroft's efforts to raise the public spirit."

"And so you agreed to come out of retirement to take the case?" I said. "To assist the nation in its hour of need?"

"Indeed. I explained to Mycroft that I would do so on the strict understanding that my old friend, Dr. John Watson, was to meet me from my train and accompany me for the duration of my investigation."

I admit I felt a sudden flush of pride that Holmes should issue such a stipulation on my behalf. "But how did you know that I didn't have a previous engagement?" I asked.

"My dear Watson," said Holmes, with an appraising look. "Has Mrs. Watson not been in the country for some months, ever since the zeppelin raids began in earnest? Has your old regiment not patronised you with talk of advisory positions? Have your efforts to throw yourself into your literary pursuits not ended in dissatisfaction?"

"Why… yes," I replied, deciding not to encourage a lengthy explanation of how he had reached his assertions. It was clear that Holmes had lost none of his acute observational abilities. "You are correct on all counts."

"Then, Watson, are you not ready for an adventure?"

"More than you could ever imagine, Holmes," I said, with feeling.

"Excellent!" he proclaimed, animated now. "And how fitting that it should begin at one of our most familiar haunts, a place to which we have both become greatly accustomed over the many years of our acquaintance."

"Baker Street?" I ventured, my heart warming at the very thought of the place.

"Indeed not, Watson!" he replied, with obvious relish. "We are going to the morgue."

I sank back into my seat, my enthusiasm suddenly dampened. "I can hardly wait," I said.

It felt peculiar to return to a place that had once been so familiar, such a part of my life both professional and personal, and yet which, at the end of my career as chronicler of Holmes's investigations, I had been overjoyed to leave behind me. It smelled the same: the tang of spilled blood, the musk of decay, the chemical stench of carbolic and bleach.

As a medical man and a retired soldier I was far from squeamish around the dead – I had carried out more than my share of dissections over the years, just as I had witnessed the mutilated remains of combatants on the battlefield. Yet something about the proximity of so *much* death left me feeling plaintive, morose. Perhaps it was that I most often had recourse to visit the place in order to play my part in the investigation of a murder, which in and of itself is a depressive business. The ingenious and elaborate methods that people devised in order to harm one another never failed to astound me.

Whatever the case, I could not claim to be cheerful to be back, although I admit to a certain frisson, a sense of feeling revivified at the thought that Holmes and I were once again engaged on a case. This, to my mind, was simply the first hurdle to be crossed.

A man was waiting for us in reception, wrapped in a vast, woollen overcoat, despite the weather. He was tall, broad around the shoulders and even broader about the waist. He wore a big, bushy beard, which had long ago gone to grey, and was standing with his arms folded across his chest, his expression brooding. He looked up when we entered, and his countenance brightened considerably.

"Mr. Holmes. You're most welcome. Most welcome indeed," he said, approaching Holmes with a hesitation akin to reverence. "My name is Inspector Gideon Foulkes." He extended his hand and Holmes took it, shaking it briskly. "I'm sure you won't recall, but we've met before, almost twenty-five years ago, during that business with the 'iron men'. I was, of course, a mere constable in those days."

Holmes smiled graciously. He was clearly not surprised that the Inspector remembered him. I suppose for many of the Scotland Yard men now in positions of seniority, Holmes was something of a mythical figure, a shadowy outsider who men like Lestrade and Bainbridge had brought in for assistance when their own abilities had failed them.

Some of them, like Foulkes himself, had even been serving constables during the height of Holmes's relationship with the force. I recalled the case he mentioned; an investigation into the mysterious "iron men" who had carried out a plague of jewellery thefts in the autumn of 1889, although I fear I had no recollection of meeting him. It pained me to consider those events had occurred over twenty-five years earlier, when we were all much younger men.

"Thank you, Inspector," said Holmes. "You know why we're here, of course?"

"Quite so, Mr. Holmes. I've been fully briefed," replied Foulkes. "I've made all of the necessary arrangements."

"Excellent," said Holmes. "Then if you would be so kind as to lead on…?"

Foulkes paused, as if a little put out by Holmes's lack of niceties or conversation, but then nodded thoughtfully, as if remembering that he should have expected no less. "Of course," he said.

He glanced in my direction and I smiled warmly. His reciprocating smile told me that he appreciated the gesture. "If you'd care to follow me?" he said, beckoning toward a side passage that would lead us from the reception lobby and into the morgue proper.

We trailed after him in silence.

Foulkes led us deep into the warren of white-tiled corridors and chambers. Everything was lit with the harsh brilliance of naked electric bulbs, causing the tiles to gleam like the porcelain scales of some vast, dormant beast.

The passages were abuzz with activity, and we were forced to stand aside whilst two porters shuffled past us bearing a litter. The corpse on the stretcher was blackened and burned, barely more than the skeletal remains of a man, but I found myself unable to avert my gaze, fascinated by the dead man's ghastly visage, the blank stare of his empty eye sockets.

The porters scurried away down the passage with barely a word or a nod of acknowledgement. I could hardly blame them for such minor infractions, however – if ever there was a soul-destroying job, it must be this. As a doctor I had long ago vowed to heal people, to find ways to help them continue to *live*. Consequently, in a place such as this, I always had the sense of arriving too late. By the time a person's corpse had found its way to the morgue, the only job left was to clean up after them.

We resumed our trek through the maze of rooms. After a short while I noticed that the tiled walls had given way to a series of canvas screens, and realised that the place where Foulkes had brought us was, in fact, a much larger chamber that had been segregated to create a series of smaller partitions. There must have been ten or more separate booths, each of them occupied by people both living and dead. The familiar sounds of autopsy and medical examination mingled with the muffled voices of the surgeons muttering to one another.

Foulkes navigated his way around these small pockets of industry and we followed on behind him, until, finally, we came to a side room toward the far end of the chamber, in a quiet corner away from the bustle. Here, the corpses of the three suicides had been laid out for us on adjacent marble slabs.

I had never felt the charnel-house atmosphere of the place more acutely than I did upon sight of those three unfortunates. Their remains were displayed like carcasses in the back room of a butcher's shop: naked, uncovered, their dignity unpreserved.

Holmes immediately shrugged off his coat and, without even a courteous glance over his shoulder, held it out behind him, clearly intending for me to take it. With a sigh I did what was required, accepting it and folding it over my arm.

Unbuttoning his cuffs and pushing his sleeves up to his elbows, Holmes quietly set about the task of examining the bodies.

They were each of them in a rather sorry condition. Foulkes, clearly gritting his teeth, talked us through them in turn. "Captain John Cummins," he said, indicating the remains of the man on the slab nearest to the wall.

"The man who threw himself into the tiger enclosure at London Zoo," I said. That much was evident from the condition of the corpse. Even a cursory glance made it clear that the animals had done for him: his throat had been ripped out by the powerful jaws of a beast, leaving unsightly ribbons of torn, glistening flesh. Hunks had been removed from his upper left arm and his right thigh, and perhaps most disturbing of all, his ribcage was exposed on the left side, where the tigers had worried at the flesh, trying to get at the organs. The body was already beginning to show signs of decay.

"Quite so, Dr. Watson," confirmed Foulkes. "The zoo attendants got to him as soon as possible, but clearly, he was beyond help."

"Hmmm," murmured Holmes noncommittally.

Foulkes eyed Holmes with what appeared to be a measure of nervousness, as if worried that he might have said something wrong. Nevertheless, he forged ahead. "This is the second victim," he said, stepping back and indicating the female remains. "Miss Mary Temple, a former suffragette and proponent of the women's liberation movement. She threw herself in front of an Underground train during the early morning rush."

"Good Lord," I said, beneath my breath. She might have been a pretty young woman once, but it was now almost impossible to tell. The impact of the engine had shattered almost all of her bones and bruised her flesh beyond recognition. Her body looked as if it had been crushed by an immense weight. Additionally, the train's wheels had severed her right leg near the hip, leaving a ragged, sickening wound. The limb had evidently been recovered and – now blackened with soot and dried blood – lay on the slab close to where it should have been, as if willing itself to be reattached. The woman's eyes were closed, but this was no peaceful slumber.

"Finally," went on Foulkes, moving to stand beside Holmes, who appeared to be paying little, if any, attention to what Foulkes was saying, "this Mr. Herbert Grange, MP. Grange worked at the War Office, interviewing German expatriates. As I'm sure you're aware from the many lurid newspaper reports, he took it upon himself to take a swim in the Thames earlier this week."

Grange's body was that of a man in his late thirties, but it was now grossly bloated and discoloured from the time it had spent in the water. The hair was lank; the lips, having taken on a bluish tint, were curled back in a horrible parody of a smile, and the flesh was pale and blubbery.

Holmes paced between them, stooping to examine each in turn, paying close attention to the hands, the lips, and the eyes. He seemed unconcerned by any of the obvious wounds. At one point he looked up and caught my eye, perhaps in an attempt to draw me in and seek my opinion on the bodies, but I was giving little away, and he swiftly returned to his examination.

His eyes were as sharp and observant as ever, as he circled the bodies, drinking in every detail, every clue. To Holmes a corpse was an open book waiting to be read, as telling as a written confession, and perhaps more reliable at that. From an examination of the body Holmes would be able to discern the person's final movements, their emotive state, their financial situation – even the nature of their last meal, all without need of an autopsy. At least, I hoped he wasn't about to press me to roll up my sleeves and set about a detailed medical examination. It had, after all, been many years since I'd had cause to apply myself to such gruesome work.

"No," he announced, dismissing the dead captain with a wave of his hand. He turned his back on the slab. "And no again," he said, regarding the remains of Miss Temple. He crossed to the final body, that of Mr. Herbert Grange, MP. "This one, however. This one is of interest." He leaned closer, so that his nose was almost touching the dead man's face.

"No?" echoed Inspector Foulkes. "In what sense do you mean 'no', Mr. Holmes?" He looked decidedly confused, and I felt a certain measure of empathy for the man.

"I mean, Inspector Foulkes, precisely what I say," replied Holmes. "Those bodies are of no interest to me. It is plainly evident that there is no connection between these deaths. The manner and cause by which they met their respective ends is abundantly clear, if one simply cares to look closely enough at the facts."

I winced at Holmes's cutting tone. "Perhaps, Holmes, you could share with us your observations?" I said.

"Must I explain my reasoning?" said Holmes, with a heavy sigh. "It's devilishly tiresome."

"I fear, Mr. Holmes, that if I am expected to dismiss these deaths as you imply that I should, I must have your reasoning," said Foulkes. "If nothing else, there are the families to think of."

"Very well, very well," said Holmes. He gestured to the mangled corpse of Captain Cummins. "Consider the late captain. Had he not recently returned from the front?"

"Well… yes," confirmed Foulkes.

"Where he undoubtedly witnessed scenes of the most appalling nature. Is that not enough to shake a man's commitment to the cause? To make him consider surrender, if it is perhaps the swiftest path to the cessation of hostilities?" The questions were, of course, rhetorical. We stood in silence for a moment, waiting for Holmes to continue.

He moved deftly between the slabs until he was once again standing over the body in question. "Now consider the evidence. There are exceedingly dark rings around the eyes, a tell-tale sign of insomnia. This man was troubled. He had not slept properly in weeks." He lifted the dead man's right arm, indicating the hand. "See here: the cuticles on both hands have been picked away until they were raw and bleeding – suggestive of a decidedly nervous disposition. And then, of course, there is the simple fact that any man in his right mind would not hurl himself into the tiger enclosure at London Zoo." The timbre of Holmes's voice had grown during the course of his explanation. "No, sir. I put it to you that this is, indeed, a clear case of suicide, brought about by a malaise of the mind, inspired by Captain Cummins' recent exposure to the horrors of the war."

"Shell shock?" I ventured.

"Precisely, Watson," confirmed Holmes. "And thus of little interest. I see no conspiracy in this man's death, other than that which one man conspires to do to another upon the field of battle, and the anguish which necessarily ensues."

Foulkes nodded, slowly and deliberately, considering Holmes's words. "And the woman?" he asked.

"Quite the opposite," said Holmes, "but no more interesting because of it." He moved across to where her body lay on the adjacent slab. "The corpse is clearly in unenviable condition, but it is plain enough to see that Miss Temple had enjoyed a far more ordered and serene existence in her final days. She had taken a position in a munitions factory, preparing shell cases for the men at the front; she lived an admirably structured life; she had recently discharged her political concerns and aired them to the nation in her letter to *The Times*. She was a woman with a bright future ahead of her."

"But her letter to *The Times*, the one of which you speak – it essentially amounts to a suicide note, does it not, a statement to support her cause? She renounced her support for militant activism and then threw herself beneath the wheels of an Underground train," said Foulkes.

"Indeed not, Inspector," said Holmes, a little harshly. "If the woman had intended the missive to be, as you suggest, a suicide note, would she not have thrown herself beneath the train the very day it was published? The delay of a day suggests quite clearly that she was not, as you imply, attempting to draw attention to her cause by underlining her letter through her actions. By the time her death was reported, the edition of the aforementioned newspaper containing her heartfelt message was already serving as a wrapper to a thousand fish suppers."

"Then you suspect murder?" said I.

"I do not," said Holmes. "Tell me, Inspector – which train was Miss Temple awaiting when she took her unfortunate tumble from the platform?"

"The 8.22 from Tottenham Court Road," replied Foulkes.

"Ah," said Holmes. "As I expected. A busy train, Inspector?"

"One of the busiest," replied Foulkes. "Hundreds of people all anxious to begin their working day."

Holmes nodded. "Then it is clear. Miss Temple's death is naught but a tragic accident. Her letter, as you suggest, was not a suicide note, but an attempt to begin anew. In this, Miss Temple was simply following the example of Miss Pankhurst in setting aside all thoughts of violent protest. The very fact that she had taken up a position on the production line of a munitions factory proved her point – for Miss Temple, the battle was won. The war has achieved precisely what the Suffragettes have been striving for: raising the acceptance of women in society."

Holmes stopped for a moment, peering across at us, each in turn. "There is no evidence of suicide in this matter, Inspector Foulkes," he said. "Only an unfortunate accident: a young woman, anxious to do her bit for the war effort and attempting to cross town to work, was jostled on a busy platform, lost her footing, and fell into the path of the 8.22."

"But surely…" began Foulkes, before trailing off. He gaped at Holmes, utterly flabbergasted. He opened his mouth as if to speak again, and then appeared to think better of it.

I, of course, had grown used to Holmes's more theatrical outbursts, and despite our time apart, did not find myself in the least bit surprised by his swift and precise deductions. Nor was I doubtful of their verisimilitude. I knew they could be supported by a score of further deductions that he had not seen fit to mention. "What sets this third death apart, then, Holmes? Why is Herbert Grange so different?"

I could see the appreciation in Holmes's eyes, the twist of his lips. He'd been anticipating this question. "Isn't it obvious, Watson?" he said, animated. "Isn't it clear? Recall, if you will, what

I said of brother Mycroft in the motorcar. He is the instigator of this little adventure, and he rarely acts without cause. I do not doubt for a moment that Mycroft is aware of the true nature of these unfortunate deaths and that – given his position of influence – Mr. Herbert Grange is the man whose demise he truly wishes me to investigate."

"But why, Holmes?" I said, confused. "Why go to all this trouble? Why infer a connection where there is clearly none?"

"Because Mycroft suspects foul play. Because he wishes to keep the wolves from our door, and because he does not want the world at large to know that he has called me here to London with the specific objective of investigating Mr. Grange's unquestionably suspicious death. The suicides are our cover, Watson; a concealment, a falsehood." Holmes tapped his index finger thoughtfully against his chin.

"Then what you are saying, Mr. Holmes, is that you believe Mr. Grange to be a victim of murder?" asked Foulkes.

"That would be somewhat presumptuous, Inspector," replied Holmes, who had returned to studying the corpse of the parliamentarian, his back to us. "I fear the body offers little in the way of motive. Where it is clear to me that Captain Cummins was accountable for his own death, and Miss Temple was not, with Mr. Grange I find myself in need of further data. Only then will I be able to establish the truth."

He turned abruptly to face Foulkes. "You mentioned that Mr. Grange was engaged in somewhat delicate work for the War Office, did you not?"

"Indeed," confirmed Foulkes, "he was interviewing expatriate Germans now living in London."

"Excellent," said Holmes. He clapped his hands together, as if to indicate our audience was over. "Then, Watson, to the War Office it is!" He made for the door, without the slightest word of thanks to Foulkes, nor even a glance back over his shoulder to see if I was following.

I glanced at Foulkes and offered him a reluctant shrug. I was about to speak, when he held his hand up to silence me. "No need, Dr. Watson. Just know that, should you require my assistance, leave word at the Yard." He paused, puffing out his chest. "And know also that you can rely on my absolute discretion."

"Thank you, Inspector," I said, stepping forward and shaking him firmly by the hand.

"Right then, Doctor," said Foulkes. "I think you'd better hotfoot it after him, or mark my words, he'll be halfway to the War Office before he notices you're not with him."

I laughed. "You know, Inspector, I'm not at all sure if that would be a bad thing." I secured my hat on my head, and took off after Holmes.

CHAPTER THREE

To my untrained eye, the War Office building on Horse Guards Avenue was something of a monstrosity. Architecturally speaking, of course, it was a triumph of neo-Baroque design, with high, decorative domes, sculpted window frames and artificial pediments. To my mind, however, it represented everything that war was not: glorious, a thing to be celebrated – cultivated, even. It even *looked* like a ruddy cathedral.

As I stood there on the pavement looking up at the building, I found it strange to consider that inside that vast edifice, the Secretary of State for War, Lord Kitchener himself, was going about his business, planning our efforts abroad. As an old soldier, I was a believer in war being a matter for professionals. I had found Kitchener's rhetoric troubling, his exhorting young men with no experience of military life to join up as if they were volunteering for a football match.

I had not spoken to Holmes regarding his opinions on the war; he did not often interest himself in the murky world of politics. To Holmes a villain was a villain – be they a petty thief, a blackmailer, or a foreign country with which we were at war. I believed the reason he was in London, taking leave of his retirement, was because he felt duty bound to do his bit for the war effort, to use his considerable intellect in assisting his brother to resolve a matter that might yet prove to have far-reaching implications for the morale of the nation.

Of course, there was also the distinct possibility that he was simply bored, and the mystery surrounding the death of Herbert Grange was nothing but a timely diversion. Truthfully, that was the real reason I'd so far avoided enquiring after his thoughts on the matter – in case I found myself frustrated by the self-centred nature of his response.

"So," I asked of Holmes. "How does one gain entry to the War Office? I don't imagine it's as simple as strolling up to the front door and asking to be let in."

"Oh, I don't know, Watson," replied Holmes, with a sly smile. "I often find the direct approach elicits the most satisfactory result. Let us not overcomplicate matters." With that, he tugged determinedly on his lapels, and then, exuding complete confidence, strode right up to the front door and went in.

I hurried behind him, shaking my head in amusement.

Two soldiers stood just inside the doorway – guards, I presumed – and they eyed us without interest as we crossed into the lobby.

I took stock of the lobby. It was everything one would expect from the exterior appearance of the building: opulent and ostentatious. A polished marble floor had been laid in neat, geometric patterns, portraits of former military commanders were hung prominently in a series of alcoves, and a vast chandelier hung on a silver stem from the high, vaulted ceiling. A series of doors opened onto what I assumed to be a network of offices and corridors leading deeper into the building.

There were two Chesterfields against the far wall, and a mahogany reception desk in the centre of the room, behind which stood a middle-aged man in a neat black suit. His hair was thinning, and beneath a clump of wispy grey strands his pate gleamed in the sunlight. His features were craggy and careworn, as if he'd spent a lifetime outdoors, toiling in the sun, and had now, approaching retirement, been co-opted into manning the reception desk of this establishment. It occurred to me that he was probably a retired solider like myself.

"Good morning, gentlemen?" he said, as much a question as a greeting.

"We are here," announced Holmes, "to represent the interests of Mr. Mycroft Holmes. I am Mr. Sherlock Holmes, and this is my associate, Dr. John Watson."

The man raised an eyebrow, and glanced from one of us to the other. "I take it then, gentlemen, that your visit relates to the unfortunate circumstances surrounding the death of Mr. Herbert Grange?" asked the man, who I now took to be a most well-informed butler-cum-receptionist.

"You surmise correctly, sir," replied Holmes, with a gracious bow of his head. "We have some questions regarding his last known movements, and I wish to examine his office if you would grant me leave."

The man gave a curt nod. "Please wait, Mr. Holmes, Dr. Watson, while I consult with my superiors."

He reached for a telephone receiver, which he plucked from its cradle between finger and thumb as if it were something distasteful. He dialled a number, and waited. A moment later, I heard the crackle of a voice on the other end, although I was unable to discern the precise words.

"Mr. Bates," said the receptionist. "I have two gentlemen here, claiming to be representatives of Mr. Mycroft Holmes."

A pause.

"Yes, that's right, Mr. Sherlock Holmes and associate. They wish to speak with someone regarding the death of Mr. Grange." He listened intently, and then placed the receiver back in the cradle.

"Sergeant Bates will be with you momentarily," he said.

"My thanks," said Holmes.

We moved away from the reception desk while we waited, so as not to be overheard.

"Well, Holmes," I said. "That was somewhat easier than I expected. Although I wonder if invoking the name of your brother might perhaps count as cheating."

Holmes allowed a smile to twitch at the edge of his lips.

"A truly great detective makes use of all the many weapons in his arsenal, Watson. My brother is nothing if not comprehensive. Mark my words, his fingerprints are all over this matter. I have no doubt that we are expected."

As if in confirmation of Holmes's theory, the door opened and a man in a black suit appeared. He approached us, his eyes lowered. "You are very welcome, sirs," he said. "My name is Bates. Sergeant John Bates, retired." He puffed out his chest as he delivered this piece of information, clearly proud of his former career. It was heartening to see. "I am to remain in your company for the duration of your visit. I shall escort you to the late Mr. Grange's office. You may ask your questions of his secretary, Miss Millicent Brown."

"Most satisfactory," said Holmes.

The man inclined his head. "If you'd like to come this way," he said, beckoning for us to follow. He showed us through another door, which opened onto a long corridor. The floor was lined with plush red carpet, the walls with yet more portraiture. I couldn't shake the notion that the figures in the paintings, peering down at us with their strict military bearing, were watching our every movement.

"Afghanistan?" I ventured, catching up to the fellow as he led us past innumerable offices, some of them apparently inhabited, others silent and empty.

"Yes, sir," said Bates.

I nodded. "Yes, me too." I smiled. "It seems a long time ago, now."

"Yes, sir," confirmed Bates. He stopped abruptly, and I nearly stumbled as I caught myself from marching on ahead of him. "This is Mr. Grange's office, gentlemen," he said, indicating a glass-panelled door. A small, brass name plaque confirmed his assertion. He knocked twice, and then turned the handle, poking his head around the door.

"Ah, Miss Brown. I hope you'll be amenable to helping two gentlemen who have come to enquire about Mr. Grange's unfortunate…" He trailed off, struggling to find the appropriate words. "Well, they wish to ask you some questions."

"I've already spoken to the police, Sergeant Bates," came the quiet, hesitant reply. "But if you think it might help, then of course. Please, show them in."

Bates pushed the door open for us and waved us through. I found myself leading the way.

The first thing I noticed was the distinct scarcity of any personal effects; the room was sparsely furnished and felt decidedly unlived in. Two oak desks, two chairs, a poster map of Europe and a filing cabinet were the sum of the room's contents, aside from a low bookcase under the small window in a far corner. The bookcase held what appeared to be legal texts and Parliamentary reports, although I was surprised to see a rather ornate amber paperweight on the bottom shelf, into which had been etched a five-pointed star. Given the stack of papers on Grange's desk, I was surprised that he hadn't made better use of such an object. Craning my neck to see through the window, I could see the identical windows of other offices on the opposite side of a triangular courtyard. Clearly Grange had had neither elegant digs nor much of a view.

The second thing that struck me was the sheer winsomeness of Grange's secretary, Miss Millicent Brown. She was a remarkably handsome woman; young, in her mid-twenties, with startling rust-coloured hair tied back from her long, pale neck, and a smattering of delicate freckles across her nose. She was dressed in a smart blouse and grey jacket, and was standing behind her desk on the left of us as we entered the room.

"Thank you for agreeing to see us, Miss Brown," said Holmes. "I understand this must be a troubling time for you. My name is Sherlock Holmes, and this is my associate, Dr. Watson."

The woman's expression changed so dramatically at the sound of our names that I had to resist the urge to laugh. Her eyes widened in shocked recognition, and her bottom lip began to tremble uncontrollably. "M… M… Mr. Sherlock Holmes?" she stammered, before sitting down on the edge of her chair and looking decidedly lost.

Compassion overrode any sense of amusement I had felt. I went to her side. "Are you quite well, Miss Brown?"

"Oh, yes, quite well," she said, although her tone was unconvincing. Her eyes flitted from me to Holmes, and then back again.

I glanced up at Bates. "Could I trouble you to fetch Miss Brown a glass of water?" I asked.

Bates nodded and went immediately from the room. It was clear to see that the woman was out of sorts. This, I supposed, was in no small part down to the recent death of her employer, but it also seemed that the appearance of Holmes and me had thrown her into disarray.

"Forgive me," she said, after a moment. "It's just – to have you both here, it suddenly makes it all so real." She put a hand to her mouth. "He's really dead, isn't he?" She peered up at Holmes, a pleading look in her eyes.

"How long had you and Mr. Grange had an understanding, Miss Brown?" said Holmes, gently.

"An understanding?" I blurted, surprised. I quickly realised my transgression and found my manners, although I felt my cheeks flush with embarrassment. Once again, Holmes had managed to see to the root of the matter within moments.

"But how…?" began Miss Brown.

Holmes smiled, but managed to refrain from showing off too overtly to this clearly distressed woman. "I observe the sterling-silver pen upon your desk, marked with the initials 'M.B.' It is clearly less than a year old – the nib shows wear consistent with only a few months' use, and the casing is not yet tarnished. It was evidently an expensive object, far beyond the means of a secretary. A gift from an admirer, then. This, along with the unusual proximity of your desks, the onyx mourning ring upon the third finger of your right hand and your obvious distress, lead me to infer that you and the late gentleman had a relationship beyond the confines of the War Office."

Miss Brown gave a sad, knowing smile. "You're right. Of course you are. We have been courting for almost a year," she replied. "We were to be married, once the war was over. He didn't want to wait, but I couldn't do it, not with all this going on." She waved her arms as if to encompass not only the room, but also the entire War Office, and everything it represented. "I couldn't bring myself to be that happy when we were sending so many young men to their deaths. When even my friends and neighbours were at risk of dying in their sleep, with the zeppelin raids…" She broke off into a sob, and I passed her my handkerchief. She dabbed ineffectually at her eyes.

"I can't believe he'd do something like this," she said, between stifled gasps. Her body shuddered, wracked with misery. My heart went out to the poor girl. "Why did he do it?"

"That is what we are here to establish, Miss Brown," said Holmes, not unkindly. He paced up and down before Grange's desk, thoughtful for a moment. "So, if I am to understand you correctly, Miss Brown, you believe Mr. Grange's actions on the day of his death to be… shall we say, *uncharacteristic?*"

"If you mean, did I have any notion or indication that he intended to kill himself, Mr. Holmes, I did not. I thought we were happy…"

"Nothing in the weeks or days leading up to Mr. Grange's death gave you any cause to suspect he may have been troubled? No nervousness, unexpected telephone calls, erratic behaviour, cancelled trysts?" Holmes had tented his hands beneath his chin, and continued to pace up and down, a distant look in his eyes.

"No, nothing like that. He was a busy man who often found himself pulled from pillar to post, but there were no signs of anything unusual," replied Miss Brown. "Just his work here, and the typically punishing schedule of meetings in Whitehall. That is, until the last day. The last time we spoke he did not seem himself…"

She broke off as we heard the sound of the door opening, and Bates appeared with the requested glass of water, which he handed to Miss Brown. She took a sip, and placed the glass on her desk beside her typewriter. Bates retreated to stand in the opposite corner of the room, watching us all attentively.

"And, forgive me for being indelicate, Miss Brown, but he shared no concerns with you during your time together as a man and a woman? No personal considerations?" asked Holmes.

Miss Brown glanced anxiously at Bates, and then shook her head. "No. Everything seemed normal."

"I understand there was some recent furore over a speech given in the House that many considered to represent a pro-German attitude?" said Holmes.

Miss Brown shook her head. "Mr. Grange was a kind and

generous man, Mr. Holmes, and he counselled mercy. He believed that people should not be deemed innocent or guilty simply by virtue of the place they were born, but by their actions. His speech was not pro-German, any more than it was anti-British. He argued against the targeting of German civilians, that is all; whilst at the same time condemning the German command for authorising the zeppelin raids on London. He believed soldiers should fight wars, not the poor, the infirm, or women and children."

"He sounds like a wise and honourable man," I said.

"Indeed," said Holmes. "Which makes it all the more intriguing that he should suddenly end his life in such an apparently erratic manner." He stopped pacing for a moment before Miss Brown's desk. "I would appreciate it if you could outline for me, sparing no detail, no matter how small, the full circumstances surrounding your final conversation with Mr. Grange. You said that he did not seem himself?"

Miss Brown took another sip from her glass. "Yes, of course," she said, "although I fear there is little to tell. The discourse was quite prosaic, at least it seemed so at first…" She stopped and took a deep breath. "Oh, I suppose I should really start at the beginning."

"Thank you, Miss Brown," said Holmes. "In your own time."

"It was approaching midday," she said. "The morning had passed much like any other. Mr. Grange had been here, in the office, since around half past eight, and he'd conducted three interviews, for which I'd taken extensive notes."

"And the nature of these interviews?" prompted Holmes.

"Mr. Grange was responsible for interviewing naturalised German citizens, Mr. Holmes – people who were either German natives who now resided in England, or had been born British citizens to German parents."

"To assess their allegiance, I presume?" I interjected.

"Yes, that's right," said Miss Brown. "It was his job to ensure that none of those people were working against us from within our own borders."

"And of the three interviews he conducted that morning," said Holmes, "were any of the interviewees suspected of anything untoward?"

Miss Brown shook her head. "No, not that I can recall. Herbert—" she stumbled over his name, and then corrected herself. "Mr. Grange, encouraged them to go about their business once their interviews had been concluded."

"Have you made typescripts of these interviews, Miss Brown?" asked Holmes.

"Not yet," she replied. "What with everything…" She cleared her throat, and I saw that she was perilously close to breaking down again.

"We understand," I said, patting her shoulder and glancing at Holmes. "It's a trying time." Bates was still standing in the corner, watching. His expression seemed fixed, regimented, as if he didn't wish to be considered to be either corroborating or denying her story.

"Nevertheless, I wish to help in any way that I can," she replied. She took a deep breath, bucking herself up. "As I've already mentioned, it was approaching midday, and just as soon as the last of the interviewees had been escorted from the building, Mr. Grange returned to the office and suggested he take me out for lunch."

"How did he seem to you at that point, Miss Brown?" said Holmes.

"Buoyant," she replied. "Reasonably upbeat. He was talking about a new café that had opened up just around the corner, how he'd spotted it the previous day and decided he'd like to take me there to try it out."

"I assume you jumped at the opportunity?" asked Holmes.

"That's just it," she replied, her brows creasing. "I said that I had a little too much work to do that afternoon, and that I'd be quite happy to remain here in the office with my sandwiches and apple."

"He was somewhat deflated by this news?" I suggested.

She shook her head. "No. Well, perhaps. That's when things became a little odd." She got up from her chair, and I stood aside to let her pass. "He went to the window and noted that it looked like rain anyway, and that perhaps it was best that we go another day." She touched her hand to her hair in an innately feminine movement. "Herbert knew how I don't like to be caught out in inclement weather. I was about to agree when he seemed to be overcome by a sudden – well, illness, I suppose. He put a hand to his head, like this," she held her fingers to her right temple, "and staggered across here." She paced across the room, retracing his steps. "He mumbled something along the lines of 'My God, they're here. They're in here.' He looked horrified. Panicked, even."

"How did you respond to this sudden alteration in his behaviour?" said Holmes.

"I rushed to his side, of course, to check that he was alright. He shrugged me off. He didn't appear to be in any pain, but he was clearly distraught." I noticed Miss Brown was trembling as she recounted the harrowing events. "I asked him what he meant, who 'they' were, but he was inconsolable. He simply looked at me, grabbed me by the top of my arms, and said: 'I won't be responsible for the loss of the spirit box.' That was it. He didn't look back, or say goodbye. Didn't even stop to collect his coat. He simply stormed from the room in a great hurry, and that was the last I saw of him."

"Good Lord," I said, unable to contain my astonishment at such a bizarre and unexpected tale.

Holmes appeared animated, still pacing, and I could see from the look in his eyes that he was fascinated by this new and unforeseen development. "The 'spirit box,'" he said. "Do you have any notion of what he meant by that?"

"I fear not," replied Miss Brown, returning to her seat. "I've never heard of it before. Do you know what it is?"

Holmes sighed. "I do not," he said, "although it may yet prove to be of great consequence to the case. Permit me another question, Miss Brown. When Mr. Grange exclaimed 'they're here', who do *you* believe he was referring to?"

"Well, the Germans, of course. Who else?"

"Who indeed," replied Holmes, cryptically. He was standing before Grange's desk, looking down upon scattered reams of paper, his back to us. "And you believe he meant that they were here, in the War Office?"

"It's so difficult to tell, Mr. Holmes," replied Miss Brown. "He… he wasn't himself. Some change had come over him, and at the time I was more concerned with his health than what he was actually saying." She sighed. "I've gone over it a thousand times since, and I can only suppose that's what he meant by it, yes." I watched as a tiny tear formed in the corner of her eye, and then rolled down her cheek. She caught it with the back of her hand. Another followed a moment later. "I can't help thinking…" Her voice cracked. "I can't help thinking that if I'd only agreed to go to lunch, none of this would have happened." The tears came in a sudden flood, and she put her hands to her face, turning away.

"I think we've asked enough questions today, Holmes," I said levelly.

He gave a curt nod of acknowledgement. "There is just one other thing, Miss Brown, if you'll forgive me."

She choked back her sobs and, with as much dignity as one can muster in such situations, dabbed at her eyes with my handkerchief and straightened herself up. She turned to Holmes. "Yes, of course. What is it?"

"The interviews that Mr. Grange has been conducting. How

many should you say you'd transcribed?"

"Why, all of them, save the final three," she replied. "Around forty or fifty, I should think. They're over there, in that filing cabinet."

"Excellent," said Holmes. He glanced at Bates, "Sergeant Bates, I shall need your permission to remove these transcripts, but I feel it necessary in the pursuit of this matter that I investigate all possible avenues. I'm sure you'll understand."

"Of course," replied Bates. "There'll be some paperwork to see to, but my instructions were to provide you with full and unencumbered access to Mr. Grange's files."

"Most satisfactory," replied Holmes. He approached the filing cabinet, pulled out the top drawer and began removing the files, heaping them untidily onto Grange's desk. "Miss Brown," he said as he worked, "I trust it is not too much of an inconvenience to request your timely assistance in transcribing those final three conversations? I believe their contents may be fundamental in helping to understand this most singular matter."

"Of course," she replied. "I will set to work immediately, and have them sent to you tomorrow."

"Very good," said Holmes. He had finished extracting the contents of the filing cabinet and now had a heap of manila folders about a foot high, balanced precariously on the late man's desk. He gathered them up into his arms. "Dr. Watson will provide you with the address."

With a sigh, I searched in my pocket for one of my address cards and placed it upon Miss Brown's desk. She glanced at it, and then stood, as Holmes crossed the room with the folders, heading for the door. "Mr. Holmes?" she said urgently, as if panicked that she might miss her chance. "Do you believe that Herbert was under some form of influence when he did what he did? I'm not sure if I could bear it if you thought otherwise…"

"I believe there is a distinct possibility that he was, Miss

Brown," replied Holmes, with a sad smile. "However, I do not care to speculate until I am in receipt of all of the facts." He hesitated in the doorway, where Bates was holding the door open for him. "Come along, Watson. There's work to be done."

"My thanks to you, Miss Brown," I said to the sad, pretty woman, who was still standing behind her desk. "I will endeavour to inform you just as soon as there is any news to share."

"Thank you, Dr. Watson," she said. She was holding herself together with remarkable dignity, although I knew that the moment the door was closed, she would once again lose herself in floods of tears. I decided to leave her my handkerchief. It was the very least I could do.

Holmes had gone ahead and was waiting for me in the lobby while Bates – presumably – saw to the paperwork for the files Holmes wished to remove.

"A devilish business this, Holmes," I said wearily, as I came to stand beside him before one of the alcoves. He was staring up at the portrait of a mustachioed man in full military dress.

"Indeed, Watson," he murmured in reply. "Indeed." He touched his index finger to his lips. "There is much still to learn regarding Grange's interests, his habits, what sort of man he was. I cannot help but feel the answer to this puzzle lies outside this office, amongst matters more personal or private."

"You're referring to this 'spirit box', are you not?" I said.

"Quite so, Watson," he replied. "Intriguing, is it not? So intriguing in fact, that I will ask for your forbearance for just a short while longer. There is one further stop I wish to make before we retire for the evening – the home of Mr. Herbert Grange."

I nodded my acquiescence. "Very well," I said. "I'll leave you here to await the return of Bates with your files, and in the meantime I shall prepare Carter for the worst."

Holmes laughed. "Watson?" he said.

"Yes, Holmes?"

"It is good, is it not, to be once again concerned with a new mystery?"

I grinned. "Yes, Holmes," I said. "It most certainly is."

CHAPTER FOUR

Herbert Grange's house was a relatively modest property for a man of his standing; a mid-terraced home just of Theobald's Road. The small front garden was not yet mature, but a row of glorious red roses spilled over the dwarf wall, poking out through gaps in the cast-iron railings.

There were no lights on in the front room, although the curtains had been closed in the bay window. It simply looked as if nobody had arrived home from work that day; as if the house was still waiting for Grange to return. The thought made me shudder, recalling images of his bloated, distended body. If it hadn't been for the soft yellow glow leaching out through the glass panel above the front door, offering evidence of recent occupation, the place would have seemed entirely unwelcoming. Clearly, however, Inspector Foulkes had arrived before us.

Holmes had telephoned ahead to Scotland Yard, requesting that Foulkes meet us at Grange's house, and judging by the light in the hall and the automobile parked in front of the building, he'd already arrived.

My stomach was grumbling, and I hoped what remained of the evening's endeavours would not take long. I was sure that both Holmes and I would benefit from a hot meal at my club.

Despite this distinct lack of sustenance, I could not avoid the fact that I'd enjoyed myself more that day than I had in quite some years. It felt good to be working with Holmes again, not only because I had missed my friend dearly during the months since our last adventure, but because I felt that, finally, I was able to do some good. The war had left me feeling helpless and old, but Holmes's arrival and insistence on my help had reminded me what it was to be useful. To be a man who made a difference.

I glanced across at him, only to discover he was already climbing out of the motorcar, despite the fact we had not yet come to a complete stop. I mobilised myself quickly in order to keep up.

"You should come inside with us, Carter," I said to our driver, as I opened the door and climbed down into the road. "You'll catch your death out here." The sun had long since set, and the bright, clear skies of earlier had given way to a chill and starry evening.

"Oh, don't worry about me, Dr. Watson. I'm quite happy to wait for you out here. I've a good book and a warm coat. You go about your business, and I'll be right here waiting for you when you're ready."

"If you're sure?" I said, offering him a final chance to change his mind.

"Perfectly sure, Dr. Watson," he replied.

I took him at his word, hurrying round the vehicle to catch up with Holmes. "Decent chap, that Carter," I said.

"Quite," replied Holmes. "Shame about his heart."

"His heart?" I queried. "What the devil do you mean, Holmes?"

Holmes issued a disapproving tut. "Watson, I should have thought to a medical man it was obvious. Our driver suffers from a chronic weakness of the heart. Consider the facts: pale skin, breathlessness…"

"The very fact he's here, in London, rather than at the front…" I cursed myself for my poor observation. "I should have seen it. Poor boy."

Holmes said nothing, but took the steps up to the house and rapped loudly on the door with the brass knocker. It was cast in the shape of a rather undignified, impish face, its mouth fixed open in a screaming grimace.

Footsteps followed, and a moment later the door yawned open and Inspector Foulkes stood in the light, his considerable figure cast in stark silhouette.

"Evening, gentlemen," he said. His voice sounded muffled, and it took a moment before I was able to discern that he was speaking around the mouthpiece of a pipe, which he'd clenched between his teeth. "This is something of an unconventional hour to be making house calls."

I offered him an apologetic shrug from behind Holmes.

"Well come in, come in." He stood to one side and ushered us both over the threshold.

"I understand, Inspector, that Herbert Grange lived alone," said Holmes.

"That's correct, Mr. Holmes. He was a bachelor," replied Foulkes.

"No lodgers, tenants, housekeeper?"

"The housekeeper comes in on Monday, Wednesday and Friday to take care of the washing and cleaning. I gather Mr. Grange had no love of home cooking and preferred to eat out." Foulkes shook his head, as if finding it difficult to comprehend such a notion. Holmes had already pushed on past him and was at the other end of the hallway, taking stock of his surroundings. "There were no lodgers or other inhabitants," added Foulkes.

"Very good," said Holmes. "Now, if you'll give me leave?"

"Be my guest," said Foulkes, with a gregarious shrug. "Take as long as you need." At this, I felt my stomach grumble once again. "We've disturbed nothing. The house is as it was the day Grange died."

"Excellent," said Holmes. He passed along the hallway and disappeared down the short flight of steps to the kitchen.

Foulkes glanced at me, realised that I was not about to follow Holmes, and gestured for me to join him in the sitting room instead while we waited.

The room, and from what I could gather the rest of the house, was well appointed. Grange had obviously lived comfortably, and lived well. The house had the well-worn feel of a place that had been *inhabited*. Trinkets clustered on the mantelpiece, and on top of the sideboard stood framed photographs of people I took to be close friends and family.

Papers were spread out on a small table beside a high-backed chair in the bay window. A cut-glass decanter and a half-finished tumbler of whisky had been placed on top of them.

The curtains were drawn, but I had the distinct impression that the room was indeed very much how Grange had left it, as if he had simply got up from where he'd been sitting and left for the day, with every intention of returning later.

"So, Dr. Watson," said Foulkes, "did you manage to turn up anything useful at the War Office?"

I shrugged. "With Holmes, even the most trifling detail might be the key to unlocking a mystery, but I fear his method is not to reveal anything until much later in the game."

Foulkes nodded. "Keeps his cards close to his chest, does he? Can't say I blame him. Although I admit, Doctor, this whole business has me somewhat baffled. I mean – a suicide is a suicide, is it not? No matter the victim or how much it pains us to acknowledge the rather unseemly deed. I cannot see that there is much of a mystery to unravel."

"I rather fear that if the matter has piqued Holmes's interest – and, indeed, that of his brother – then there will be layers to this case that have yet to become apparent," I replied.

We lapsed into silence for a moment, both standing by the fireplace, contemplating the implications of what I'd said. After a while I noticed that my back was beginning to ache, and cursed myself for not taking more care. I wasn't getting any younger, and I'd pushed myself harder that day than I had in months, if not years. That was the thing about spending time with Holmes, I realised – being caught up in a new case, dashing about like we had when we were younger – it felt a little like old times. There was a joy in that, of course, but nevertheless, I had to remind myself that I no longer had the stamina I once did.

"Do you mind if I sit?" I said. "It's been something of a trying day."

"Not at all," replied Foulkes. "Help yourself."

I chose the armchair by the window and slumped into it gratefully. Foulkes, in the meantime, had drifted over to the sideboard, where he was taking in the unsmiling faces in the photographs. I cast around, looking for anything of interest.

The papers on the small table caught my eye and I reached for them, sliding a handful out from beneath the decanter, careful not to spill the remains of Grange's drink in the process. I transferred them to my knee. They were, it seemed, a series of bizarre colour photographs.

Clearly the subject was Grange himself, sitting in a repeated pose across six photographs: a head-and-shoulders shot. His expression was decidedly serious, perhaps even vacant, as he stared, unseeing, into the lens of the camera. The photographs had clearly been taken in sequence; although his pose had not altered, there were minute alterations in the curve of his lips, the direction of his eyes. Most unusual, however, was what could be seen above Grange's head.

In every print there were strange shapes and cloudy patterns, like some sort of gaseous aura surrounding the man. The pattern changed from photograph to photograph, but it was clearly present in all of them. I peered more closely. Within these patterns were striations, segregated bands like the pattern of a rainbow, and just as colourful. They were unlike anything I had ever seen. How the photographer had managed to achieve such colour and vibrancy in his prints, I could not say.

"What do you make of these?" I said to Foulkes, holding them aloft.

He turned, saw what I was looking at and crossed the room to stand over me, looking down on the photographs. "Yes. Damned unusual, aren't they?" he said. "Some sort of double exposure, I presume. A sequence of portraits that have gone wrong."

I shook my head. "I don't think so, no. Look at Grange himself. His image is sharp and clearly in focus. If the photographs were double exposed, it would be evident here, as well. And besides, look at his countenance, his posture. He's not posing for a studio portrait. It's as if he's not really there. He looks – well, *haunted*, I suppose. He doesn't look engaged. No, this is something else."

"Then what?" said Foulkes. "I suppose it could be some sort of gas or vapour, swirling around above and behind him. But what about those colours? How did the photographer achieve that?"

"Good point," I said, intrigued. I simply couldn't fathom the look on the man's face. Had he been planning his own death, even here, in these strangely crafted shots? Did he know what was coming?

I looked up at the sound of footsteps in the hall outside. "Let's see what Holmes makes of them," I said, getting to my feet.

As expected, Holmes appeared in the doorway a moment later. He looked pleased with himself.

"Well?" said Foulkes.

"This," said Holmes "is in no way the home of a man who planned to commit suicide. If his death was premeditated, it was not by Grange himself. I have studied the habits of many diverse victims in my time, Inspector, and a man who does not intend to return home from work does not leave the remnants of his breakfast on the kitchen table, his bed unmade and entries in his diary for events still to be fulfilled."

"Yes, I had that sense too," I said. "The place feels as if he simply got up and went to work in the usual sort of hurry; that he intended to return home later to see to it all."

"Precisely, Watson," agreed Holmes. "It is the tendency of suicides, in my experience, to put their homes in order before committing the fateful deed. It brings a note of finality to proceedings, helps them to prepare." He paced back and forth as he spoke, his eyes flicking from the mantelpiece, to the sideboard, to the ticking clock. "It is my belief that Grange fully intended to return home from work on the evening upon which he died."

"Then you *do* suspect foul play," said Foulkes.

"It is the only logical conclusion," said Holmes.

"Murder, then?" I suggested.

Holmes shook his head. "Perhaps by proxy," he replied. "I do not for a moment believe that anyone but Grange himself had a hand in arranging his plunge into the Thames, but as to whether he was in his right mind, and whether another had placed an undue and unwelcome influence upon him – well, that reminds to be seen."

"Though you suspect that to be the case?" said Foulkes.

"I suspect nothing," said Holmes, a little sharply. "I deal only in facts. To draw any conclusions at this juncture would be tantamount to guesswork. I had assumed that Chief Inspector Bainbridge might have impressed such cardinal principles upon his men before he retired."

Foulkes flushed a bright shade of cerise.

I coughed, drawing attention away from the rather embarrassing conversation.

Holmes peered at me inquisitively. "Do I take it, Watson, that you have found something worthy of consideration?"

I glanced down at the photographs in my hand. "Well... I... oh, goodness knows," I said. "See what you make of these, Holmes."

I crossed the room and handed him the bundle of prints. He leafed through them with interest.

"Well?" I prompted, after a short while. Holmes glanced up at Foulkes. "Inspector, have you any indication that Mr. Grange might have shown a particular interest in matters of the spiritual or the occult?"

Foulkes looked perplexed. "No, not at all," he said. "I've heard or seen nothing to support that claim."

Holmes gave a brief nod of acknowledgement. "Indeed, quite the same can be said of his home. I see no evidence here – these photographs aside – of a particular fascination with such *trivia*." This last word was accompanied by a derisory snort, indicative of perhaps Holmes's most unsavoury trait: his lack of empathy and his distinct inability to engage in the idea that others might find comfort in notions or beliefs that he himself had previously disregarded.

"Yet, here are the photographs," I said, a little haughtily. "And clearly you take them to be examples of the sort of spiritualist material that we have often seen purported to present evidence of the supernatural realm." I was referring, of course, to the many cases Holmes had dismissed over the years when, upon allowing a visitor to seek consultation in our Baker Street sitting-room, they had gone on to produce folders full of similar works, asking for Holmes's assistance in contacting a late family member, or laying an errant spirit to rest. He had never had time for such nonsense, and while I consider myself a typically open-minded chap, as a man of science I had been forced to agree with him.

Nevertheless, the manner of his rejection had always left something to be desired, particularly when handling the rather sensitive needs of a person who had recently been bereaved.

"Poppycock," said Holmes, as if to underline my thoughts. "Hokum."

"Nevertheless, I *am* right," I pressed.

Holmes sighed theatrically. "Quite so, Watson. Quite so. These photographs do, indeed, appear to have some connection with that murky world of showmanship, extortion and irrational credulity."

"An indicator, perhaps, of his state of mind, close to the time of his death?" I suggested.

Holmes shrugged. "All evidence points to the contrary, Watson, as I have already outlined. No, there is something more going on here."

"Have you ever seen anything like it?" asked Foulkes. "This halo effect around the subject's head. The colours…"

"They are quite singular," agreed Holmes. "The ingenuity behind their creation is remarkable."

"I was just saying to Fou—" I started, breaking off suddenly at the deafening *crump* of a detonation from somewhere nearby. The house trembled around us, the windows rattling in their frames.

"Good Lord!" bellowed Foulkes. "What the devil…?"

The echo of the explosion was still ringing loudly in my ears. It had been very close, no more than a few streets away. I looked at Holmes. "Zeppelins," I said.

Holmes went to the door, as if to head out into the street.

"Wait!" I called, sternly, and to my surprise he stopped, his hand upon the doorknob. "Stay inside," I added. "There'll be more bombs to come." He backed away, crossing the room to stand beside me.

As if to ratify my point, the sound of another nearby explosion caused us all to flinch. This time it was close enough to make my teeth feel as if they were rattling inside my skull.

"They're damn close," I said. "And coming this way." I crossed to the window and parted the curtains, peering out into the night sky. Sure enough, the silvery lozenge of a German zeppelin drifted lazily across the sky, under-lit by the wavering pillars of searchlight beams. From somewhere close by the dull thud of anti-aircraft fire started up, like the roar of distant thunder. The zeppelin seemed unconcerned by this noisy banter, however, continuing on its slow pass over the city.

Oily smoke over the rooftops marked the trail it had left, from tumbling incendiary devices, and worse, explosives like the two that had just been deployed.

"I'd suggest you step away from the window, Dr. Watson," said Foulkes. "If another of those ruddy bombs goes off, you could find yourself on the receiving end of the blast."

"Yes," I said, allowing the curtain to drop and backing away. "Of course, you're right." I looked to Holmes. "I think we'd better lie low until it's passed over. We'll be in more danger if we try to make a run for it. Shall we see if we can rustle up some tea?"

Holmes looked distracted. "What? Yes, of course," he said, although I knew that he hadn't really heard me. He'd been thinking about the bombs, about the people trapped in the burning buildings, the imminent danger. I'd never seen him quite like this before – the look of sheer impotence on his face. He clearly wanted to *do* something, but there was nothing he *could* do.

We'd faced danger together countless times before, of course, but this time the enemy was not simply a criminal out for revenge, or a murderer attempting to flee. There was no master plan at work here, no trail of clues to uncover. This was not an enemy that Holmes could understand and outwit, but rather an implacable, faceless foe, and the realisation of that, I believe, was quite startling to him.

In all the years he'd been hiding away in Sussex with his bees the world had changed, and there, in Grange's house that night, his disassociation with the modern age was brought to the fore in sharp relief. Where Foulkes and I had remained in London, and had consequently witnessed the horrors of the war first hand, Holmes had only read the reports in the newspapers, or heard them recited on the wireless. Witnessing them directly had momentarily stopped him in his tracks.

"I'll do it," I said, deciding to give him a moment. I started toward the door, but as I did so there was a momentary stillness. Then a bomb exploded in the street outside.

The percussive *boom* of the blast was like a terrifying thunderclap, and the force of it bowled me forward, sending me sprawling across the sitting-room floor. I landed face down on the burgundy rug, jarring my elbow and knocking the wind from my lungs. It felt as if I'd been shoved between the shoulder blades.

I rolled onto my side, trying to catch my breath. My hands were smarting, and my ears were ringing so that I couldn't hear anything but the sound of my own heartbeat, thumping ten to the dozen.

I propped myself up, gasping, trying to get a measure of what had occurred. Holmes was on the floor beside me, stirring and in the process of picking himself up. He had a small cut on his left cheek, but otherwise seemed unharmed.

Foulkes was on the other side of the room, close to the sideboard, and had already regained his footing. He was dusting shards of broken glass from his trousers.

The bay windows had shattered in the explosion, and a spear of broken glass – a jagged shard about as long as my arm – had skewered the chair I'd been sitting in just a few minutes earlier. I swallowed. If I hadn't moved, or if Foulkes hadn't urged me to step away from the window, it would have been buried in my chest now.

Fragments of glass were scattered all across the floor, and the edges of the curtains were on fire. I scrambled to my feet, skidding on broken shards, and rushed over to the window. "Help me!" I called to the others, grabbing the nearest smouldering curtain and tugging it down from the pole. The pole itself came away from the wall with my frantic wrenching, and I hastily bundled it all up together, tossing it out through the now empty window frame into the front garden. I realised Foulkes had joined me and was following suit.

Within a moment or two, the fire was safely confined to the garden.

I sighed with something akin to relief. My hearing was starting to return in stuttering episodes, increasing in frequency, and I was thankful that we were all still alive and mercifully uninjured.

Through the blasted frame, I took in the scene of utter devastation in the street outside. Many of the houses hadn't been as lucky as Grange's – the roofs and frontages had been severely damaged and small fires licked hungrily at exposed beams. Desperate people were spilling out into the street, laden down with their children and armfuls of their prized possessions. A portion of the road itself had largely disappeared; in its place was a crater the size of an omnibus, the tarmac cracked and splintered around the lip. Thick smoke hung in the air.

The ringing bells of ambulances were converging on our location, mingling with the sorrowful cries of children and the dispossessed.

I looked up, searching for the perpetrator. Searchlights still pierced the sky, but the zeppelin was now receding into the distance, its havoc wreaked, at least on this small area of the city. I had no doubt that there would be more to come before the night was out.

I would be glad to get home, although I guessed that Carter might have to abandon his vehicle for the night and join us on foot, at least until we could pick up a hansom.

And that's when it dawned on me. *Carter.* He'd been outside in the motorcar during the blast.

Panicked, I shoved Holmes out of the way – he had come to

stand beside me at the window – and rushed to the door. I hurtled along the hallway, flung open the front door and charged down the garden path toward the waiting automobile.

The sight that greeted me was one that I would never forget.

The blast had hit the vehicle with such force that it had tipped it over so that it lay on its side, half up on the pavement. The driver's door was buckled, so that it had pinned Carter in, trapping his legs beneath the steering wheel. The roaring heat of the explosion had scorched the vehicle so comprehensively that the paint had bubbled from the metal panels. The seats were still smouldering where the leather and stuffing had burned. And Carter, that poor, poor boy, had been torched alive.

The flesh of his face was now a charred and blackened mess, but I could see the fixed expression of horror, the scream of anguish frozen forever in the set of his jaw. I couldn't help but recall what I had said to him when I'd left him out here by himself, less than an hour earlier: "you'll catch your death". It was an old expression, but it had proved horrifyingly prophetic.

I sank to my knees, tears welling in my eyes. I felt responsible for the lad, as if I'd somehow let him down. I should have pressed him harder to come inside, *demanded* that he did as I said. But it was too late, now. There was nothing to be done. Carter had become another victim of the war.

I realised Foulkes and Holmes were standing behind me, and felt Holmes's hand on my shoulder. He helped me up, and the look on his face was one of heartfelt sorrow. "That poor boy," he said.

Around us, the ambulances and fire engines had started to arrive on the scene, and the firemen were beginning to round everybody up.

"You should go," said Foulkes. "Get home before you become embroiled in all of this."

"We can't!" I said. "I'm a doctor. I could help."

Foulkes shook his head. "You're in no fit state to help, Dr.

Watson, and besides, the ambulances are here. There are plenty of doctors and nurses on hand. If anything, you should consider getting *yourself* looked over."

"I am quite well," I said, although in truth, I was wincing with every intake of breath.

"The Inspector is right, Watson," said Holmes. "We can be of little use here. We should take our leave and repair to Ealing, where we can recuperate without distraction. We are neither of us as young as we used to be."

I glowered at Holmes, but in truth I knew he spoke sense. I noticed he still had the photographs of Grange, tucked under his left arm. "We still have a case to solve, and I am resolved now, more than ever, to see it through," he said. "That boy gave his life in pursuit of Mycroft's cause. I shall see the matter resolved."

"What of Carter?" I said. "We can't just leave him here. Who's going to speak to his mother?"

"I will remain here and see to the necessary arrangements, Dr. Watson," said Foulkes. "Rest assured, I won't leave until the boy has been extracted from the wreckage and taken to the morgue. I will see to it that the family is informed."

"Very well," I said, with a heavy sigh. I could see there was no point arguing, and in truth, my every instinct screamed at me to get as far away from the place as possible.

"Thank you, Inspector," said Holmes. "We shall be in touch."

"See that you are, Mr. Holmes," said Foulkes.

"You're a good man, Inspector Foulkes," I said. "Bainbridge would be proud."

"Thank you, Dr. Watson. Now go, before that lot rope you in to start answering questions."

I nodded, and with one last look at the terrible, charred remains of our driver, I turned and walked away, leaving Holmes behind me to catch up.

CHAPTER FIVE

I came downstairs the next morning to find Holmes sitting in my favourite armchair, poring over the documents we had taken from the War Office the previous day. They were scattered all about him on the floor, many of them covered in pencil marks and scrawled notes. The fire was burning in the grate, despite the clement weather outside. Three teacups were abandoned on the hearth, beside the remains of my crumpets from the previous day. I grimaced at the sight of them.

Holmes glanced up momentarily as I came into the room. "Morning, Watson," he pronounced. He returned to his reading without waiting for my acknowledgement.

"Haven't you slept, Holmes?" I asked.

"A little," he replied.

"Really, Holmes. At our age…"

I saw him grind his teeth, measuring his response. "Old habits die hard, Watson. Particularly when there's a case to be solved. You know my methods."

"Mmmm," I murmured disapprovingly in reply. In truth, I

had not slept well myself. Images of the burnt-out motorcar and the remains of that poor young man had haunted me every time I closed my eyes. I was plagued by the look of sheer, unadulterated terror on his face.

I felt as if I should have done something. I should have considered him, alone out there in the street, instead of cowering inside the building, thinking only of myself. Perhaps if Holmes and I had got to him earlier... He couldn't have been more than – what – twenty years old? It was no age to die. Yet, I reflected, his story was no different to the thousands whose lives were being forfeited in the trenches every day. Just like my nephew, Joseph. The war itself was the real culprit here. We had invited death into our lives, and now it was wreaking chaos.

The journey home from Grange's house had proved increasingly harrowing, following the trail of destruction left behind by the Kaiser's zeppelins, not to mention the ever-present threat of more incendiary devices tumbling from the skies above. It was a simple matter to map the route of the bombers across the city, following the guttering fires, the crumbling buildings, and the screams. Black smoke had formed a pall across the rooftops, and the stench of death hung heavy in the air.

I had tried to help, offering my medical services to the fire crews who had scrambled to attend to the bombsites, but there was little I could do. Those who had been caught in the blasts were already dead, and I was grateful to discover that many had escaped with their lives, if not their possessions. They would be moved on to shelters elsewhere in the city, distraught but grateful for their lives.

With little else to be done, Holmes and I had struck out towards Ealing on foot, and had been forced to walk some miles before finally picking up a cab.

As a consequence I was bone tired, and felt a dark shadow of depression threatening to overwhelm me. Left to my own devices, I was sure that I might sink into a well of grief and self-pity, and the very notion appalled me, bucking me up. I made a conscious decision to banish such black thoughts. There was a case to be solved. There was work to be done.

Holmes was still intent on the papers upon his knee. "Have you discovered anything?" I asked, as I collected the detritus from the fireplace.

Holmes sniffed. He shook his head. "Nothing of consequence," he replied. "At least, not yet. I need those other transcripts. There is a pattern here, I'm sure of it. It's simply that I cannot yet discern it. The picture remains incomplete. Additionally, without my index the work is much more difficult. Many of these names are familiar to me; minor criminals, petty thieves, that sort of thing, but I fear I'm going to have to rely on Inspector Foulkes to confirm it."

I could see his frustration in the set of his jaw. He must have been at it for hours. There were dark bruises beneath his eyes from lack of sleep. "Coffee," I said. "And breakfast." It occurred to me that neither of us had eaten since before we'd met at Victoria Station.

Holmes waved a dismissive hand, without looking up.

"Now then, Holmes, I'll have none of that. I'm speaking now as your doctor, as well as your friend. It's time to eat." I waited for a moment, but there was no response. So, grabbing the bull by the horns, I headed to the kitchen, where I rolled back my shirtsleeves and set about preparing a hearty spread of grilled kidneys and bacon, with a side of buttered toast. Years of experience told me that, despite his protests to the contrary, Holmes would soon attack this food if it were placed before him.

I was not wrong, and within half an hour we were both sitting at the breakfast table lining our stomachs in preparation for the day ahead. My culinary skills leave a lot to be desired, but my simple offering seemed to suffice.

"As I see it, Holmes," I said, around a mouthful of bacon, "we have two potential lines of enquiry. The transcripts from the War Office, on which you're already engaged, and those eerie photographs we recovered from Grange's home last night." I paused while I gulped down a welcome mouthful of coffee. "Have you any notion what they might be, what they might represent?" I'd intended to ask him this on the way home the previous evening, but events had somewhat disrupted my plans.

"I fear not, Watson," he replied, in what I took to be a rare moment of modesty. "It is clear to me that these unusual prints bear some manner of relationship to the field of spiritualism and the occult, but I am not yet convinced of their exact purpose. It is most likely they represent a form of elaborate hoax, a way of extracting money from a vulnerable or gullible man."

"I'd wondered much the same," I said, for although I was perhaps more disposed to matters of the spiritual than Holmes – who was at heart a cold, clinical logician, prepared only to accept the empirical evidence of his eyes – I had found myself assuming the photographs to be the result of a parlour game or an artistic experiment, rather than a true likeness of anything from the spiritual realm.

"The problem," said Holmes, "is that all evidence suggests that Herbert Grange was neither vulnerable *nor* gullible." He underlined his point by stabbing fiercely at a piece of kidney, which he proceeded to chew on thoughtfully while staring into the middle distance.

"Nevertheless," I said, following this train of thought, "surely if someone *was* attempting to extract money from Grange it represents a potential motive for his suicide. Blackmail, I mean. Perhaps they had a hold over him, something we have yet to discern. Or perhaps he did actually believe whatever spiritualist nonsense they were peddling. We can't ignore it."

"Quite so, Watson," replied Holmes. "Quite so."

"The pertinent question is surely, then: who is behind them?" I placed my cutlery on the empty plate before me and pushed it away across the table. "Who is the man or woman behind the camera? The difficulty is in getting to the bottom of that."

"We both know a man with the knowledge to be able to assist us in this matter," said Holmes, "or at the very least, to aid us in identifying the purpose of the photographs, if not, perhaps, their origin."

"We do?" I replied, momentarily perplexed.

Holmes's thin lips formed a forced smile, as if the idea was, perhaps, a little unsavoury. "Consider," he said, "Horburton Fen."

"Ah!" I exclaimed. "Of course. Sir Maurice Newbury. He's exactly the man we need." Newbury was an old acquaintance, an agent of the Crown and an expert in all matters pertaining to the occult. I had worked with him on a number of occasions – including the aforementioned affair at Horburton Fen, investigating a series of ritual murders and a satanic coven of witches – and found him to be a most excellent, reliable fellow. I understood that Holmes, however, would likely feel differently about the situation. He had never put much stock in talk of the supernatural, and I didn't imagine he was about to start now. Nevertheless, as Holmes well knew, it wasn't so much a question of whether either of *us* believed in whatever hokum was behind the photographs, but whether Grange himself did. Holmes's hope was that Newbury might be able to help us understand the context of the photographs, no more.

Whatever the case, I found the notion of catching up with Newbury after all this time most appealing, and I said so to Holmes.

He responded by withdrawing his cracked old briar pipe from his coat pocket and stuffing it full of shag.

I had visited Newbury's home once before, during the adventure I have previously chronicled as "The Case of the Night Crawler",

and so, after fishing out my address book, I was able to search out
the location of his Chelsea home for the telephone operator.

A quick call established he was not at home, but his valet –
who, despite it being over ten years since I'd visited, appeared to
remember me when I gave my name – helpfully informed me that
Newbury was to be found at his office in the British Museum. I
recalled then that Newbury maintained a post at that august
establishment, for the times when he was not actively pursuing
an investigation for the Crown. A further telephone call to his
secretary there confirmed an appointment for later that morning.

While I tidied away the remnants of our breakfast, Holmes
also made use of the telephone to call his brother Mycroft, with
the express purpose of informing him of the sad death of his
driver the previous evening. Their call was brief and somewhat
stilted, although I made a point of not overhearing the content of
their conversation.

When he was finished, Holmes came to find me the kitchen.
He was already wearing his coat and gloves, and was holding a
manila folder containing Grange's photographs. "To the British
Museum, then?" he said.

"Yes, I suppose so," I replied. "It'll be good to see Newbury
again after all this time."

Holmes offered me an enigmatic smile in response.

I have always been fond of the British Museum. I believe it
symbolises the cultural wealth of our nation – indeed, of our
empire. It represents perhaps the greatest collection of historical
artefacts in the world. I would often enjoy whiling away afternoons
there with my wife, touring the exhibits and soaking up the
atmosphere of ancient lands.

On occasion I have wondered whether, if Holmes had not

given himself entirely to his chosen profession of consulting detective, perhaps he might have made an exemplary historian. Not that he showed a particular interest in such matters, I hasten to add – indeed, it was fair to say that he was quite ignorant of much of what is generally considered historical fact. Unless, that was, those facts happened to pertain to a particular criminal investigation. Ask him to name the successive kings and queens of England, for example, and he would be quite flummoxed.

No, it was more that I understood the pursuit of historical data to be a series of puzzles to be solved, of mysteries to be unravelled. I was certain that if Holmes had chosen to put his mind to it, he might have caused quite a stir in the field. Knowing him as I did, however, I understood that he would find such work meaningless, and that the lack of empirical evidence and reliance on supposition would drive him to distraction.

Newbury, of course, had a deep affinity for such matters, and although I'd never been certain whether it was simply a cover for his more practical work for the Crown, or a genuine attempt to establish an academic career, his interest in the field seemed most genuine. Where Holmes would dedicate his time to producing a monograph on the identification of tobacco ash and its application in criminal investigation, Newbury was more likely to be concerned with Neolithic stone circles and their use in ancient fertility rites. In this, they could not be further apart.

I admit to feeling a certain amount of anticipation at seeing Newbury again. This was partly because I looked forward to rekindling an occasional acquaintance I had much enjoyed during the last decade and a half, and partly because I was interested to see how Holmes would acquit himself. He had originally been critical of my association with Sir Maurice and his assistant, Miss Veronica Hobbes, writing Newbury off as a credulous charlatan who put too much stock in the affairs of the supernatural. Indeed, during the aforementioned investigation into the mysterious machine that later became known as the "night crawler", Holmes had entirely refused to engage with the man, leaving it to me to act as a go-between.

Years later, however, we once again crossed paths with Newbury during the episode I have laid out as "The Witch of Horburton Fen", and this time, in coming face-to-face with a man I believe Holmes once considered a rival, his earlier scorn had given way to a begrudging respect. Newbury had been fundamental in the successful wrapping up of the case, aiding Holmes in bringing an errant vicar to justice. Then, as I suspected Holmes imagined now, the supernatural elements of the case had proved to be quite the opposite, with a perfectly rational – if somewhat distressing – explanation. What was more, at no point during the investigation did Newbury fall back on any ungrounded beliefs, or preach to us the likelihood of a supernatural cause. He approached the matter in much the same way as Holmes, examining each and every clue, deciphering its meaning, and refusing to make suppositions until all the data was in place. This, I knew, had impressed Holmes immeasurably, and as such his overall attitude towards Newbury had softened, to the extent that now, unexpectedly, he was counselling a visit to seek the man's advice. Wonders, I decided, would never cease.

Holmes had remained silent throughout our journey, but now, as our cab came to a stop before the main gates of the British Museum, he turned to me, his expression warm but serious. "I'm sorry for your loss," he said quietly.

Caught off guard, I mumbled an acknowledgement, fighting back an upwelling of unseemly emotion. He nodded once, and then turned and climbed out of the conveyance. I followed suit, but as I did, I noticed that my hands were trembling. It was, I realised, one of the kindest gestures that Holmes had ever made, in all of our years as friends. I swallowed and reached for some change to pay the driver.

The museum grounds were quiet, with only a handful of people milling around the courtyard. It wasn't surprising, given the events of the evening before. With so much clearing up to do, and the lingering threat of death at the hands of the zeppelin bombers, the last thing that people wanted to do was lose themselves in the artistic endeavours of the past. The present was simply too pressing.

We crossed the forecourt in the shadow of the monolithic building, and I found myself thinking how grateful I was that the edifice had so far avoided becoming a target of the enemy bombs.

At the top of the steps, close to the main entrance, I stopped to speak with a doorman. He looked rather harried, as if he had somewhere better to be. "We have an appointment with Sir Maurice Newbury," I said. "I wonder if you could point us in the right direction?"

"Across the main lobby," he said, "and then follow the courtyard around to the right. You'll come across a flight of steps. Can't miss it. Sir Maurice keeps an office in the basement."

"My thanks to you," I said.

Newbury's office was along a dimly lit corridor at the bottom of the stairs. At first I thought the doorman has given us the wrong directions; we seemed to be down in the bowels of the museum, amongst the dusty storerooms and disused offices. There were numerous doors stemming off the corridor, each of them with opaque glass, but lacking nameplates. We checked them one by one as we traversed the length of the corridor. Holmes was the first to spot it, the final door, about as far from the museum proper as you could get. Here, a small brass plaque was etched with a legend: "Sir Maurice Newbury".

Holmes rapped on the door, and then opened it without waiting for a response. He strode in, all sense of proper decorum ignored.

Shaking my head, I followed after him.

Inside, the office was not at all what I'd been expecting. Instead of a musty old room full of long-abandoned files and papers, there was a rather homely space containing a fireplace, stove, bookcase, filing cabinet and desk. The walls were adorned with an array of ancient weapons, including a mace, a rather deadly looking morning star, an elaborately engraved shield and a primitive axe, the head bound to the shaft with what looked like twine. On the left was a door to an antechamber, presently closed. There was no sign of the secretary I had spoken to that morning.

"Hello?" said Holmes.

There came the disharmonious sound of chair legs scraping across tiles from the antechamber, and through the glass partition I saw the silhouette of a man getting up from behind a desk. Moments later the door opened, and Newbury stood in the opening, a broad grin on his face. "Dr. Watson!" he said, with what sounded like genuine pleasure. "It's good to see you after all this time." He came forward, proffering his hand. I took it and he clasped mine firmly. He had aged well: his hair was still the same raven black as it had been almost ten years earlier, with only a peppering of grey; the lines on his face looked distinguished rather than careworn, and he was still lean. He must have been in his early fifties. I guessed he still continued in active service. "And you, Mr. Holmes," he continued, releasing my hand and turning to Holmes. "You are most welcome."

"Thank you for agreeing to see us, Sir Maurice," replied Holmes. "I am hopeful you can assist us with a rather delicate matter. It falls within your area of... specialist expertise." He teased out the last two words, as if more comfortable with the euphemism than explaining himself outright. "I know we can rely on your discretion."

"Of course," said Newbury. "I'm more than happy to help in any way that I can. But first, I have an important question."

"Go ahead," said Holmes, with the merest hint of a frown.

"Excellent!" said Newbury, clapping his hands together abruptly. "How do you take your tea?"

"So, what of Miss Hobbes? I hope she is well?"

We were gathered around Newbury's desk in the adjoining room, each brandishing a steaming teacup. Holmes, to my surprise, had accepted Newbury's offer of tea, and Newbury had set to work at the stove, boiling up a pot of water. It was a primitive thing, clearly decades old, but Newbury handled it like an old expert. This was evidently a ritual he cared profoundly for, and as we watched, he warmed the pot and measured out the leaves from a battered old caddy.

"She is quite well, Dr. Watson," replied Newbury. "I'll be sure to pass on your regards. I fear she's currently engaged in an undertaking for the Secret Service Bureau, otherwise I know she would have been delighted to see you." He looked plaintively at the empty desk across the room. I could see that it pained him to consider his friend – well, I wasn't sure exactly *what* she was to him, but he evidently cared deeply for her – out there somewhere, probably engaged in an initiative to influence the outcome of the war. Whatever it was, it couldn't have been less than dangerous work, given the political situation. I wished her well, wherever she was.

Holmes set his teacup down upon on the surface of the desk, indicating that it was time to address the real reason for our visit. He took the manila folder from his inside pocket and handed it to Newbury. "Inside this folder, Sir Maurice, you will find a series of photographs. They are of an unusual nature. I have so far been unable to ascertain their purpose, and, thus, who might have taken them."

Newbury opened the folder and extracted the sheaf of photographs. He spread them out on the desk, looking at them each in turn. Upside down – for I was sitting across the other side of the desk from Newbury – they appeared even more disconcerting than they had before. As he laid them out in sequence, it looked as if the central figure of Grange was surrounded by a ghostly aura that moved in each shot, swirling into different patterns as if it were a living – or at least *animated* – thing.

"Fascinating," said Newbury, clearly impressed. "Where did you obtain these?" He glanced up, looking directly at Holmes.

"The subject's home," replied Holmes, giving little away. I presumed that he was withholding the details of the case not because he doubted Newbury's discretion, but because he did not want to colour his opinion before it was proffered.

"Your client?" said Newbury.

"In a manner of speaking," said Holmes.

Newbury grinned. "Very well, I'll play along with your game, Mr. Holmes. I know precisely what these are, and exactly who took them."

Holmes leaned forward in his chair. He folded his hands on his lap. "Indeed?" he said.

"They really are wonderful examples," continued Newbury. "Perhaps the best I've seen." He selected one and picked it up, holding it up to the light. "This one in particular. The aura is really quite pronounced." He glanced at me, and smiled impishly. He was toying with Holmes. I couldn't contain a grin of my own.

Holmes cleared his throat. "The subject in the photographs is the late Mr. Herbert Grange, MP. He'd been engaged in vital work for the War Office until his untimely demise just two days hence. I have been asked to temporarily take leave of my retirement to investigate."

"Oh, yes, the chap who threw himself into the Thames," said Newbury. "I read about it in *The Times*. Poor fellow, to be reduced to such a state that the only recourse is the swirling depths of the river."

"It was undoubtedly instigated by an as yet unidentified third party, Sir Maurice," said Holmes. "I have little doubt of that. The means by which it was achieved, however..."

"Are another thing entirely," finished Newbury. "Well, gentlemen, I can tell you this much: the photographs you have in your possession are the work of a man named Mr. Seaton Underwood. He calls them his 'spectrographs', and he has spent many years developing the machine that makes them possible, his 'spectrograph generator.'"

"Yes, but what exactly are they supposed to represent?" I asked.

"Underwood is obsessed with the notion that the human soul can – and does – exist independently of the body, Dr. Watson. He purports that these images," he turned the photograph so that I might see, and ran his finger around the halo surrounding Grange's head, "represent a photograph of the subject's living soul."

I glanced at Holmes, who raised a sceptical eyebrow. "And do you, Sir Maurice, give any credence to these claims?"

Newbury shrugged. "I remain doubtful," he said, "although I do not claim to have investigated Underwood's process in any detail."

Holmes nodded, clearly approving of Newbury's rationalist approach.

"But what would Grange be doing with such things?" I said. "It seems unlikely that a man of his position would engage in such unfounded nonsense." I realised then that my derisory words might have seemed discourteous to Newbury, who had dedicated so many years of his life to the research of such phenomena, but he simply smiled and laughed.

"I think you might be surprised, Dr. Watson, how many otherwise rational men have expressed an interest in occult or spiritual matters, particularly during times of uncertainty and unrest," replied Newbury. "Although, I grant you, there is another possible explanation."

"Go on," pressed Holmes, listening intently.

"Seaton Underwood is the charge of Lord Foxton, of Ravensthorpe House."

"The well known reformist?" I said, surprised. I was well aware of Foxton from the newspapers, a member of the House of Lords who had worked with Asquith's Liberal government on the welfare reforms.

"Quite so," said Newbury. "Underwood's family were killed in a tragic accident when he was a boy – an accident, I understand, that involved certain members of Foxton's own family. He took the child in, raised him as his ward. He's had a privileged life, but he's also been indulged."

"So you're suggesting that Grange may have met Underwood through Foxton?" said Holmes.

"Precisely," replied Newbury. "I understand that Ravensthorpe House is quite the destination for those who wish to rub shoulders with the political elite. Foxton has cultivated an enviable circle of friends. It would not surprise me to discover your friend here was one of them."

"And Foxton could, therefore, have encouraged Grange's interest in Underwood's work?" I reasoned.

Newbury shrugged. "It's possible," he said, "but more likely that Foxton sees the spectrographs as a harmless diversion, a parlour game to amuse his well-heeled guests."

"Which has the added benefit of placating his ward," I added.

"Then we shall make it our business to pay Lord Foxton a visit, I think," said Holmes.

"I can arrange it, if you like?" said Newbury. "Foxton and I share a mutual acquaintance in Professor Archibald Angelchrist. It may help to grease the wheels. Foxton is notoriously difficult to gain access to. Unless you're part of his inner circle, that is."

"Excellent!" said Holmes. "Most excellent. Your assistance in this matter is greatly appreciated, Sir Maurice."

"It's my pleasure," said Newbury. He rose to his feet, shuffling the photographs back into the envelope and handing it to Holmes. "I'll send word once I've managed to arrange things with Archibald. Will I find you at Baker Street?"

"Alas, no," I said. I withdrew a card and laid it upon the desk. "Baker Street is long given up to new tenants. Here's my card."

Holmes tapped the index finger of his right hand thoughtfully against his pursed lips. "There was just one other question, Sir Maurice."

"Yes?" replied Newbury.

"Does the term 'spirit box' mean anything to you?"

Newbury frowned. "I have heard the term used before, Mr. Holmes. I believe it refers to a practice originating in the West Indies, in which the soul of a person is captured and trapped within a small wooden casket, the eponymous 'spirit box'. Influence is then asserted upon the person through ritualistic endeavour. The victim becomes suggestible, carrying out the bidding of the shaman who owns his soul..." Newbury trailed off. "Have you reason to believe that someone might have attempted to employ such a device to unduly influence Herbert Grange?"

"It's possible," said Holmes. "On the day of his death, he was overheard by his secretary mumbling the words 'I will not be responsible for the loss of the spirit box'. I must add that, given your enlightening explanation, it remains a potential line of enquiry, despite my reservations. I would be very interested to hear what Mr. Seaton Underwood had to say on the matter."

Newbury nodded. "Yes. It does seem rather coincidental, given the nature of those photographs. Nevertheless, first you would have to believe that such methods held some measure of validity. That's a significant leap of faith."

"And one that I am not, at this stage, prepared to make," said

Holmes. "Although that does not preclude the notion that *others* might believe it to be true, and act accordingly." He extended his hand and Newbury shook it. "Thank you for your time, Sir Maurice. I will await your call."

"Yes, thank you," I echoed. "It was good to see you again after all this time."

"Indeed it was, Dr. Watson," said Newbury. "I'll be in touch."

"Where to now?" I asked Holmes, as we climbed the steps out of the museum basement, emerging into the harsh daylight of the courtyard. I cupped my hand around my eyes while they adjusted to the sudden change.

"Back to Ealing," said Holmes. "There is much to be done, and by now Miss Brown should have sent over the missing interview transcripts. Whilst the origins of this mystery might be rooted in the supernatural, I'll wager there's a corporeal villain at the heart of it, and those transcripts may yet hold the key to identifying him." And with that he was off, moving with the speed and vitality of a man half his age. The game was, as he was occasionally wont to say, most definitely "afoot".

CHAPTER SIX

My house in Ealing seemed somewhat dark and gloomy upon our return. The grandfather clock in the hallway measured the seconds with a deathly monotony, and there seemed to be no life in the place.

This, I supposed, was a symptom of my wife's absence, but in many ways highlighted what my life had become during the course of the last few months. I had fallen into a miserable pattern of existence. I had allowed myself to wallow in my grief at the death of my nephew, and it had taken the reappearance of my old friend, Holmes – or rather the agency of his brother and the emergence of a new case – to realise it. Silently, I cursed myself, and vowed that, when this was over – when Holmes had returned to his bees in the Sussex Downs – I would not allow myself to fall afoul of such self-pitying again.

Miss Brown had been diligent, and the last three interview transcripts had been delivered in our absence. They'd been pushed through the letterbox in a large, brown envelope. The address had been handwritten upon the envelope in neat print, and the lack of a postmark was evidence that it had been delivered in person, rather than trusted to the vagaries of the Post Office. I wondered for a moment how Miss Brown was coping with her grief.

Holmes had been animated upon laying eyes on the transcripts, and after shrugging off his coat – which he flung untidily across the telephone table in the hall – he kicked off his shoes, stoked the fire and sank once again into my favourite armchair to read. With a shrug, I set about organising some tea. Years ago I had learned that there was little else to do when Holmes was so absorbed.

Upon returning with the tea tray a short while later I found him buried in innumerable pages of typescript. He was examining each page in turn, holding them so close to his face that the tip of his hooked nose was almost touching the print. I decided that I would make a gift to him of a pair of reading glasses before he left London, knowing full well what he would make of such a gesture.

I slumped into the armchair opposite Holmes and perused the newspapers for a while, skimming over page after page of reports from the front, of impossible-sounding death tolls and descriptions of the myriad horrors faced by the young men in the trenches.

Closer to home, I read of the devastation wreaked by the raid of the night before, and couldn't help but think again of poor Carter, and of the near miss we'd had at Herbert Grange's house. I found it all thoroughly depressing, and it threatened to dampen my spirits even further. I tossed the papers aside with a muttered curse.

Holmes, I noticed, had failed to drink his tea. He was still absorbed in his reading but I could stand the silence no longer. "Well, Holmes?" I said, a little huffily. "What do you make of it all?"

Without lifting his eyes from the page he was reading he held up his left hand, extending his slender index finger in a gesture intended to encourage my silence. I gave an impatient tut and rose to my feet, indignant at being treated in such a manner in my own home.

"A fresh pot of tea, if you will, Watson," said Holmes, "now that you are up. I fear this one is rather tepid." He reached for the still-full cup and saucer on the table beside him and held it out for me. Still, he did not look up from his reading.

I collected his teacup, fighting the urge to overturn it on his lap, and retreated to the kitchen. A short while later, upon returning to the sitting room, I found Holmes of an altogether different disposition.

The papers were now scattered untidily around his feet, having been introduced to their kin from the previous day. Holmes was reclining in the chair, one knee crossed atop the other, and a smouldering pipe clenched between his teeth. He smiled brightly when he saw me standing in the doorway. "Ah, Watson, my good man. Have you brought biscuits?" He looked at me inquisitively. "One should always accompany tea with biscuits, in my opinion."

"You have that smug look about you, Holmes," I said, ignoring his remark. I set the tea tray down on the occasional table, rattling the cups in their saucers. "I see that you have discovered something in those transcripts. No doubt it confirms a fact that you had already anticipated, but for which you were lacking proof."

"Bravo, Watson!" said Holmes, removing his pipe from between his teeth. The end appeared chewed and decidedly unsightly. "Most perceptive." He accepted the fresh cup of tea that I proffered. He raised a dubious eyebrow at the evident lack of biscuits, but a fierce warning look from me brought the matter to a brisk close. With a sigh, he took a long draught from his cup.

"Well?" I prompted.

"Well indeed," said Holmes. "I have now examined each of the transcripts provided by Miss Brown, concerning Herbert Grange's interviews with the German nationals resident in the capital. I found them most enlightening."

"To what end?" I asked. "You said earlier that you were sure there was a pattern."

"Quite so, Watson. The particulars of the individuals are of little consequence, it seems – bakers, clerks, mechanics and factory workers," said Holmes. "However, when all the facts are considered together, one particular line of enquiry presents itself. It seems that the same man employs three of the individuals in question, here in London: a banker by the name of Henry Baxter. He is the Head of Investments at Tidwell Bank, one of the partners."

"I've never heard of the man," I said.

"Indeed not," said Holmes. "It appears he specialises in catering to the European elite – counts, viscounts, dukes and lords. Only the richest of men."

"And why is that in and of itself suspicious?" I queried.

Holmes shrugged. "As you know, I do not put great stock in coincidence. Of the three men whom Grange interviewed that fateful morning, the second of them was another of Baxter's employees. Could it be that one or more of these men had something to hide? Something they were holding back in fear that Grange might arrange for their incarceration or deportation?" He tapped his chin thoughtfully. "I see the possibility of motive, Watson, if not yet the means by which the killer might have enacted his crime."

"I see your point," I said. "Then what next?"

"A trip to Tidwell Bank, I think," said Holmes. "To speak with Mr. Baxter regarding his employees." He took another sip of his tea. "But first, I really must press you for that biscuit."

Tidwell Bank was, as Holmes had previously suggested, a rather upmarket establishment, a far cry from the sort of place I might typically visit to transact my financial affairs.

The lobby was more like that of a grand hotel than any bank I had ever seen, with a marble floor laid out like a black-and-white chequerboard, a grandiose crystal chandelier, baroque stone window frames and plaster busts of figures from classical myth, nestled amongst rows of aspidistras. Nine identical oak desks, laid out in three neat rows, completed to the picture. Behind each of these desks sat a male clerk dressed in a formal black suit.

"May I help you, gentlemen?" I turned to see a woman in a long, grey gown, sweeping across the lobby toward us. It appeared we were the only customers.

"Good afternoon, madam," said Holmes. "I telephoned ahead. We have an appointment to speak with Mr. Baxter."

"Very good," she said, clearly surprised. "Allow me to just check the diary. Your names, if I may?"

"I am Mr. Sherlock Holmes, and this is my associate, Dr. John Watson," said Holmes.

She crossed to a narrow lectern that stood just to the right of the entrance, and leafed through an appointment book resting on top. "Ah, yes," she said, her demeanour immediately softening. "A last-minute arrangement." She smiled. "If you'd like to come with me, I shall show you to Mr. Baxter's office. He's expecting you."

I glanced at Holmes, who offered me a thin smile before following the woman. She led us into a small waiting room adjoining an office and rapped at the door, then opened it without waiting for a response.

Baxter's office was as opulently appointed as the rest of the building, and as the receptionist showed us in, I found myself drawn in by the décor. Four bookshelves were lined with the neat leather spines of old tomes, although from across the room I found it impossible to discern their gilded titles. A glass-fronted case held a range of oddities, including a porcelain phrenologist's head, a trophy, and a photograph of the Giza pyramids in a silver frame. Maps of Europe were pinned to the walls, and a tall, thin man sat behind a desk, reading a newspaper.

"Mr. Baxter, your three o'clock appointment," said the receptionist.

Baxter was a slender man of around forty, with long, willowy limbs, and a pale, drawn face. Neatly trimmed blonde hair was beginning to recede from his forehead. He placed the newspaper he had been reading upon the desk, and rose to meet us. "Mr. Holmes, Dr. Watson, welcome, welcome!" he said, exuberantly. "Please, make yourselves at home." He beckoned us to two chairs, and as we sat, he took Holmes's hand in his own and shook it vigorously. "I could barely believe it when my clerk informed me of your intended visit. The great Mr. Holmes! I've long been an admirer of your work. And, of course, thanks in no small measure to your beautifully written accounts, Dr. Watson," he said, as if recognising his unintended slight. He proffered his hand and I took it. It was slightly cold to the touch. Holmes cast me a shrewd, sidelong glance.

Baxter sat in the chair behind his desk and seemed to study Holmes for a moment. "But tell me, sir – I understood that you had retired?"

Holmes's lips curled into a smile, as he seemed to process this sudden rush of enthusiasm. "I fear a man of my profession never quite retires, Mr. Baxter, so much as stops for an indefinite period of time."

Baxter guffawed heartily. "A man after my own heart, what?" he said. His accent and manner marked him out as the alumnus of one of our better-known public schools. Probably Eton or Harrow, I decided.

"Thank you for making the time to see us, Mr. Baxter," said Holmes. "This is quite an establishment. I imagine your time is very precious."

"Quite so, Mr. Holmes," he replied. "Yet, it would seem

prudent to make time for such an occasion. Am I to assume you wish to question me regarding a case?" He looked hopeful, as if the very thought of being put to the question by Holmes was sort of badge of honour.

"In a manner of speaking," replied Holmes.

Baxter reached into his jacket pocket and withdrew a small silver cigarette case. It was clearly an antique, battered and worn, and tarnished by fingerprints. He popped the clasp and withdrew a cigarette, offering them to both Holmes and me. We politely declined. He shrugged and placed the case down upon his desk, atop a pile of loose papers, which were held in place by a small half-globe paperweight, made from polished amber and neatly engraved with a five-pointed star. It looked remarkably similar to the one I had seen at Herbert Grange's office.

Baxter struck a match, touched the flame against the tip of his cigarette and inhaled deeply. He allowed the smoke to billow from the corner of his mouth, along with a satisfied sigh. As he reached up to withdraw the cigarette from his lips, I noticed there was dirt encrusted beneath the fingernails of his right hand. "So, gentlemen, please tell me – in what way can this simple banker be of assistance?"

"We are following a particular line of enquiry regarding the unfortunate death of Mr. Herbert Grange, MP," said Holmes.

"Ah, yes. I read the account in *The Times*. Such an appalling waste of life," said Baxter. "I'm sure you'll agree."

"Indeed," replied Holmes. "May I ask, did you happen to have a personal acquaintance with Mr. Grange?"

Baxter shook his head and took another draw on his cigarette. "I did not. I knew of the man, of course – he was quite a figure in Parliament and political circles, but I don't believe I was ever fortunate enough to meet him myself."

"But some of your employees did," prompted Holmes.

Baxter gave a curious grin, the left side of his mouth twitching in amusement. "Ah," he said. "So now it becomes clear. You're here to quiz me on why I should have so many German nationals in my employ. The men whom Grange interviewed at the War Office prior to his death."

"Precisely," confirmed Holmes.

"Well," said Grange. "It's like this. I'm in the business of investments. People entrust their money to me, and it is my role to not only protect their interests, but to generate a healthy return. But this is no ordinary bank, Mr. Holmes. I cater to a very particular clientele, the rich elite of Europe: counts and countesses, dukes and barons, princes and merchants. Why, only this week I have entered into an arrangement with an exiled prince from Romania, a man of some infamy."

"So these Germans on your staff, Mr. Baxter," said I, "they are employed to deal with your overseas customers?"

"Precisely that, Dr. Watson," replied Baxter. "I find it helps to have native speakers of all the major European languages in my employ. It lends a certain authenticity to proceedings, and allows my clients to feel at ease. And, of course, smoothes any transaction that might need to take place with other interested parties in those countries."

"And where do you make your investments, Mr. Baxter?" said Holmes.

"Oh, here and there," replied Baxter, with a shrug. "I'm sure you'll understand, I cannot disclose all my secrets."

"Quite so," said Holmes, reasonably. "But please, answer me this – would any of the three German men in your employ have reason to wish Herbert Grange ill?"

Baxter looked thoughtful. "I do not believe so, Mr. Holmes," he said. He stubbed out his cigarette in a cut-glass ashtray on his desk. "My men have been vetted most thoroughly. I select only the best.

Their allegiances are eminently clear to me. I do not believe Herbert Grange could find them wanting, and therefore see no possible motive for their wishing him harm." He cast about, as if looking for something, and then shrugged and continued. "Indeed, Mr. Grange was their ticket to remaining in this country. Without him, they faced possible imprisonment and loss of income. They needed his approval. His death could only complicate matters. It seems unlikely to me, then, that the finger of suspicion might fall on them in any way."

He paused for a moment, touching his index finger against his lips. "But of course! How naïve of me. I take it then, Mr. Holmes, that you believe Mr. Grange's death to be suspicious in some way? The newspapers reported it as suicide, but perhaps you suppose he was murdered?"

"No, Mr. Baxter," said Holmes. "It is clear to me that Herbert Grange did, in fact, take his own life. Of that there is no question. What as yet remains unanswered is the reason why."

Baxter smiled. "The human mind is a wondrous thing, Mr. Holmes, but I fear even *your* celebrated deductive powers may struggle to comprehend the emotional intricacies that would drive a man to take such a terrible step. To my mind it has less to do with logic and fact, and everything to do with the irrational and unexplained. I'm sure, being a medical man, Dr. Watson would agree." He glanced at me, as if seeking approval. I remained impassive.

"You sound as if you might even believe that a man in such a position might be influenced by otherworldly forces, Mr. Baxter?" said Holmes, raising an eyebrow.

"Perhaps so," replied Baxter. "Although I fear it would be almost impossible to prove either way."

"How interesting," said Holmes. I sensed the judgement behind the comment.

There was a moment of silence while Baxter lit himself a

second cigarette. "I take it, Mr. Holmes, that you wish to interview the three men in question?" The sudden change in the topic of the conversation was palpable.

"That will not be necessary at this time," said Holmes, much to my surprise. "Although in due course, I may yet prevail upon you to that end, if the need arises."

"Of course," said Baxter. "You can count on any assistance that it is in my power to give."

"My thanks to you," said Holmes. "Then perhaps if I might venture one further question?"

"Be my guest," said Baxter. His expression was earnest, but I couldn't shake the feeling he was toying with us for his own amusement, drawing things out.

"Do you happen to have a personal acquaintance with Lord Foxton, of Ravensthorpe House?"

"As a matter of fact, I do," said Baxter. "Although it is most definitely a case of acquaintance and not friendship."

"Indeed?" queried Holmes. The way Baxter had said it made it sound as if there was no love lost between the two men. I wondered what had occurred to create such a definite rift between them.

"Oh, it's not as if we're at each other's throats," said Baxter. "We just didn't quite hit it off, that's all. I've been to one or two of his parties, although admittedly, not for some time. I find him a bit staid, if I'm honest. A little too stuck in his ways. Why do you ask? Do you believe Foxton is in some way connected to Mr. Grange's death?"

"Far from it, Mr. Baxter," replied Holmes. "Forgive me, it was simply inquisitiveness on my part."

Baxter laughed. "An admirable trait in a consulting detective, eh?" he said. Holmes inclined his head in acknowledgement of the compliment.

"Well, I do believe that we have taken up enough of your valuable time, Mr. Baxter," said Holmes, rising from his seat. "My thanks to you. We shall call again if we need to speak to your men."

"Very good," said Baxter. "A pleasure to meet you both. I hope you'll forgive me if I don't show you out." He indicated the spread of papers on his desk. "I fear I have ledgers to balance."

"Good day to you, then," I said.

"Good day."

I held the door open for Holmes and we quit the bank through the waiting room, nodding our thanks to the receptionist as we crossed the foyer to the main doors.

Once we were outside, out of earshot of the clerks, I turned to Holmes. "What did you make of the man?"

"To my mind, Watson, Baxter is an admirable example of his kind," said Holmes.

"Really?" I said, somewhat incredulous.

"Quite so," said Holmes. "I have yet to meet a banker who is not a perfidious wretch, and Mr. Baxter, it seems, is no exception. I'd wager he counts amongst his clients some of the more notorious criminals in Europe, and that his portfolio of 'investments' would not stand a great deal of scrutiny in a court of law. And there is the small matter of his gambling habit. Not a laudable quality in a man who has control over other men's money."

"Gambling? What on earth makes you say that?" I asked.

"The newspaper, Watson. Open to the racing section, and yet no significant gatherings are held today. A true adherent, then. Together with the fact that his cigarette case bore the initials 'F.W.S.' and was therefore not his own – taken in a card game, I'd wager – I'd say that Mr. Baxter likes more than the occasional flutter."

"Then you feel he is worthy of further investigation?" I said.

"I do. I cannot yet put my finger on it, Watson, but mark my words: Mr. Henry Baxter has a role to play in the proceedings yet to come."

"Yes. I had a sense of that too," I said. "He seemed to be holding something back. And did you happen to notice the paperweight on his desk?" I ventured. "Almost identical to the one we saw at the War Office, on Grange's bookcase."

Holmes laughed. "Yes, I wondered if you'd notice that, Watson. Excellent!"

"You think there might be something in it?"

"Indubitably," said Holmes, in his usual, dismissive fashion. "Come now. Let us discover if our associate, Sir Maurice, has made the necessary arrangements for our trip to Ravensthorpe House. A party could be just the thing to revitalise the spirits, eh, Watson?"

My heart sank. "If we must, Holmes," I said.

CHAPTER SEVEN

Newbury had been as good as his word, and upon arriving back at the house I found a note on the mat, informing us that arrangements had been made to visit Lord Foxton's house that very evening.

Holmes seemed most animated by this development and immediately repaired to the second bedroom, for what undertaking I could not begin to imagine.

We had a couple of hours to spare, however, before necessity dictated a journey across town, and so given the opportunity I reclaimed my favourite armchair and sat for a while with my notebook and pen. It was my intention to set down all that I could recall of proceedings so far. I had a notion that in detailing an account of this new adventure with Holmes, I might in some way break the deadlock I had otherwise encountered with my writing. It felt good to have the words flow once more, and before long I had lost track of time, covering page after page with my spidery, inky scrawl – I have, after all, the handwriting of a general practitioner – which I planned to later transcribe on my trusty typewriter.

"I see, Watson, that you have once again found the use of your pen."

I glanced up from my work to see Holmes standing over me, looking immaculate in a formal black dinner suit. His hair was brushed neatly back from his forehead, his collar was buttoned and dressed with a bow tie, and he had even taken the time to fold a handkerchief and place it neatly in his breast pocket. It seemed most unlike Holmes.

I frowned, and then glanced at the clock. I realised with horror that time had indeed run away with me, and that I risked making us late for our appointment. With some bluster I set down my pen and paper, and stood, stretching my tired back. "Well, I must say, Holmes – you still scrub up rather well," I said, attempting to wipe a smear of ink from my fingers.

Holmes inclined his head and offered me a look of wry amusement. "It seems that scrubbing will indeed be necessary in your case, Watson," he said.

I glanced at my hands. The ink had become deeply ingrained. "Well, give me five minutes and I'll be with you," I said. I hurried off to see to my ablutions, leaving Holmes laughing, loudly, in the sitting room.

Minutes later, and feeling a little out of breath, I found Holmes in the hallway, waiting to help me on with my light overcoat. "I've a carriage waiting," he announced. "We shall be perfectly on time. Fear not, Watson."

"Fear nothing!" I replied, a trifle brusquely, as we bundled out of the house and into the waiting hansom.

Dusk was settling over London, and the pleasantly sedate journey across town served as a reminder of all that had changed since the last time my friend and I had taken such a conveyance together. Motorcars were not yet in abundance, but were growing in popularity, thundering along the cobbled lanes and parping riotously at any pedestrians daring enough to get in their way.

All around us work was being carried out repairing buildings damaged in the bombing raids. London was changing – *times were changing* – and I had not yet decided whether there was a place in it for a curmudgeonly old soldier such as myself. Perhaps Holmes had been right after all, retiring to the country to escape the altering landscape, and perhaps with it, the terrible, creeping feeling of irrelevance that comes with age.

I hadn't yet managed to shake the pronounced feelings of guilt that had worried away at me all day, following the death of Carter the previous night. I knew there was little I could have done for the man – he had insisted, after all, in waiting for us outside in the automobile – but I was nevertheless troubled by those fateful last words I had exchanged with him, warning him that he would "catch his death" out there in the cold. Today, those words felt like some unholy prophecy, a curse that I had inadvertently invoked when I'd left him out there, alone, to die.

Holmes, as perceptive as he ever was, seemed to know what was troubling me. "There are never the right words, are there, Watson, for times such as this?"

"What's that, Holmes?" I said, feigning ignorance.

"The boy," he replied. "The driver who died last night. It troubles you."

I was silent for a moment, listening to the rattle of the hansom's wheels on the cobbled road, the *clop clopping* of the horses' hooves. "Does it not trouble *you*, Holmes? Surely you cannot mean to tell me you are not affected by the death of that boy."

"This war," he said, glancing away, peering out through the window at the buildings passing by, "it eats away at you. I can see it, Watson, like a parasite that has inveigled itself in your mind. You think of little else." He turned to look at me, his eyes piercing. "You feel your loss keenly, and for that, I am truly sorry."

I stared at Holmes, aghast. "Once again, you speak of Joseph," I said. It was a rhetorical question, and Holmes did not deign to answer it. "How did you know?"

Holmes waved a dismissive hand. "The matter is elementary."

I bristled. "I assure you, Holmes. The matter is *far* from elementary."

"Forgive me, Watson. I meant no offence," he said. His tone was regretful.

I sighed. "No. Of course you didn't. It is I who should apologise to you, Holmes. I fear the subject is still a little raw. Thank you for your condolences."

We lapsed into silence, rocking gently in the carriage as we trundled on towards Lord Foxton's house.

Ravensthorpe House was a rambling old mansion on the outskirts of the city, set amongst sweeping acres of lush parkland. As we crawled up the gravel driveway in our carriage, I peered out of the window, spotting a herd of deer bounding gracefully across a grassy expanse in the distance. Beyond that, a large belt of dark, wild woodland appeared to stretch away for miles.

The driveway was bordered by an avenue of stately oak trees, and through their boughs I caught stuttering glimpses of an enormous lake to our left, its surface sparkling in the fading light. A rowing boat appeared like a tiny speck on the horizon, drifting on the glassy surface.

The whole place felt serene and timeless, as if it had remained this way, untouched, for centuries. It was a far cry from the drab streets of the city.

We pulled up in a large courtyard at the front of the building, and clambered down from the carriage. Three motorcars were parked in the shadow of the house – all of them sleek and black and near invisible in the dusk. These, I presumed, were the conveyances of the other guests. I hoped one of them might be Newbury himself. Time in his company always seemed to lift my mood.

Holmes paid our driver, and as the carriage trundled away, back toward the city, I stood for a moment and regarded the property that would play host to our investigations that evening.

It was most impressive: a manor in the Late Baroque style, likely dating from the beginning of the eighteenth century. The portico was reached by a set of stone steps and flanked by three columns on either side. Serried ranks of sash windows punctuated the tall, broad front of the building, and electric lights blazed within, welcoming and warm. The front door stood open, and the strains of a distant gramophone could be heard from within.

"Shall we?" said Holmes.

"Indeed," I said. "It's been a long time since I've attended anything quite so formal. I hope I can remember how to keep out of trouble."

Holmes grinned. "Now, Watson," he said, with mock derision. "Where would be the fun in that?"

He mounted the steps to the portico and rapped loudly on the door. It was opened by an elderly man, who had a shock of white hair, thinning but still full despite his advancing years, and whose dress marked him out as the butler. He had a kindly face, liver-spotted and creased from years of smiling. I surmised he must have been in his late seventies or early eighties.

"Good evening to you both, gentlemen," said the butler, a little out of breath. "My name is Brown. May I ask – are you expected this evening?"

"I believe so," I answered. "My name is Dr. John Watson, and this is my associate, Mr. Sherlock Holmes." I decided for once that Holmes could be *my* associate for the evening. "I understand a friend of ours, Sir Maurice Newbury, made arrangements for us to meet with Lord Foxton."

"Very good, sir," said Brown. "You are, indeed, expected. I've been asked to show you through as soon as you arrive. But first, allow me to take your coats." He extended his hand, which trembled slightly with a mild palsy. I slipped off my overcoat and handed it to him. Holmes did the same.

While the old man fussed with our outerwear, shaking out imaginary creases, I took stock of our surroundings. Inside, the house was as magnificent as I'd imagined, although tastefully presented, and not at all ostentatious. Nevertheless, one couldn't help but feel the presence of old money permeating the place – the portraits that hung on the walls in the hallway were just that little bit too faded to be recent fakes or reproductions, and much of the décor looked tarnished and original, as if it had been purchased when the house was first built and had been used by the family ever since.

Alarmingly, a large, stuffed polar bear, rearing up on its hind legs, stood at the bottom of the stairs, as if guarding against unwelcome guests. Both Holmes and I regarded it warily. The butler saw our expressions and smiled.

"Ah, that's Bertie. He's been a guest at the house for some years. Shot by the previous Lord Foxton on an expedition to the Arctic."

"Fascinating," said Holmes. To my surprise, he sounded genuinely interested.

Brown nodded. "If you're ready, then, gentlemen, I'll take you through."

"Please do," I said, grinning at Holmes.

Ponderously, Brown led us across the hallway, which narrowed on the right as it ran alongside the staircase. A passage led to a suite of adjoining rooms, from which we could hear the undulating chatter of male voices, accompanied by the clinking of glasses.

"The other guests have already arrived," said Brown. "You'll find them through there. I'm sure Sir Maurice will be anxious to introduce you." So, Newbury *was* here. The night was certainly looking up. "Please do call if you find yourselves in need of anything."

We thanked Brown and made our way into the drawing room, where a number of Foxton's guests were gathered in a small cluster before the fireplace. Others lounged about on the sofas, deep in discussion, or stood by the window, sipping at drinks and making idle chitchat. I counted approximately ten other guests. Some of their faces seemed familiar, but I couldn't quite place any of them. Politicians, I imagined, whose likenesses I had seen in the newspapers.

"Dr. Watson, Mr. Holmes!" I turned to see Newbury coming towards us, his hand extended in greeting, a warm smile upon his face. "I see you received my note. It's most excellent to see you."

"Likewise," I said. I shook Newbury's hand. He was looking well, if perhaps a little merry with the pre-dinner drinks.

"Over here," he said, waving enthusiastically for us to join his little group by the window. "There's someone I'd like you to meet."

We followed him over to where he'd evidently been conducting a conversation before we came in. There were two other men, who both greeted us warmly. One was a portly chap wearing a black formal suit and a dicky bow, with a neat side parting and a bushy black beard. He introduced himself as Percy Cranston, a solicitor.

The other was a short, thin fellow in his late sixties, clean-shaven, with greying hair and a dappling of liver spots around his left temple. He had a hawk-like nose, a deeply lined forehead, and sharp, interested eyes. In contrast to Cranston he was wearing a tweed suit with a relaxed, open collar. He took my hand and shook it graciously.

"This is Professor Archibald Angelchrist," said Newbury. "A dear old friend. We've been through rather a lot together, over the years. Quite a raft of adventures."

"It's a delight to meet you, Dr. Watson," said Angelchrist. His voice was gentle, his words exceptionally well enunciated. "I've enjoyed many of your written accounts of your investigations," he said. "It's quite a remarkable achievement, to have documented so many interesting cases."

I laughed. "And those are just the ones Holmes has allowed me to publish," I said. "I have boxes overflowing with more. Perhaps one day they'll see the light of day."

"Hmmm," murmured Holmes, with a smile. He reached around me to grasp Angelchrist by the hand. "A pleasure," he said. "I understand we have you to thank for seeing to this evening's arrangements?"

"Hardly a trial," said Angelchrist. "Foxton's rather an admirer. In fact, I barely had to mention your name before there was talk of having you both over."

"Well, all the same, we're indebted to you," I said.

"The pleasure is all mine," said Angelchrist. "In truth, I've been anxious to meet you, Mr. Holmes. Your brother has told me a great deal about you."

"You know Mycroft?" said Holmes, with a note of genuine surprise.

"For many years," replied Angelchrist. "He's been a good friend to me, and I still see him regularly."

I, myself, had had only limited contact with Mycroft Holmes over the preceding decades, but the thought of him being a good friend to anyone seemed quite remarkable. He was an outwardly indolent fellow, who nevertheless had an intellect at least on a par with his brother's, yet chose to apply it in a spectacularly different way, involving himself in the governance of the country at the very highest level.

"Now, now, gentlemen," said Cranston, pushing forward and causing Angelchrist to step to one side to avoid his considerable bulk. "First things first. You both look as if you could do with a drink." He waved his hand and I looked round to see a footman making a beeline for us, carrying a tray of drinks. Cranston handed Newbury his own glass and snatched two champagne flutes off the tray, passing them to Holmes and me. He dismissed the footman with a cursory "Thank you." He grabbed his glass back from Newbury and clinked it against mine in a rather informal salutation, before draining it.

Newbury caught my eye and offered an apologetic shrug, and I chuckled, realising now why he might have seemed a little tipsy when we'd first arrived. I decided to sip at the drink in an effort to eke it out – the last thing I wanted was to find myself too inebriated to comprehend anything that might constitute a clue in our ongoing investigation.

"So... do you visit Ravensthorpe often, Mr. Cranston?" I ventured, unsure what else to say to this giant of a man.

"Percy," said Cranston. "Please, call me Percy." He glanced around, then placed his empty glass surreptitiously on the windowsill. "And no, this is my first time here."

Angelchrist offered me a look that seemed to suggest it might well be Cranston's last, too.

Cranston turned to Holmes, who had been watching the man's buffoonery with a sphinx-like gaze.

"So you're the famous sleuth, sir?" He chuckled at Holmes's silent inclination of the head. "Do much sleuthing these days?"

Holmes raised an eyebrow. "I have been retired for many years, Mr Cranston," he replied. "Although one never truly rids oneself of certain habits."

"What, peering through magnifying glasses and haring after criminals?" Cranston guffawed. "I'd have thought you and Dr. Watson here were a little long in the tooth for such business."

Holmes smiled thinly. "While it is true that I do not engage in the more vigorous pursuits of my younger days, I was in fact referring to the habits of observation." He steepled his long fingers under his aquiline nose. "Take your suit jacket for instance."

Cranston looked down at the black affair, as did we all.

"From this item of apparel alone I can deduce that you have are left-handed, have put on seven pounds, four ounces within the last eleven months, and have acquired a new valet."

Cranston looked rather taken aback, while out of the corner of my eye I could see Newbury and Angelchrist exchanging conspiratorial smiles. Holmes himself had taken on an expression of perfect innocence that didn't fool me for a moment. No matter how old he got, my friend would never grow out of the habit of showing off. In many ways, it defined him.

"How could you possibly know all that?" Cranston asked. He extended his arms, turning them over and examining them, as if expecting the jacket fabric to yield its secrets.

"Oh, quite straightforward, I assure you," said Holmes. He turned to Newbury. "Sir Maurice, would you care to clarify how I know Mr. Cranston is left-handed?"

Newbury cocked his head. "The cufflink, I believe."

"Indeed." Holmes smiled. "Mr. Cranston, you are wearing plain sterling-silver cufflinks, manufactured, I believe, within the last five years, given the modern style. The right one is still in fine condition, yet the left has several small scratches across its face, such as would be made by repeated movement across the surface of a desk while writing, not to mention other small knocks that befall one's dominant hand." Cranston examined the item in question, and I saw that it did indeed show signs of wear, abrasions that were missing from the right cufflink.

"What about the other things you mentioned?" Cranston had lost some of his earlier bravado and was looking quite put out. "And I think you'll find I've gained no more than three pounds."

Holmes shook his head. "Seven pounds, four ounces. I saw the tailors' name and address sewed into the lining when you handed us our champagne. The tailors in question, Messrs Brentley and Shunt, have only been at their new South Molton Street address for eleven months. Therefore the jacket is no more than a year old. Yet it is tight under the arms and hangs an inch wider at the stomach than it should. Brentley and Shunt are exemplary craftsmen, therefore we must assume that you no longer fit the suit, rather than imagine that they fitted it incorrectly."

Cranston unconsciously held his hands guardedly over his pronounced stomach. "What about Fenwick? I admit, I've only had him for two weeks. But how did you know?"

Holmes smiled again, clearly enjoying himself. He leaned forward and indicated an area of cloth below Cranston's right earlobe. "Observe, gentlemen, the slight indented line in the fabric at Mr. Cranston's shoulder. Its shine denotes that this was the previous site of the shoulder crease, made by a valet repeatedly pressing the suit in an identical fashion. Yet the fresh crease tonight is a quarter-inch below its older fellow. Clearly this suit has been pressed by a man to whom it was previously unfamiliar, or else he would have automatically pressed the crease in the same manner as he had so many times before. A new valet. That, or your man has taken to drink."

Cranston looked momentarily confused, then laughed uproariously. "Well you've clearly not lost your touch, Mr. Holmes!" he exclaimed. Holmes took the compliment with good grace, and I felt almost young again. It was good to see my friend at work.

"Now, Sir Maurice," said Cranston, putting his arm around Newbury's shoulder. "I've been wanting to ask you about the British Museum, and a particular monograph you wrote regarding the ritualistic practices of the Ancient Britons."

I saw Newbury force a smile, and took the opportunity

to extract myself from the conversation. I sipped at my drink, angling myself out of Cranston's line of sight, before turning my attention to Angelchrist.

I knew very little of this genial man, other than what Newbury had told me – that he was a former agent of the British Secret Service Bureau, and had been instrumental in forging the organisation during the early days of the century. As Newbury had already intimated, the two of them had been involved in a number of adventures together, along with Sir Charles Bainbridge, the former Chief Inspector of Scotland Yard and agent to the Crown, and a man for whom I had the utmost respect.

"I understand from Sir Maurice that you're close friends with Sir Charles Bainbridge?" I said.

"Quite so," said Angelchrist. "Charles is a very dear friend."

"Is he well?" I enquired. "Holmes and I had the pleasure of working with him on a number of cases, many years ago now, but since his retirement I've heard very little of how he's faring."

"I'll pass on your regards," said Angelchrist. "He'll be delighted, I'm sure. He's quite well – although I fear the word 'retirement' is perhaps a little strong. He's currently scouring the Norfolk Broads in search of a feral child who's said to be attacking the farmers and their livestock. It's an odd business. Word is, a witch raised the child in the woods, and somehow cursed the boy, altering him through some ghastly ritual, so that he's now a strange amalgam of man and beast." He waved his hand dismissively. "If you believe that sort of thing. No doubt Bainbridge and his young protégé are having a whale of a time."

I laughed, finding myself beginning to relax. It was good to hear that Bainbridge was keeping active, even if his present investigation sounded somewhat bizarre.

"So, Mr. Holmes, I understand from Newbury that you have an interest in Seaton's spectrograph machine?" said Angelchrist.

"Although your reputation would suggest that you are not, yourself, a dabbler in arcane matters. Unless your time in Sussex has served to change your mind, of course?"

"Indeed not," said Holmes. "I fear I do not put great stock in those things that cannot be properly observed. Faith, to me, is a form of blind weakness, and although I am aware of the comfort it can offer others of a more... *spiritual* persuasion, I put my confidence in empirical evidence and logic."

Angelchrist grinned. "Then what, if I may be so bold, is your interest in Seaton's work?"

"It's related to a case we're investigating," I said. "The apparent suicide of Herbert Grange. You might have read about it in the papers?"

"Read about it?" said Angelchrist. "You haven't been able to move in London's political circles without hearing all kinds of salacious gossip about the poor fellow."

"Did you know him?" asked Holmes.

"A little," confirmed Angelchrist. "I've seen him here a few times."

"Was he good friends with Lord Foxton?" said Holmes.

"I don't believe so. He seemed to me like one of those chaps who are always on the periphery. Invited along because of his position, but had very little to say. Still, I understand he was a great proponent of change and reformation, and I'm all for that," replied Angelchrist. He sipped at his drink. "Perhaps that's why Foxton took to him. What's that got to do with Seaton, though?"

"Perhaps nothing," said Holmes. "We found some of Mr. Underwood's photographs at Grange's house, and consulted Sir Maurice as to their purpose. He suggested we come along and see the machine for ourselves."

"Ah," said Angelchrist, with a sly wink. "I'd wager he's looking for a little demonstration himself. I showed him my own photographs and his eyes veritably lit up."

"You've participated?" I said, surprised.

"Oh, I think you'll find most of the men in the room have given it a go in recent months. It's a jolly good parlour game, that is all, although a word to the wise – don't let Seaton hear you say that. To him, it's a deadly serious business…" Angelchrist appeared momentarily distracted, peering over my shoulder at something or someone behind me. "Ah, Lord Foxton?" he called. "A moment of your time?"

I turned to see a stately looking man of around fifty, who'd clearly been walking past and had come to a stop at the sound of Archibald's voice. He was lithe for his age and dressed in an immaculate black suit. His dark hair was swept back from his forehead, with a light dusting of grey at the temples.

"Hello, Archibald," said Foxton. "Good to see you. Now, this must be Mr. Holmes." To Holmes's evident surprise, Foxton clasped him heartily on the shoulder. "How very good to meet you. I've long been an admirer of your methods. I hope you have no objection, but I've taken the liberty of placing you beside me at dinner. I'm keen to hear more about your work."

"I'd be delighted," said Holmes, most graciously.

Foxton turned on the spot, extending his hand. "And correct me if I'm wrong, but you must be Dr. Watson?"

"Quite so," I said, taking his hand.

"You're most welcome," said Foxton, with a broad, genuine grin. "It's not often I have such interesting guests." He lowered his voice to a conspiratorial whisper, leaning closer. "It'll be nice to have something other than business to discuss, for a change."

"Mr. Holmes is terribly interested in Seaton's machine," said Angelchrist. "He's seen some of the photographs the boy's produced, and I gather they've rather snared his interest." Angelchrist glanced at Holmes, a wry smile on his lips. "Is there any chance, you think, that we might be able to persuade Seaton to offer up a little demonstration?"

"Of course, gentlemen!" said Foxton enthusiastically. "I'm sure Seaton would be only too happy to demonstrate his machine. In fact, I'd wager he'd be grateful of a new audience. Most of the chaps here have already seen it, and he's short of willing subjects." He looked from me to Holmes. "In fact, why don't I show you through now? That way you can talk to Seaton all you want before dinner, and then afterwards I won't feel bad about monopolising your time."

"Perfect," said Holmes.

"I'll keep Percy here company in the meanwhile," said Angelchrist, with the considered sigh of a martyr, "so that you and Newbury can take a proper look at the machine."

"My thanks," I said. I could see just how much of a sacrifice he was making – Newbury had been backed up against the window, and looked as if he were about to lift the sash and dive through at any moment. I watched as Angelchrist expertly manoeuvred himself into the conversation and allowed Newbury to withdraw.

"Right, gentlemen," said Foxton, when we'd gathered a moment later. "Seaton has a workshop on the other side of the house. This way." He set off in the direction of the main hallway.

I followed behind, glancing over my shoulder to see Angelchrist already deep in conversation with Cranston, his expression reminiscent of a startled deer.

CHAPTER EIGHT

Underwood's rooms comprised a series of three interlinked chambers in the east wing of the house, set apart from rest of the manor. As we entered through a side door, following behind Foxton, it became abundantly clear why. Their appearance was quite extraordinary.

What had once been Raventhorpe's second drawing room or study had become… well, it was difficult to describe. The place was positively bursting with ephemera.

Bookcases lined two of the walls, but had long ago been filled beyond their intended capacity, and had since begun to disgorge themselves, giving rise to heap after heap of leather-bound tomes and pamphlets on every waypoint in the paranormal and mystical sphere: mesmerism, magnetism, spiritualism, hypnotism, transmigration of spirits, the art of the medium, and many other queer and arcane subjects. There were also substantial volumes on physics, chemistry and the organic sciences. A large globe sat in one corner, partially obscured by a red velvet drape. A human skeleton was wired up on a frame just inside the doorway, staring forlornly at us as we filed into the room, and at least five or six colourful birds hopped around in assorted cages, some hanging from the ceiling, others propped on tables or stands.

Most unusually, the windows had been plastered over with pages and pages of scrawled notes, diagrams and photographs, some of them now terribly faded and illegible from their exposure to the sun. The light was provided by a series of electric floor lamps, placed at random intervals around the room.

It seemed to me more like a lair than a place of scientific endeavour, although in many ways I was reminded of those hazy days at Baker Street, and the proliferation of Holmes's books, notes, specimens and chemistry equipment which had cluttered up the place. Underwood's rooms had the same sort of chaotic, obsessive quality that can only be born of years of dedication to a cause. The main difference was that Underwood had expanded to fill the space afforded to him by virtue of living at a manor house.

A thin, gangly man, with sandy hair – whom I took to be Underwood – was hunched over a small upright desk, peering into the lens of a microscope. He was wearing a stained white shirt, which had come untucked from his trousers and was hanging loose around his waist. He looked dishevelled and somewhat wild.

"Gentlemen, I'm delighted to present my ward, Seaton Underwood," said Foxton.

Underwood looked up, and the expression of displeasure on his face was impossible to miss. Despite Foxton's claims to the contrary, he was clearly not grateful for being disturbed in the midst of his studies. He surveyed us quickly, and then returned his attention to his microscope.

Foxton gave a polite cough, and Underwood, clearly in deference to Foxton's wishes, got up from where he was sitting and came over to greet us.

"Gentlemen," he said, with a forced smile. His voice was thin and reedy, and he had the look about him of a man who had seen very little daylight in recent weeks. His flesh was pale, and his eyes were bruised pits, dark and unseemly. I'd seen men of this countenance many times during my years as a medical man, and I would not have been surprised to discover he was a habitual abuser of laudanum.

I glanced at Newbury – a man I knew to have previously indulged in such filthy habits – and the look on his face told me that he agreed with my evaluation. Holmes, no doubt, would have already deduced the same.

Foxton introduced us, and explained to Underwood that we were interested in seeing a demonstration of his spectrograph generator.

"Ah, yes. More parlour games," said Underwood, bitterly.

"I assure you, Mr. Underwood, that I have more than a passing interest in the work you are doing here, and have little time for parlour games," said Newbury, smoothly stepping in and redirecting the conversation. "My name is Sir Maurice Newbury."

Underwood's eyes seemed to light up in recognition. "How interesting," he said. "I am aware of your work, Sir Maurice."

"And I yours, Mr. Underwood," replied Newbury. Underwood smiled, his mood clearly softened by Newbury's masterful flattery. I glanced at Holmes, whose expression was giving little away. "I've seen the results of your labours, Mr. Underwood – prints of your 'spectrographs' – and was hopeful you might spare us a moment for a demonstration. My friends and I," he turned to us, indicating Holmes and me with a wave of his hand, "would be most grateful."

"Yes, yes, of course," said Underwood, suddenly animated. "If you'd like to come this way." He ushered us around a long table covered in photographic prints – which I now knew to be spectrographs – and through an open door into an adjoining chamber.

Here the clutter was less apparent, but the eccentricity continued. Two bookcases lined the far wall, also overflowing with mouldering volumes. Heavy velvet curtains had been pulled across the windows, causing the room to be cast in a sort of perpetual gloaming, with only a single electric lamp to light the expansive room.

A camera rested on a tripod beside a wooden table, piled high with jars of chemicals, processing trays, papers and – to my immediate surprise – an amber paperweight, identical in every way to the ones we had seen in both Baxter's and Grange's offices. I kept my own counsel for the time being, knowing that Holmes would have already seen it, too. Surely this implied an even stronger connection between Underwood and Grange than the photographs we had found at Grange's house.

"This is the machine itself," said Underwood, proudly, indicating his creation with a wave of his hand. "My spectrograph generator." I turned to regard it. The machine comprised a sturdy wooden chair, roughly hewn, with an assemblage of hoops and wires affixed to it, standing before a black fabric backcloth. It looked disturbingly like the electric chairs used in the United States to execute criminals.

"Remarkable," said Newbury, with genuine interest. He crossed to the machine, peering closely at the workings. I hung back, along with Foxton and Holmes, who seemed happy to allow Newbury to lead the questioning, at least for the time being.

"If you'd care to take a seat, Sir Maurice, I will gladly give you a demonstration," said Underwood, crossing to his camera rig.

Newbury shook his head. "I'd find it much more interesting to observe, if it's all the same," he said. He glanced over at us. "How about you, Dr. Watson? Would you be willing to serve as our guinea pig?"

"Me?" I exclaimed, a trifle too loudly. "Well… I…" I stammered.

"An excellent suggestion, Sir Maurice," said Holmes, stepping in quickly before I was able to recover my wits and talk my way out of it.

"Oh, very well," I said, feeling less than enthusiastic.

"Nothing to fear, Dr. Watson. Seaton has had me in that chair numerous times over the last year," said Foxton. His cavalier tone revealed that he did not take the matter as seriously as Underwood did. Yet there was also a note of disapproval in his voice.

Underwood approached me, looking me up and down as if sizing me up. "This way, Dr. Watson," he said. He ushered me toward the machine, and I could feel the childlike excitement positively dripping off him. "I prefer to work with my subjects alone," he said. "I do not usually admit spectators. To capture a person's essence is a most serious business, and I find it best to avoid distractions of any kind. Optimal results are achieved when the subject is fully engaged." While I kept silent, I couldn't help but be extremely grateful that I wasn't going to undertake this experiment with only this strange young man for company.

I spent a few moments examining the strange device but couldn't make any sense out of it. There were all manner of odd mechanical and electrical components fixed to the back of the thickset wooden chair, connected to three wire hoops. It looked somehow primitive and incredibly sophisticated all at once, and most definitely the product of a disturbed mind.

"Just take a seat there," he said, "while I set up the tripod."

I glanced at Holmes, feeling more than a little sheepish, but Holmes nodded, encouraging me to continue. Newbury was standing beside him, clearly fascinated, watching Underwood's every move.

With a shrug, I climbed in amongst the metal hoops and took a seat. It was damned uncomfortable, and the roughly hewn wood scratched at my lower back through my jacket.

Underwood busied himself setting up the camera and tray and then, with a beaming smile, he rushed over, flicked a switch on the machine and turned off the floor lamp. We were thrust into darkness.

The machine issued a weird electrical hum, like the buzzing of some malign insect, and then the metal hoops began to vibrate around me. I felt a tingling sensation, as if someone was attempting to tease the hair from my scalp. It grew in intensity, and I squirmed, seriously considering getting up out of the chair.

Just as it was about to become unbearable, there was a sudden explosion of light as Underwood took his photographs, and then he hurried over, flicked the switch on the chair and turned the lights on again.

I blinked, trying to clear the temporary stains of light from my retina.

"Got you," said Underwood, as he took my arm and helped me out from the guts of the bizarre machine. I was feeling a little queasy by this point and stumbled, unsteady on my feet. Underwood caught me and guided me to another chair, mumbling something about "momentary disorientation".

He went off to fiddle with the camera, promising that he'd return shortly with the developed plate.

Newbury and Holmes were at my side almost immediately.

"How do you feel, Dr. Watson?" asked Newbury, enthusiastically.

"Wretched!" I said, rubbing at the top of my head. It was still tingling, as if I had a bad dose of pins and needles in my scalp. "It's like being eaten alive by a swarm of ants."

"The sensation will pass in just a moment," said Foxton, from over Newbury's shoulder. "You'll suffer no ill effects. And trust me, it will be quite a souvenir that Seaton is producing for you."

"It's most intriguing," said Holmes. "What does the machine actually do?"

"Agitates the spirit," mumbled Underwood. I saw he had his head and shoulders beneath a velvet cowl, as he hunched over the table, developing the print. "So that it may be photographed."

"It certainly *feels* agitated," I said ruefully. "I've felt nothing like it in all my years."

Newbury laughed. "I admit, I find myself quite anxious to see the results."

Holmes pressed his point. "Agitates the spirit? By what means?"

Underwood gave an audible sigh. "One cannot reveal all of one's secrets, Mr. Holmes," he said. "But if you must know, the machine generates a magnetic aura at a very specific frequency, which interacts with the psychical field surrounding one's physical form." Underwood straightened up, casting his velvet shroud aside with a flourish. He was holding a print between a pair of metal tongs. The paper was curled and still dripping with solution. He pinned it to a line of string above his head, which I'd failed to notice earlier due to the dim light. "Additionally, I have employed certain… ritualistic elements into my construction of the device, drawing on the practices of an obscure druidic tribe. Together, these elements ensure the continued success of the process. It has taken me many years of constant iteration and refinement to achieve such success."

Holmes sniffed, but said nothing.

I could see that a smudged image was beginning to emerge on the print. I got to my feet, feeling a little steadier, and crossed to where Underwood was standing, looking up at the photograph.

"Good Lord," I exclaimed, "I look quite dreadful." Unlike Grange, who had appeared notably serene and unmoved in his photographs, I was wearing a comical grimace. It was clear for all to see just how uncomfortable I'd been.

As I watched the picture resolve, however, I was struck by the appearance of a series of colourful smears around my head and shoulders. These gaseous shapes were vibrant in colour – pink, green and violet – and appeared to completely encircle my head, like a Byzantine halo.

"How remarkable," I said. It was clear to me that the camera had picked up something that the naked eye had been unable to see. Quite how it had been achieved, however, was a complete mystery.

I sensed Holmes standing beside me. "Tell me, Mr. Underwood, what, in your opinion, do these colourful striations represent?" said Holmes.

"I believe them to be a true representation of a human soul," replied Underwood. "More specifically, in this instance, the soul of Dr. Watson, presented in all its myriad aspects so that it might be properly catalogued and measured." He paused, eyeing us each in turn. "It is my life's work, gentlemen. It is proof positive that the soul exists independently of the body."

It was a beguiling notion, and – if it could be proved – utterly revolutionary. What did it mean for all of those loved ones we'd lost over the years, such as Joseph, so recently deceased? Not since my early school days had I given any credence to the notion that a person's soul might live on outside the confines of the physical body.

This photograph, however, I could not explain. The colourful markings had appeared as if of their own accord.

"Impressive, is it not?" said Foxton.

"Exceedingly," I said.

"Mr. Underwood, might I enquire as to whether you've performed any similar experiments using animals as test subjects?" enquired Newbury.

"Indeed I have," replied Underwood. "A dog, a cat, and any number of species of bird."

"And your findings?" prompted Newbury.

"Inconclusive," said Underwood. "Although I must add that none of the beasts subjected to the machine have generated a spectrograph. I intend to carry out further tests, but if I was to speculate, I would suggest that it only works on human beings."

A gong sounded elsewhere in the house, announcing the

imminent arrival of dinner. It was late, and I was surprised to note just how hungry I was.

"Ah," said Foxton. "I fear I must drag you away to less diverting matters." He started toward the door.

Holmes extended his hand to Underwood. "Thank you, Mr. Underwood, for your time. It has been most… enlightening," he said.

"Indeed," agreed Newbury. "Fascinating."

I nodded my agreement.

"You are most welcome," said Underwood, with a short bow.

"Now, gentlemen, I fear I must hurry you," said Foxton. "I've ignored my other guests for too long, and Brown will be fussing over dinner arrangements." He glanced at Underwood. "We'll talk later, Seaton," he said.

Underwood nodded and turned his back on us, staring up at my picture, hanging alone on the line. I felt a shiver pass along my spine, and went after the others, hurrying to catch up.

Dinner was a pleasant affair, which passed in a blur of fine food, red wine and the companionship of both Newbury and Angelchrist. I was delighted to find myself sitting between them, and they spent the evening regaling me with tales of their exploits back at the turn of the century, when they'd both been working for different agencies – Newbury for the Crown and Angelchrist for the government – but insisted on pooling their resources and secretly working together, along with Bainbridge and Newbury's assistant Miss Hobbes.

I was treated to talk of rampaging terror birds, creatures in the sewers, diabolical doctors and terrorist plots. The stories, I gathered, must have grown in the telling, as the London they described was a far cry from the one I remembered. Newbury expounded a theory on this very subject, however, explaining how the city of London was, in fact, a different place to each and every individual who walked her streets, that her intricacies were hidden in the way she was perceived, and that the city responded to each person accordingly, divulging her true nature only to those who knew how to look. By this time, however, I'd imbibed far too much wine, and the implications of his theory were quite lost on me.

I admit that for the first time in many months, I was able to relax and enjoy myself, putting all thoughts of the war, and of Joseph, out of mind – at least for a few hours.

Holmes spent the rest of the evening deep in discussion with Foxton, who seemed a jovial, generous host, and genuinely interested in hearing more of Holmes's methods, and as the evening drew on, even his theories on the hive intelligence of bees.

Percy Cranston had made friends – and I use the term most loosely – amongst a group of merchant bankers, and had settled at the other end of the long dining table, mercifully out of earshot.

Seaton Underwood was nowhere to be seen, and I gathered the young man must have taken his repast in his rooms.

As the evening wore on and people began to peel away, I found my thoughts turning to home, and was only too happy to accept the offer of a lift from Newbury, who explained that he had his automobile parked in the driveway. Angelchrist made his excuses and left with two other men, and I gathered from his sudden change in demeanour that he still had business of some sort to attend to. I admired his dedication, as well as his stamina. I was ready for very little save for my bed.

We gave our thanks to Lord Foxton for his hospitality and bid him goodnight, and after Brown had retrieved our coats, made our way out into the crisp night. The cold breeze was reviving, although it had the effect of reminding me quite how much wine I'd enjoyed with my dinner.

I settled into the back seat of Newbury's sleek-looking

motorcar, and found that even my usual trepidation around such vehicles was dispelled.

Holmes took the passenger seat, while Newbury slipped into the driver's seat a moment later. He turned the key in the ignition, gunned the accelerator, and we slid away along the driveway, the headlamp cutting a narrow beam through the darkness.

"Well, Holmes?" I said, once we'd passed through the gates at the edge of the estate, purring out onto the road that would take us back toward the city.

"A most enlightening evening," said Holmes. "Did you note, Watson, the rather conspicuous presence of an amber paperweight, marked with a five-pointed star?"

"I did," I confirmed. "Resting on a pile of books, close to that infernal contraption."

"Quite so," said Holmes. "Tell me – what do you make of Underwood's so-called 'spectrograph generator'?"

"Truthfully, I am at a loss," I said. "I find it difficult to assess the veracity of his claims. Difficult to believe them, too. Yet…" I paused for a moment, trying to articulate my sentiment, "Yet without further evidence, I cannot be sure either way." I sighed. "They're probably just hokum. Parlour games, just like Foxton intimated."

"And you, Sir Maurice?" said Holmes.

I saw Newbury eyeing at me in the rear-view mirror. "I found it quite remarkable, Mr. Holmes, for many reasons – the sheer invention on display, the vibrancy of those colours he's achieved in his prints – yet I cannot bring myself to draw the same conclusions as Mr. Underwood. Whatever those vaporous structures are in his pictures, I am sceptical they represent a schematic of the human soul."

Holmes nodded, but said nothing. We burred along the road, heading toward the distant lights of London.

*   *   *

Newbury dropped us back in Ealing a short while later, wishing us a good night. I offered him a nightcap, but he seemed as anxious as I was for bed, and suggested I telephone him in a day or two when we'd had time to pursue our other leads. We waved him off from the gate as he roared away down the street.

"So, you remain unconvinced that the spectrographs are connected to Grange's death?" I said, as I turned my key in the lock and bustled into the house. Holmes stepped in behind me, draping his coat over the end of the banister.

"To speculate is to commit the worst of follies, Watson," replied Holmes. "I need more data before I am able to assemble a full picture."

"But you do believe that Grange was somehow involved with both Underwood and Baxter, and indeed, that they are similarly involved with one another?" I said. "Surely the photographs and the paperweight are evidence enough of that."

"I do not doubt there is a connection," said Holmes, "nor that Grange was part of *something* – although I do not believe he was directly involved in whatever devilry has gripped young Underwood. There is much still to be considered. For a start, the question remains: why is Mycroft so interested in the fate of this one man, Grange?"

"Couldn't you simply ask him?" I ventured.

"I fear not. To do so would only risk damaging whatever subtle web he is weaving. No, we need to play our part, and trust that Mycroft can look after his own." Holmes entered the drawing room and, in the pale moonlight that was pouring in through the open curtains, searched out his pipe and tobacco pouch. I foresaw a night of deep contemplation ahead.

"Subtle web?" I ventured.

Holmes nodded. "There's a reason my brother brought us into this matter in the way that he did, painting a picture of three unexplained suicides, and talking of his fears for the spirit of the nation. To bring him into it now might disrupt the intended outcome of his plans."

I shook my head. "I've never been able to understand your relationship with your brother, Holmes. It seems darned odd to me that a man can't simply pick up a telephone and ask a simple question."

Holmes laughed, throwing back his head and causing me to flush hotly with embarrassment. "Oh, my dear Watson," he said, after a moment. "It is not a matter of what information Mycroft may or may not be in a position to divulge, but more a case of what *he* needs of *us*. If we were to discern from him the other fragments of this puzzle at this delicate stage in our investigation, we risk altering our behaviour, and therefore unduly affecting the behaviour of the other players. Be under no pretence, Watson: lies, secrets and duplicity are at the heart of this matter. We must trust no one, save for our own council."

I sighed. Clearly, whatever game was being played here was somewhat beyond me. "A subtle web indeed," I said, resignedly. I resolved to leave the politicking to Holmes.

"Then what next? Surely that paperweight represents a clear line of enquiry?"

"Quite so, Watson," replied Holmes. "I think it would serve us well to clarify the connection, if any, between Baxter and Underwood. You may recall Baxter's words to us at the bank, Watson – that his relationship with Lord Foxton was most definitely one of 'acquaintance and not friendship'. I cannot help but wonder if there is more to that than Baxter would have us know."

"What do you suggest?"

"That we get closer to Baxter, observe his movements," said Holmes. "A great deal can be learned about a man through the careful study of his habits."

"Very well," I said. "Until tomorrow, then, Holmes. I fear my bed is calling to me."

Holmes struck a match, carefully lighting his pipe. "Good night, Watson," he said, between puffs. He settled back into my armchair, closing his eyes, his pipe clenched between his teeth.

I observed him for a moment, considering how good it was to see him after all this time, and then, smiling, I quit the room, pulling the door closed behind me.

CHAPTER NINE

The next morning I allowed myself to lounge in bed for a while, whilst Holmes pottered around the house. I heard him in the kitchen, clattering pots and cursing. The shrill whistle of the kettle followed this, and then, a short while later the front door opened and closed, and I realised he'd gone out.

I rose, saw to my ablutions, and dressed. As I had discerned, Holmes was nowhere to be seen, and an empty teacup rested on the coffee table beside my old, comfortable armchair. I sank into it for a few moments, considering the morning ahead of me.

Today was the day of Carter's hastily arranged funeral. Mycroft – being the brother who, of the two siblings, had at least a modicum of empathy – had sent word, correctly surmising that I would wish to pay my respects.

Holmes, it seemed, had other plans, although as to what they were, he had not enlightened me.

I could not be angry with him for very long, however. I knew more than most that he found engagement with the real world a troublesome business. Indeed, I believe that his desire for solitude was the real motive behind his relocation to rural Sussex, despite his protestations to the contrary. His fascination with his bees was genuine enough, of course – his monographs were a testament to that – but his retirement was also a symptom of his need to retreat from the world at large. I remember thinking, on that day he first informed me of his plans to retire, that he had simply had enough of London and her errant children. I couldn't, in all honesty, blame him.

Whatever the case, Holmes was not a man who engaged in society, so much as observed it from the periphery. Of course, this played to his advantage in so many ways, allowing him to adopt an aloof, uninvolved perspective when involved in a case, or to question those attitudes that appeared so natural to the casual observer, but might prove crucial in getting to the bottom of a mystery. Only, such a perspective brought with it a terrible curse, for Holmes was perpetually on the outside of life, and never quite able to come in.

I glanced at the carriage clock on the mantel. It was approaching ten o'clock, but despite having not eaten since early the previous evening, I found I had no appetite. My mind kept on returning to thoughts of young Joseph, and I couldn't help but wonder – what if Seaton Underwood was right? What if the human soul really *was* capable of existing independently of the physical body? Could that mean that somewhere my nephew was at peace, having left his corporeal existence far behind him?

As a medical man, and after long years at Holmes's elbow, I have always valued empirical evidence over blind faith in such matters. Now, however, presented with something *akin* to evidence, I had begun to wonder. Had I been wrong all these years? The notion offered me the slightest glimmer of comfort. It was attractive to consider that Underwood's spectrographs might have some veracity, that for those whose names filled the casualty lists day after day, there might be something beyond the finality of a bullet.

Framing my thoughts in such a way helped me to brave the morning's endeavours, and so, after forcing myself to eat a slice of toast and marmalade, I changed into my formal attire and left for St. Bartholomew's church, where the service was to be held.

Carter's funeral passed without incident, and while it was a rather humble affair, the eulogy was delivered with great respect by the minister. Mycroft's office had provided a truly spectacular wreath, and while I had thought Mycroft himself might have put in an appearance, it was clear he was engaged with other matters.

In many ways I felt like an interloper at the graveside, being the only mourner who was not a member of the boy's family, but a word with his mother at the close of the ceremony made everything clear – Carter's young friends were all far away in France, busy with their own struggles of life and death.

I returned home feeling more morose than ever, to find Holmes had once again taken up residence beside the fireplace. He was puffing on his pipe, and he looked up when I entered the room. "Ah, Watson. I trust you gave the family our best regards?"

"I did, Holmes," I said. "Although I am unsure whether they really heard my platitudes. It is a universal truth that no parent should be forced to outlive their children." I sighed, crossing the room to switch on the lamp by the window.

"You are a good man, Watson," said Holmes. "Better than most." I stared at him, speechless, waiting for him to qualify his statement with the expected barb. It did not come. "Do not allow the misery of this world to encroach any further upon your good nature," he went on. "It would be a grave loss indeed. We may yet have need of your fortitude."

"I… I…" I started. "Well, thank you, Holmes," I said, finally finding my words. "I can't tell you how much that means to me." I coughed, disguising a sudden, unseemly show of emotion. I had never once heard him compliment me in such a fashion.

Holmes waved the stem of his pipe in my direction. "Good, good, Watson. Then perhaps," he said, "you might see to another pot of tea while you're about. We must fortify ourselves before the evening's pursuits." He looked up at me expectantly.

"By George," I said, laughing. "You don't change, Holmes."

"See to it that I might yet say the same of you, Watson," he replied, as I slipped my jacket off and headed to the kitchen.

"So, this is what you were up to all morning, Holmes," I said, blowing into my cupped hands for warmth.

It was around five o'clock in the afternoon that same day, and Holmes and I were lurking on a street corner in Belgravia, carrying out a clandestine surveillance of the home of Henry Baxter. I was wearing only a light suit, and the breeze was up, the air unseasonably cold. I longed for my gloves, or better still, the warmth of my fire. My old war injury had begun to play up in the cold, and so I'd brought my walking stick along with me to lean upon.

Holmes smiled. "Quite so, Watson. I was able to develop a clear picture of Baxter's early morning routine." He looked pleased with himself. "He rises around seven thirty, washes and shaves, and takes his breakfast in his dressing gown at eight. Following this, he opens the morning post, brought to him on a silver platter by his valet. He then dresses. At a quarter to nine his driver brings the motorcar around to the front of the house, and Baxter leaves for the short drive to Tidwell Bank."

I sighed. "You're going to have to explain to me, Holmes, what possible use this information might be. It sounds like a perfectly normal morning routine for a well-to-do businessman."

"Ah, yes, Watson. But that, in itself, tells us something, does it not?" said Holmes, tapping his chin with his index finger.

"And what would that be?" I asked. I fear I was feeling somewhat perturbed, having been dragged out for an evening of standing around, spying on people, and was taking my crotchety mood out on Holmes. I was getting too old for this sort of business, and my bones were beginning to ache.

"Now, Watson," continued Holmes, apparently oblivious to my curmudgeonly demeanour, "I'd wager the hour is near." He turned to regard the house. He did not elaborate any further, and I decided not to press the point. We were here, and we had a job to do. I might not like it, but I would see it done. I studied the building, attempting to discern anything of interest.

Quillcroft House was an ostentatious sort of place, recently built to the modern design. It was a detached residence, standing in a small but well-tended plot. Two rather pretentious stone lions lounged atop the gateposts, eyeing unwary visitors.

The curtains of the upper windows were open but there was no sign of movement. The downstairs windows revealed nothing more than the occasional glimpse of a passing housemaid.

I blew into my cold hands again, waited, and watched.

Half an hour passed. I was still feeling the cold, and beginning to wish that I'd remembered to bring my trusty old hipflask along with me, when we saw a sleek motorcar come rattling down the road and pull up outside the house. It was a smart, distinctive model in racing green, with white trim around the windows.

We both ducked lower, anxious to remain out of sight.

The vehicle's door opened, and a man whom I immediately recognised as Baxter stepped down from the footplate. He thanked the driver, slammed the door, and the machine purred away, leaving a trail of oily exhaust fumes behind it.

Baxter glanced from left to right, and then opened his front gate and passed through, allowing it to swing shut behind him. Moments later, he had disappeared inside the house.

"Well, that was worth waiting for," I muttered sarcastically.

Holmes – who had moved us into the neighbouring garden and was crouched behind a conifer – shushed me and waved his hand for me to stay down.

"Very well," I whispered, returning to my stooped, uncomfortable position beside him. "But I'm not sure how much longer I can put up with this, Holmes. It's a rum state of affairs, a younger man's game. Couldn't we have some of Foulkes's men out here, keeping an eye on the place and reporting back to us with the details?"

I glanced at Holmes. If he'd heard my brief tirade he showed no sign of it. He was utterly absorbed in his observation of the house and street.

"Holmes," I said, "Holmes?"

"Look, Watson," he said, ignoring me and pointing toward the other end of the street. A lone figure was walking in our direction, on the other side of the road. He was a dark-haired man, tall and thin and wearing a long raincoat, the collar of which was turned up, obscuring much of his lower face. He walked with a slight stoop.

Holmes and I waited in silence, watching as the man drew steadily closer. The man seemed familiar. I squinted, attempting to discern his features – and then it struck me. I *had* seen him before. "Is that…?" I whispered.

"Yes, Watson," replied Holmes, the words barely audible on his breath. "It's Seaton Underwood."

"Well, I'll be," I muttered.

Underwood stopped at the gate to Baxter's house and,

parroting Baxter's earlier ritual, glanced in both directions along the street before opening the gate and walking to the front door. He rapped loudly three times and stood back, stamping his feet on the bottom step.

A few moments later the door opened, and an elderly woman – whom I took to be Baxter's housekeeper – opened the door and permitted him entry.

"Well," I said, straightening my back, "that's an unexpected development. Proof positive that there's a connection between the two men, just as you suggested. I wonder what the devil they're up to?"

"What the devil indeed," said Holmes, with a sly look.

"What now?" I asked, hopeful that, with this new development, Holmes had all he needed to cogitate on our next course of action, preferably from the comfort of my armchair back in Ealing.

"I have a suspicion, Watson, that it won't be long until they're on the move," said Holmes. "If they leave together, we must follow them and discover their destination. It could be vital."

"Very well," I said, containing a sigh. I could see Holmes was onto something, and I admit, I was as anxious now to see the matter through as he was.

Around twenty minutes later, just as I was beginning to grow impatient, two figures emerged from the house. They both had their collars turned up, but it was easy enough to see that it was Baxter and Underwood, leaving together just as Holmes had anticipated they might.

Beside me, Holmes stirred. I glanced at him, and he put a finger to his lips. He crept along the length of the garden hedge, peering over the top at the two figures as they exchanged a few indecipherable words and set off, taking a right turn at the bottom of Baxter's garden path.

We waited a few moments and started after them, trailing at

a reasonable distance. We kept to what shadows there were on a summer's evening, hanging back from our quarry.

The two men walked side by side, deep in conversation, but they talked in hushed tones, and aside from the occasional burst of laughter, I was unable to hear any of what passed between them.

We followed them for about a mile through the quiet streets, which grew steadily busier the closer we came to Knightsbridge. Most of the men we passed were office workers, slowly drifting home from their jobs in the City, wearing hassled expressions and lugging briefcases under their arms. The occasional automobile or carriage rumbled by, but Baxter and Underwood paid them no heed. They were tracing a familiar route, I realised, comfortable in each other's company and falling into a regular, steady rhythm. They seemed unconcerned that anyone might be following them. All of this, I knew, was a sure sign that they had walked these streets together many times before.

Up ahead, Baxter and Underwood turned a corner and Holmes waved for me to hurry. We dashed after them, rushing along the side of a large hotel. I was fearful that we might lose them in the street, or that they might take an unseen turn into an alleyway or building.

As it transpired, the two men were still within view when I reached the corner, and what was more, were standing outside a familiar building: the entrance to Tidwell Bank.

Baxter was fishing in his pocket for a ring of keys, which he withdrew a moment later. He selected one and opened the front door and entered, beckoning Underwood inside. He then proceeded to lock the door behind him.

Holmes waited for a moment, and then beckoned me on. We strolled hurriedly past the building, glancing in through the barred windows as we walked. Inside the bank the lights remained off, and there was no sign of either Baxter or Underwood.

We paused at the other end of the street, huddling into a brief conference.

"What the devil are they doing visiting the bank at this hour?" I said.

Holmes consulted his pocket watch. He showed me the dial. It was approaching seven o'clock. "I have a suspicion, Watson, that the answer to that question will provide the insight we need to get to the bottom of what truly happened to Herbert Grange."

"Then we should go after them?" I ventured. "Knock on the door until Baxter lets us in?"

Holmes shook his head. "We are unprepared for such a confrontation. No, I believe further investigation is required. Tomorrow, if you are willing, you might return to Ravensthorpe House and put a question to Lord Foxton, regarding Underwood's relationship to Baxter."

"Of course," I said. "And you, Holmes? Will you not come with me?"

Holmes shook his head. "Indeed not, Watson. I shall continue my observations of Baxter."

"Very well," I said.

"Good man, Watson," said Holmes. "Now, come. Let us take our leave. I'd wager there are others expected at the bank this evening, and it would not do for us to be seen. I do not wish to show our hand too early."

"That's the best idea you've had all night, Holmes," I replied, with feeling.

CHAPTER TEN

It felt a trifle strange returning to Ravensthorpe House so soon after my previous visit. Holmes, however, had insisted that I come alone. In his wisdom, he felt that Lord Foxton might be more disposed to elaborate on the relationship between Underwood and Baxter if the questions were put to him by – as Holmes put it – "a man of my mild disposition".

In truth, I suspected that Holmes was simply more concerned with the other plans that he had hinted at the previous evening. Nevertheless, this was not a new position in which I found myself – heading out alone on a mission to gather intelligence for Holmes – and the distraction was a welcome one.

I called ahead to ensure that Foxton would be able to see me that morning, and the old man, Brown, was most accommodating, explaining that if I was sure to call in the morning, rather than the afternoon, I should find Foxton available and happy to speak with me.

It was, of course, my intention also to speak again with Seaton Underwood. Holmes had tasked me with discovering whether

Underwood would admit to his evening rendezvous with Baxter, or would attempt to cover it up and provide himself with an alibi.

Upon the approach, the house looked just as splendid as it had the other night. However, as I drew closer, I began to realise my initial impressions had perhaps been a little coloured by the beautiful surroundings.

In the full light of day it was clear the building was more dilapidated than it had at first appeared. A number of the roof tiles were missing and a carpet of thick, green moss was making its presence felt, slowly subsuming the east wing like a hungry parasite. Mildew stained many of the upper windows in that part of the house, and it appeared largely uncared for and disused. Clearly, Foxton, Underwood and their servants now inhabited only a small part of the sprawling property.

Once, I would have given my eyeteeth to live in such splendour, regardless of the apparent disrepair. Now, though, I craved a more frugal existence. I had no need for such lavishness, nor for the associated difficulties it would bring. In all my years accompanying Holmes on his investigations, I had learned that such grand estates always came at a terrible price – the envy of others. Time and again, I had seen people do terrible things to one another for the slightest glimpse of a fortune.

My conveyance stuttered to a halt. Once again I had come via horse and carriage, and as I dropped down from the box, my feet crunching in the gravel, I saw Brown standing in the doorway.

I paid the driver and told him to park up and wait for me, then trudged up to the house. Brown greeted me in the portico. "Good morning, Dr., ah…"

"Watson," I said. "Dr. John Watson. We spoke on the telephone."

"Quite so, sir," replied Brown, carrying on as if I hadn't had to remind him. "Quite so. Lord Foxton is waiting for you in the library. May I take your coat?"

I handed it to him as we ambled sedately into the house.

"This way, sir," he said. He led me, once again, along the side of the staircase to where the passage narrowed, but this time took a sharp right into a further passage, and indicated a door on the left. "There you are, sir. Could I fetch you a drink?"

"A pot of tea would be most welcome," I said. "Thank you." Brown pottered off to make the necessary arrangements.

The door to the library was slightly ajar, and I rapped on it three times before pushing it open.

Foxton sat in a burgundy leather armchair, a book resting open upon his lap. He was dressed in a tweed suit, with a white shirt and mustard-coloured jumper beneath his jacket. He looked up and offered me a welcoming smile when he saw me hovering in the doorway. "Good day to you, Dr. Watson," he said. "This is an unexpected pleasure. Come in, come in."

The library was a most impressive room, filled to bursting point with books. Unlike Underwood's chaotic lair, however, this room was ordered and tidy. Foxton clearly had a system: his shelves were labelled, his books ordered by subject and author. It was a room clearly devised for a single purpose – to read in. There was no desk, no drinks cabinet, no other unwanted distractions. Aside from the books, the room contained only two armchairs and a small occasional table.

The smell of the musty old pages filled my nostrils, and I sighed appreciatively. "Ah, now this is a room I can approve of," I said, drinking it in.

Foxton laughed. "I think, if you looked carefully, Dr. Watson, you'd find a number of your own literary endeavours nestling amongst the others on the shelves."

I felt my cheeks flush with embarrassment. "Your support is much appreciated, Lord Foxton. It appears to be a superb collection."

Foxton sighed. "What is life about, Dr. Watson, if it is not about literature? To my mind, all else is a distraction. I should happily idle away the rest of my days in the company of a good book." He smiled. "Now, please, take a seat. I'll arrange for Brown to bring tea."

"Ah, no need," I said, somewhat self-conscious. "He's already seeing to it."

Foxton laughed. "Good old Brown. Ever efficient." He folded his book shut and placed it on the floor by his feet. I took a seat opposite him.

I could see now that Holmes had been correct in his assertion – Foxton and I did appear to be of a similar temperament.

"Now, tell me, Doctor – how may I be of assistance?" said Foxton. "Something to do with a case you're investigating, I presume?"

"Yes, I apologise if I was perhaps a little vague on the telephone, but I thought it best not to broadcast the reason for my visit to the rest of your household," I said.

Foxton frowned. He looked troubled. "Then am I to understand, Doctor, that your questions pertain directly to myself or my ward?"

I nodded. "Specifically, to the relationship between Mr. Underwood and Henry Baxter, of Tidwell Bank."

There was an immediate change in Foxton's demeanour at the mention of that name. His expression darkened, his eyes narrowed. "Ah," he said, and there was a palpable reluctance in his voice. "I had hoped I'd managed to nip that business in the bud." He fixed me with a look so intense that it felt as if his gaze was burrowing through me, such was his wish to underline his next point. "Mr. Henry Baxter is an odious wretch and he is not welcome in this house," he said, "or any other in which I might assert an influence."

I was about to press him further, but hesitated at the sound of a rattling tea tray from just outside the door.

"Come on in, Brown," called Foxton, and the elderly butler shouldered open the door and bustled in with the tray. The teacups bounced in their saucers and rattled noisily as a result of his tremor.

"Very good, sir." Brown set the tea tray down on the occasional table and made a hasty retreat from the room, pulling the door to behind him.

"Forgive me, Lord Foxton," I said, "but might I ask you to elaborate on your obvious distaste for Henry Baxter?"

Foxton ran a hand through his muss of silver-grey hair. "Well, yes, I suppose I must," he replied. "You see, it's all down to his relationship with Seaton."

"Relationship?" I queried.

"Such as it is." He sighed. "You must understand, Dr. Watson – Seaton is a very vulnerable young man. Are you aware of how he came into my care?"

"I am not," I said.

"It was fifteen years ago, now. My family, as you may or may not be aware, made its fortune in the woollen industry. We still own a number of mills in the Home Counties and the Midlands. Seaton's father was employed at one such mill. Philip Underwood was a good worker, a well-respected man, much liked by his peers. Handy with the machines, you see. The milling machines are prone to breaking down, and Underwood had a knack for fixing them.

"It was during one such episode," Foxton continued, "when production had been halted and one of the machines was jammed, that Underwood tried to mend it. Something went wrong – I've never been quite sure what – and he was killed as the machine started up again."

I winced at the thought of such a terrible death, although in itself, an accident in an industrial works was not uncommon. I'd heard similar stories a hundred times before.

"Underwood's wife, distraught, committed suicide a few days later. Seaton was only five years old – an orphan – and I felt responsible, you see?"

Foxton's eyes met mine, and I could see a genuine sadness in his expression. "I saw to it that the boy was placed in the care of a good local family, with an appropriate allowance. What else was there to do? I couldn't allow him to be sent to the orphanage. After all, it was my fault, *my* mill, which had taken his parents away from him. It was the least I could do."

"That's incredibly generous of you," I said. I admit I was surprised by Foxton's compassion. It seemed most progressive that a man in his position should even *care* about the orphan of a worker, let alone arrange to have the boy raised at his own expense. I could see now why Foxton had been such a prized acolyte of Asquith's during the recent welfare reforms.

"Of course, they told me I was mad – every one of them – that I couldn't blame myself for something unavoidable." Foxton shook his head. "Yet I proved them wrong. Given encouragement, the boy began to show an aptitude for science and mathematics. I arranged for his attendance at a good school, and when I heard talk of his abilities and dedication, I offered him a place here at the house during the holidays – somewhere he could continue his studies without pecuniary concerns."

"You became his sponsor?" I said.

"In a manner of speaking," confirmed Foxton. "I grew fond of the boy. We all did. I cared for him in the best way I could. I paid for his schooling, his upkeep, granted him an allowance. When he'd finished his studies he returned here to Ravensthorpe. In many ways he's lived a privileged life." He frowned. "None of that, however, can compensate for the fact he's had to grow up without a mother and father."

"The poor lad," I said, although in truth I also felt a deep sense of pity for Foxton himself, who had clearly been tormenting himself all these years for an accident that had been played out a hundred times since the growth of British industry.

"The thing is, Doctor," he said, "it left the boy scarred, impressionable; fragile, even. He's constructed his entire existence around the notion that, one day, he might be reunited with his late parents."

"It's a thought that comforts many," I said. "Christianity is predicated upon the notion."

"Yes, but belief in itself is not enough for Seaton. He wants proof. Thus his preoccupation with that damnable machine. He's fallen in with that spiritualist claptrap that seems all the rage these days. He's obsessed with the idea that the spirits of his dead parents live on – that if he can prove that the human soul truly can exist independently of the body, then he might also prove that his parents still exist in some non-corporeal form."

"How terribly sad," I offered. There was little else to be said.

"It is a sickness, I think," said Foxton, "for which there is no medicine."

I nodded, rendered mute by Foxton's unexpected openness and the strength of feeling behind his words.

"Right, tea then, Dr. Watson?" he said, deftly diverting the conversation before his emotions overwhelmed him.

"Yes, thank you," I said. "Most kind."

Foxton splashed a measure of the hot, brown liquid into a teacup and passed it to me. I saw to my own milk and sugar. "So, Baxter," I said, still hopeful that I might gain some insight into the reason for Baxter and Underwood's rendezvous the previous evening, "where does *he* fit in?"

"Baxter is a manipulator, out for what he can get," said Foxton. "He befriended Seaton during his visits to this house. He attended some of my parties, you see, before I knew him for the man he really is. He used the opportunity to ingratiate himself with my ward and encouraged him in his foolish pursuits."

"In what way?"

Foxton shrugged. "It seems Baxter believes all that rubbish. Before I knew it, he had Seaton attending séances and meetings in spiritualist circles. Seaton would return with his head full of nonsense, and as a consequence began to retreat further and further into himself. He no longer talked to me, and spent all of his time working on that machine, or reading books given to him by Baxter."

"What did you do?" I asked.

"The only thing I could. I confronted Baxter and told him he was no longer welcome here. I warned him that if he didn't sever all ties with Seaton then I would expose his little scam."

"His scam?"

"Oh yes, Dr. Watson. I'm sure that's what it was. I don't believe for a moment that the man was actually interested in Seaton and his work. Rather that he was using it as an opportunity to get closer to my inner circle and myself, to attempt to assert a political influence. Seaton is simply an unfortunate pawn in Baxter's game."

"I see," I said. I wasn't quite convinced by his logic – after all, filling a man's head with spiritualism seemed a rather roundabout way of getting closer to his benefactor – but I didn't want to interrupt Foxton's flow. "So tell me – as far as you are aware, has Seaton abided by your wishes? To stay away from Baxter, I mean."

"Absolutely," said Foxton. "He's had nothing to do with Baxter for months." I didn't have the heart to tell the man that just the previous evening, Holmes and I had witnessed quite the contrary.

"What is it that you suppose Baxter to have done?" asked Foxton suddenly, as I was taking a sip of my tea. "I understood from Professor Angelchrist that the case you were investigating was the unfortunate suicide of Herbert Grange. Is Baxter mixed up in all of that?"

"Perhaps," I said, a little guardedly.

"Angelchrist said something about murder?"

I hesitated, trying to decide how much to give away. "Holmes plays his cards very close to his chest, Lord Foxton, but as I see it, there is no question as to whether Herbert Grange committed suicide. The case is more to do with motive, and whether someone else was asserting an undue influence upon him."

Foxton nodded thoughtfully. "Well, as I explained, Doctor, Baxter is a manipulative man. It would not surprise me to discover he was blackmailing poor Herbert, or something to that effect."

I took another sip of my tea, taking it all in. The sheer contempt in which Foxton held Baxter told a story all of its own.

"You knew Grange, didn't you?" I asked.

"I did. He was a regular visitor here," replied Foxton. "A brave man, a force for good, pushing against the tide to fight for much-needed reform. Seaton was very fond of him. Grange's visits were some of the only times he could be encouraged out of those rooms of his. More than once I had to prise Grange away to introduce him to other guests."

"How interesting," I said. "Tell me, is Seaton here today? I should very much like to speak to him again."

"Alas, Dr. Watson, he's gone into town. Although I imagine he'll be back this afternoon. You're most welcome to stay and make yourself comfortable here with a good book." He smiled, throwing his arms wide to encompass the bookcases all around us.

"My thanks to you, Lord Foxton, but I fear I have a prior engagement this afternoon," I said. This was a half-truth, but I wished to return to Ealing to find Holmes and apprise him of what I had learned.

"Well, I will certainly make a point of telling him you called," said Foxton, "and you are most welcome to return to Ravensthorpe at any point that is convenient to you. Yourself and Mr. Holmes, of course."

"Thank you," I said. "For your hospitality, and for your frankness. You may rest assured that I will treat everything you have told me with the strictest confidence."

Foxton inclined his head. "I only hope I've been of some use."

"Oh, I'm sure of it," I said. I stood, and Foxton started to rise, but I held out my hand. "Please, don't disturb yourself. I can find my own way out."

Foxton nodded and held out his hand. I shook it firmly. "Good day to you, Lord Foxton."

"Good day, Dr. Watson."

Brown was industriously polishing silver in the entrance hall when I emerged from the passageway, and upon seeing me, downed his polish and rags and wordlessly loped off to fetch my coat. He returned a few moments later wearing a beaming smile. "I trust you got what you came for, Dr. Watson," he said, helping me on with my garment.

"Indeed I did. My thanks to you, Brown."

He nodded and returned to his work.

Feeling contemplative, and keen to get back to Holmes and outline all that I had heard, I hurried out to my waiting carriage.

CHAPTER ELEVEN

I returned home to find my sitting room in utter disarray.

The furniture had been completely rearranged, pushed back into the corners of the room to create a large space in the centre. A neat stack of notebooks had been overturned and now lay in a disorganised heap. A chair stood atop my desk, upon which my papers had been scattered haphazardly, and an inkwell upset. Dark blue ink dripped monotonously onto a large, stained area of carpet.

In the middle of the room was a new centrepiece, sitting proudly in the space that had been cleared: a large, oak travelling trunk.

Holmes, of course, was nowhere to be seen.

"Holmes!" I bellowed, incandescent with rage. "Holmes, are you here?"

There was no response.

I stormed from the sitting room to the kitchen, and then upstairs to the guest room. There was no sign of him. Furious, my fists bunched, I stomped back to the sitting room to examine the offending trunk.

It was old and battered, faded from years of use. The banding was wrought in black iron, and it was tied securely with a leather buckle.

Upon its gnarled surface was a folded note, tacked in place with a drawing pin. I tore it free, unfolded it and held it up to the light, mumbling to myself in consternation.

Watson,

I have arranged with a clerk from Tidwell Bank for this trunk to be collected at precisely three o'clock this afternoon. It is to be transported directly to the bank and placed in their vault as a matter of the utmost urgency. To ensure these instructions are carried out to the letter, a new account has today been established in your name. It is paramount that you escort the object to the said establishment and ensure it is deposited securely before the day is out. Do not leave until you have seen the trunk placed in the vault with your own eyes.

Following this, make arrangements to meet me outside of the bank at precisely quarter to seven this evening. I trust you will not delay.

Yours,

Holmes.

"Hmph!" I said. "Typical Holmes." Where in God's name had he happened upon such a decrepit old thing, and what was in it?

Despite my being perturbed at Holmes's presumptuousness, my interest was piqued. Whatever this was, it clearly had to be related to our investigation of Baxter. Why else should he make the arrangements to have the trunk deposited in Tidwell Bank, of all places?

Keen to know precisely what I was dealing with – and struck

by my innate sense of inquisitiveness – I unbuckled the leather straps and folded back the lid. It creaked on dry hinges.

Inside was a mountain of old, yellowed papers. I grabbed a handful and leafed through them, scanning a few lines on each page. They were brittle and covered in Holmes's scratchy handwriting, and appeared to be his notes on our old cases. I was half tempted to sit down and begin reading – I couldn't help but wonder whether Holmes's perception of events tallied with my own recollections and published accounts.

If it hadn't been for my suspicion that our investigation might hinge on the deposit of these papers at Tidwell Bank, I should have offered to store them for him in my own house. As it was, I knew that any failure on my part to follow Holmes's instructions to the letter might jeopardise our success.

I replaced the papers, closed the lid and secured the buckle.

The two men arrived from the bank promptly at three, as Holmes had outlined in his note. They were not, however, the clerks I had been expecting, but rather removal men in filthy blue overalls. Clearly, these fellows were employed by the bank to do the heavy lifting. By the look of them, I couldn't help wondering what, in Henry Baxter's case, "heavy lifting" might mean.

The chap who came to the door had a pugilist's face; battered and scarred, with a nose that had been broken numerous times and a fuzz of close-cropped blonde hair. He seemed to me to represent every cliché of a cockney strong-arm.

"Afternoon, guv'nor," he said, as I opened the door. "Dr. Watson, is it?"

"That is I," I said, perhaps a little imperiously.

"We've come to collect your shipment for Tidwell Bank. Large trunk, if I understand right?"

"That's right," I said. "You'd better come in."

Reluctantly, I showed the two men into my home, cursing Holmes beneath my breath. I'd taken a few moments to tidy the sitting room following his rather hasty rearrangement, but it was still an awful mess. "This is the trunk in question," I said. "It needs to be placed securely in the bank's vault."

The man nodded. "Oi, Reggie," he called to his colleague, who was lurking in the hallway. "Come on, give us a hand."

The other man entered the room, and for a minute they stood about, sizing up the trunk. "Right-o, Reggie," said the first man, "let's get this on the cart."

Standing at either end of the trunk they each took one of the rope handles, and on the count of three, heaved it up to knee height.

"Blimey! What've you got in here?" gasped the one known as Reggie.

"Papers," I said, trying not to laugh at the expressions on their faces. "Lots of them."

"Whatever you say, boss," said the first man, and together they shuffled out of the sitting room, down the hall, and along the garden path toward their waiting horse and cart.

"I'll just fetch my coat," I called after them.

"Oh, there's no need," said the first man, glancing over his shoulder. "We'll see it right for you. Straight into the vault, yes?"

I considered Holmes's note, his precise instructions. "Thank you," I said, "but all the same, I wish to see it placed in the vault myself."

"Very well, guv'nor, very well," he replied, obviously of the opinion that I was wasting both my time and his.

I dashed back inside and quickly collected my coat and keys, then locked the house behind me, fumbling a little with the lock in my haste. By the time I was ready to leave they had managed to manhandle the trunk up onto the cart and secure it in place with several ropes.

"I'm afraid it's not the comfiest of rides," said Smythe, whose name I had managed to determine by listening to the two men talk as they'd struggled with the trunk. "Up here with us," he said, indicating the box at the front of the cart. "You can sit beside Reggie."

"Thank you," I said, hauling myself up with some difficulty. I am not, by any means, as lithe as I used to be. Once settled, however, I reflected on the fact that I felt safer up there on the box than I had in any motorcar in which I'd so far had the misfortune to travel.

Smythe flicked the horse's reins, and at a slow, steady gait we trotted away in the direction of the bank.

Upon arrival at the bank we did not approach the main entrance, but rather a small loading yard at the rear. Here, two further horses were tied up beside a water trough, along with another wooden cart. The place seemed dank and carried the unfortunate aromas of urine and manure.

One of the clerks, a wiry young fellow with sandy hair and thin – rather ridiculous – whiskers, was standing out in the yard smoking a cigarette, evidently taking a break from his duties. He was slouching against a wall, but straightened up and dropped his cigarette, crushing it underfoot, when he saw that Smythe and Reggie had a customer in tow.

"Good afternoon," he said, in a polite but affected accent. He approached the cart as we drew to a stop, and offered me his hand in assistance. I took it gratefully, jumping down onto the straw-covered flagstones below. "My name's Mr. Scriver," he said. "How can I be of assistance?"

"I'm here to make a deposit," I replied. "My colleague arranged it over the telephone. This trunk here," I pointed to the box in the back of the cart, "I'd like for it to be placed in your vault."

"Very good, sir," said the clerk. "May I ask – do you have an account with us?"

"I do," I said, a little dubious as to how Holmes could have managed to make such an arrangement. I wouldn't put it past him to have impersonated me, and not for the first time.

"Excellent. Then if you would like to follow me," he said. He pushed open a rear door, ushering me into the bank. "You two, bring the box," he called behind him.

The door opened into a large, relatively empty space, within which there were stacked five or six wooden pallets, heaped high with boxes. They were unmarked, and I had no opportunity to ascertain what they contained as I was led away.

"There's just a little paperwork to see to Mr…?"

"Dr. Watson. John Watson," I said.

"Dr. Watson," finished the clerk. "It shouldn't take more than a moment. My desk is just through here." He showed me through another side door, which led to the familiar lobby of the bank proper.

We settled the paperwork quickly – a simple matter of terms and conditions – and then I made a down payment on the storage. Holmes had been thorough, but not thorough enough to arrange for the prepayment of his little exercise. Once again, I cursed him for saddling me with this damnable business.

"I should like to see the trunk safely secured in the vault," I told the clerk, "if it is not too much trouble?"

The man's shoulders sagged slightly, as if in recognition that it was, in fact, more trouble than he wished to admit to, but the forced smile on his face told a different story. "Of course, Dr. Watson. That's no trouble whatsoever. We'll see to it immediately." He pushed his chair back so that it scraped on the marble floor, and stood. "If you'd be kind enough to remain here for a few moments, I'll just check with the manager and retrieve the keys."

"Very well," I said. I watched him scurry off in search of his superior.

Five minutes later the clerk returned bearing a hoop of jangling keys. "Right, Dr. Watson. Everything is arranged. If you'd care to come with me?"

"Excellent," I said, getting to my feet. "Lead on."

He showed me back to the unloading area, where Smythe and Reggie had carried the trunk in from outside and were awaiting further instructions. "This way, gentlemen," said the clerk.

The two men bearing the trunk followed the clerk through a door and down a long, sloping passageway, which terminated in a small chamber, at what I took to be the basement level. I trailed behind, watching inquisitively, anticipating that Holmes might question me on the matter later.

The chamber consisted of plain, whitewashed brick and stood empty, save for a large, steel door, which I assumed to be the entrance to the vault. The clerk produced a hoop of jangling keys from his belt and began sorting through them, selecting the correct one. Duly found, he inserted it into the lock, rotated the wheel that served as a handle, and heaved the door open with a grunt of exertion.

It yawned wide to reveal what transpired to be a fairly mundane-looking inner room, full of tall wooden cabinets filled with lockable drawers, a handful of crates, and a large, brass Buddha, sitting squat on a shelf. I'd always imagined bank vaults to be filled with countless treasures – oil paintings by Old Masters and bars of gold bullion – but alas, in this instance, I was gravely disappointed.

"Go ahead," said the clerk, and the two labourers carried the trunk inside the vault and placed it neatly against the back wall.

"Now, Dr. Watson, I fear there is one final matter to attend to," he went on. "It is company policy to properly inspect any goods placed within our vault. It is important for us to ensure, you understand, that no one of a rebellious or criminal nature is able to place contraband – or, Heaven forbid, even explosives – under our noses." He smirked, as if the very idea was ludicrous, and he was simply doing his job. "Might you open the trunk for me?"

"Of course," I said. I stepped forward, unbuckled the strap, and opened the lid. It banged noisily against the rear wall. Inside were the reams of paper I had examined earlier. "For a writer such as myself, such manuscript pages are valuable beyond words," I said. "And I fear what might happen to them if there should be a bomb raid. For that matter, a single incendiary could destroy years of work!"

The clerk peered over my shoulder, rifled through the upper layers of paper, and nodded in apparent satisfaction. "A most sensible course of action," he said. "I can assure you they will come to no harm here."

I pulled the lid shut. "Then it seems our work here is concluded," I said. "My thanks to you."

"Excellent," said the clerk. He beckoned for me to leave the vault, and I did so, feeling distinctly uncomfortable. He closed the door behind me, turning the handle so that the deadbolts slid into place. "Would you care for me to arrange transport home for you, Dr. Watson?" he said, as he showed me through to the main lobby once again.

"No, thank you," I said. "I have an appointment in town later this evening, and I think I'll pass the time by paying a little visit to my club."

The clerk smiled. "Well, then I hope, Dr. Watson, that we shall see you again in the near future."

"You can count on it," I replied, unaware of just how prophetic my words would turn out to be.

CHAPTER TWELVE

Dinner at my club proved to be a lonesome affair, which served only to underline my present feelings of reclusion.

Admittedly, it was early, but the place was close to empty, with only a handful of solitary figures haunting the saloon bar, idling away a few hours with a newspaper and a drink. Long gone were the days when I could arrive here to find the place swarming with my fellow medical practitioners and strike up a conversation with any number of regulars whom I had grown to know. In those days, my fame had served me well, too – people were aware of my relationship with Holmes, of the accounts of our adventures I had penned for the delectation of the public – and I rarely found myself wanting for a dinner companion.

Now, things were quite different. Even old Brownlow, a general practitioner who had been a friend for countless years and who had been a relative fixture at the place, had stopped coming since the outbreak of war. It seemed that Kaiser Wilhelm had us all on the run, scurrying away to hide in our homes and bury our heads.

Consequently, I ate my Beef Wellington in rather a hurry,

feeling a trifle embarrassed at finding myself dining alone. Afterwards, I sat by the fire in the saloon with a tot of whisky, and contemplated the progress of our investigation so far.

I hadn't yet got a true sense of what was going on, with how Herbert Grange's suicide might have been influenced by external forces. I understood Holmes's reasoning, of course – Grange did not, on the surface, appear to be the sort of man who might have readily committed suicide, and everything we had learned about him, his state of mind and his circumstances, right up until the morning of his death, seemed contrary to his actions.

On top of all that, of course, were the paperweights. It was simply too much of a coincidence that Grange, Baxter and Underwood should all have the same unusual paperweight in their possession, particularly given its odd markings. That hinted at the connection between these different players.

Clearly, there was some further connection between Underwood and Baxter, too – subterfuge of some description, carried out in secrecy and unbeknownst to Lord Foxton – but that in and of itself was not entirely incriminating. Not, at least, until we knew the true nature of their clandestine meetings.

To my mind, the entire investigation hinged on the veracity of Underwood's experiments, and whether his interpretation of the results could be believed. If he truly *had* found a way to take a measurement of a person's soul, might he also have found a way to use that insight as a tool, a weapon, even – a means to influence their behaviour? Could that have been the method by which he affected Grange's suicide?

The thought of it seemed outlandish beyond words. Even Newbury, a known dabbler in rituals and an expert in occult matters, had seemed to think Underwood's success was dubious. Yet I could see no other way to explain the connection between the parties. Unless, of course, we'd missed something, and

Grange's death was, in fact, a straightforward matter of suicide. Perhaps the relationship between Baxter and Underwood was not a conspiratorial one, at least in the political sense, but was conducted in secret for more... *personal* reasons.

It seemed unlikely to me, however, that both Holmes and Mycroft would see conspiracy where there was none to be had. I trusted Holmes's instincts implicitly. If he saw murder, or at least intent to incite suicide, then it was there to be found.

I pondered on this for a while, warming my feet by the fire and sinking a second whisky. I might almost have drifted off, comfortable in the armchair, until, dozing, I heard the clock chime half past six, and realised with a start that I was due to meet Holmes within fifteen minutes.

Hurriedly, I collected my coat, hat and walking stick from the club's valet, hailed a passing carriage and made haste back to Tidwell Bank.

I arrived just a few moments late, around ten minutes to seven, to find the street deserted. I hopped down from the footplate, paid the driver and watched as he trundled away, the carriage bouncing over the cobbles as it creaked off.

I'd been expecting Holmes to appear out of nowhere upon my arrival, to berate me for my lateness, but there was no sign of him. I paced up and down before the bank for a few moments, my cane ticking against the paving slabs with every step. "Holmes?" I said, in a hissed whisper. "Are you there?"

There was no reply. I supposed he must have been held up.

As I waited, my mind began to turn things over, running through likely scenarios. I hoped he hadn't decided to confront Baxter already, without taking any sort of assistance. He'd been most precise about the time of our meeting in his note. Perhaps if he didn't materialise I would have to return to Baxter's house in search of him. Or worse – had my late arrival meant that I had missed him, and somehow thrown out his plans? I didn't dare consider the latter – so many times during our adventures together had the denouement of his investigation rested upon my prompt arrival upon a scene. I decided to wait in the doorway of the bank for a further five minutes before making any decision about a further course of action.

I peered in through the glass panel in the door. Inside, the lights were off, just as they had been the previous evening, and there was no evidence of current occupation. I turned my back, glancing up and down the street while leaning heavily upon my cane. There was still no sign of Holmes. I sighed. It was unlike him to be late for a rendezvous. I was beginning to think the worst.

I waited for a few moments longer, feeling a little foolish standing there in the doorway. I checked my pocket watch. It was almost seven o'clock. Holmes was a full fifteen minutes late. It struck me that, if Baxter and Underwood were to repeat their clandestine meeting of the previous evening, in a few moments I might find myself in a rather precarious position.

I had no reasonable cover story, no excuse for why I should be loitering outside the bank at such an hour. The same would be true if a police constable were to wander past on his beat, too – it was not typical for gentlemen to arrange to meet one another in the sheltered doorway of a rather upmarket bank after hours.

Just as I was about to give up and head off in search of a cab to take me back to Ealing, the gentle tapping of fingertips on glass startled me. Once again, I glanced around the front of the building, but there was still no sign of Holmes, or anyone else, for that matter. Surely I hadn't imagined it?

No – there it was again a moment later. This time I realised the sound had come from behind me. Surprised, I turned on the spot to see a shadowy figure standing *inside* the bank, standing on the other side of the door and tapping on the glass panel to get my attention.

I peered closer, and was amazed to see my suspicion confirmed. The man on the other side of the glass was none other than Sherlock Holmes.

"How the devil?" I started, but Holmes put his finger to his lips, shaking his head and urging me to remain silent. Then, with a flourish, he produced a ring of keys from his pocket, selected one, and opened the door. I stared at him, flabbergasted.

"Well?" I whispered.

"Come on in, Watson," he said by way of response. "Quickly now."

Feeling decidedly uncomfortable, I did as he suggested and stepped quickly into the darkened foyer of the bank. Holmes closed the door behind me and locked it again, slipping the keys back into his pocket.

"But how did you…?" I said, keeping my voice low.

Holmes smiled, amused. "I should have thought the 'how' was obvious, Watson," he said. "The Trojan Horse."

"Yes, yes, the box," I said, irritated that he might take me for such an imbecile. I realised now that it must have been his mode of entry, but I wasn't entirely clear on precisely how he'd managed it – or, indeed, why. "But I checked it, Holmes. I opened it up and rifled through the papers. So did the clerk."

"Oh, Watson," said Holmes. He ran a hand through his hair. "It was, of course, by means of a false bottom that I effected entry. A most simple feat to engineer. I was curled up within a small compartment beneath the papers. Damned uncomfortable, but quite necessary."

"Well, those men did comment that it was deuced heavy," I said.

Holmes laughed. "No doubt a result of those grilled kidneys you've been feeding me with, Watson."

I grinned. "But look here, Holmes. What's your game? Breaking and entering into a bank – and the vault, no less – if anyone catches us here we'll be done for. Locked up in a flash."

"Then the key, my dear Watson, is not to get caught," said Holmes. "Come on, quickly. This way." He started off toward the other end of the foyer. "Keep to the shadows and try not to make a sound. We don't know who else might be lurking here, or due to pay a visit."

"But what exactly do you hope to achieve, Holmes?" I said as we walked.

"I have a suspicion that the reason for Underwood and Baxter's little visit here yesterday evening will soon become abundantly clear." He crossed to the door. "Now, to the vault," he said.

I followed Holmes as I had followed the clerk just a few hours earlier, exiting the foyer into the loading area at the rear of the bank. The lights remained off, and there were no windows here, meaning we were navigating in near darkness.

I felt my way around one of the pallets and across to the other door, guided by a narrow sliver of light that emanated from beneath it.

The darkness here was so pure and impenetrable that I couldn't help but consider what Holmes had said, imagining the hulking shapes of other people concealed in the shadows, waiting for us to shuffle past. Waiting to strike. The hairs on the nape of my neck prickled with fear, and I clutched my cane a little more tightly.

Holmes reached the door and prised it open with his fingers. The pale electric lights had been left on in the passageway beyond. It took a moment for my eyes to adjust.

"How did you get out of the vault?" I whispered. It had occurred to me, standing at the mouth of this passageway leading down to the vault itself, that I had seen the heavy metal doors locked behind me as I'd left. There was no way Holmes could have forced his way out from within, not without a key, or at least some assistance.

"Elementary, Watson," replied Holmes. "There is an opening mechanism on the inside, a safety feature to prevent people from being accidentally trapped within. The door is designed to keep people out, not the other way around."

It occurred to me that he had taken quite a gamble in this. If the mechanism had not opened from the inside, then he might have been trapped until morning, at which point he would no doubt have been discovered and arrested.

In the small chamber at the end of the passageway, the vault door stood open. "What now?" I said. There were no other exits from the room, and I was still not entirely clear what he hoped to achieve. "Are we looking for something in the vault?"

"In a sense," said Holmes, as he disappeared through the heavy steel door.

"I wish you'd share a little more, Holmes," I said. "I can hardly help you to look if I have no idea what I'm actually looking for."

"It'll only take a moment, Watson," he said, by way of reply. "Here, help me with the trunk."

I crossed to where Holmes's trunk stood open against the back wall. Papers were scattered all around it, and a shallow wooden tray – of almost exactly the same perimeter as the trunk itself – was propped upright against the wall. This I took to be the false bottom beneath which Holmes had concealed himself. He must have lifted it out from below, tipping the papers over the floor as he forced the lid of the trunk open from within.

"Quickly, Watson. Help me to replace the contents." Holmes grabbed the false base and lowered it carefully into the trunk, as I gathered an armful of papers. I hurriedly stuffed them back into the box. Two further armfuls saw the remaining papers collected and returned to their rightful place, if a little haphazardly.

Holmes pulled the lid shut, grabbed the edges of the box,

then indicated I should help him to slide it to one side. It was considerably lighter than it had been earlier, when I'd tested its weight at my house, and together we shifted it easily.

Holmes then approached the back wall, stood before it for a moment, and began running his fingers over its roughly plastered surface.

"What the devil are you doing?" I said.

"Shhh!" came his response. He knocked lightly on the wall, drumming his fingertips and leaning closer to listen intently. Then, moving a few inches to his left, he did the same again, then again, then a third time, repeating the action until his knocking returned a different sound altogether – the sound of a hollow behind the wall.

"Ah, here we are," he said. He glanced back over his shoulder, grinning. "Stand ready, Watson. I'm not entirely sure what we're going to find down here."

He pushed at the wall and there was a quiet, mechanical *click*, as a panel in the wall shifted beneath his weight. He stood back, and a small door revealed itself, standing proud of its sunken frame. It was an ingenious piece of concealment – a door blended almost seamlessly with the rear wall of the vault.

Holmes took hold of the edge of the door and pulled it open toward him, revealing a dark passageway beyond. From what I could see, the brickwork in the tunnel was undressed, and thick with cobwebs.

"However did you fathom we'd find this here?" I said.

"Simplicity itself, Watson," remarked Holmes. "I carried out a brief study of the plans of this building earlier this morning at the British Library. They revealed that the Tidwell Bank, as well as several other buildings on this street, sits atop a large, fifteenth-century undercroft, which originally belonged to one of the many churches destroyed during the Great Fire. After emerging from my hiding place a short while ago, five minutes of exploration suggested that any obvious means of gaining access to the undercroft from inside the bank had long since been blocked. However, the space presents the perfect venue for a clandestine gathering, and it seems only logical that this long-forgotten venue is where our small group of German sympathisers would meet. Where else would you hide something in a bank, away from the prying eyes of others? The door had to be somewhere in the vault."

"German sympathisers!" I said, a little too loudly. "Is that what you believe to be going on?" I was quite taken aback by this new development. Was he inferring that Baxter and Underwood were traitors to the Crown?

"Quite so, Watson," he confirmed. "There are traitors in our midst, and more besides. Come; let us see what we might glean from below. Be on your guard."

Ducking my head, I followed Holmes into the narrow passage, pulling the door to behind me. It was dank and dirty, and the floor continued to slope down on a gradient similar to that of the passageway we had previously traversed to reach the vault. It was at least a hundred foot long, and all the while my back remained stooped as I fumbled along in the dark, following the sound of Holmes's shuffling footsteps.

Presently, a dim light became visible at the end of the tunnel – the glow of firelight or candles, rather than the sharp electric light of the rooms above. Tense, I slowed my approach, listening for any sign of activity. I could hear nothing, other than the sound of my own breathing and the scuff of Holmes's boots.

A few moments later, we emerged into a large underground chamber. It was shrouded in gloom, but I could see that the ceiling was vaulted and the bricks undressed, the floor nothing but impacted dirt and stone chippings. The space was huge, and, as Holmes had suggested, I had the impression that it extended beyond the boundaries of the bank and beneath the adjoining buildings, too. Supporting pillars stood like sentries, propping up the floor above. Much of the chamber remained in shadow.

The only source of light – that which we had seen from the mouth of the tunnel – emanated from four large church candles, each positioned on a bronze candelabra around the four corners of a rectangular wooden table. Above the table hung the black, white and red flag of the German Empire. Two marble statues of women in the classical mode, their faces pale and serene in the candlelight, stood to either side of the arrangement, garlands of holly draped around their necks.

The table's surface was covered with a red silk cloth, upon which rested an unusual array of paraphernalia, including what looked to be a ceremonial dagger with a jewelled handle; a golden chalice; strange pyramidal structures made from bound twigs; a sprig of holly; and a mouldering old book, bound in black calf's leather.

There didn't appear to be anyone else around, but the burning candles served as a warning – someone had been here very recently.

I crossed to the table, noticing a spread of photographs laid out beneath the dagger. I tugged a sheaf of them free, sorting through them, taking in the blank, expressionless faces of the men captured in each shot. They were spectrographs, taken from Underwood's machine. Some of the subjects were identifiable – Herbert Grange and Professor Angelchrist. There were others, too, men I recognised from Foxton's party.

I felt a cold sensation spreading through my gut. "What do you make of this, Holmes?" I said, holding them up for him to see. He was pacing about, taking it all in.

He came over and took the photographs from me, leafing through them. Then, dismissively, he cast the spectrographs upon the table. "One might imagine these are the accoutrements of some devilish ritual," he said, with a wave of his hand, "some occult nonsense perpetrated by Baxter."

"And the German flag," I said, my mouth dry. "It seems you were right."

"Quite so, Watson," said Holmes. "The root of this mystery has never been about spiritualism and the search for the human soul, but about political allegiance and the war."

I could hardly conceive of what had been going on down here, right beneath our noses, right in the heart of the capital. "Nevertheless," I said, "look at all of this stuff, Holmes. There's something ungodly being carried out down here, and it might well prove to be the means by which the perpetrators are influencing their victims."

"Perhaps," said Holmes, although I could tell he did not believe it. "But to my eyes this place feels more like a stage than the true lair of a cult."

"There's still the matter of this 'spirit box', too," I said. "Whatever it might prove to be."

Holmes tapped his finger against his lips thoughtfully, but didn't reply.

"I can hardly warrant it," I continued, "Baxter and Underwood, German sympathisers. Do you think Foxton's involved?"

Holmes shook his head. "No, Watson. I do not. It's Baxter I believe to be the true villain here. Underwood is a naïve and desperate young man, suffering from a broken heart and a desire to find reason in an unreasonable world. He's fallen in with Baxter, who I'd wager has manipulated him, turned him into an instrument, a means by which the members of this distasteful group might gain access to Foxton's associates."

"Good Lord," I said. "It's a despicable business. Who knows how many other men Baxter has under his power."

"More to the point, Watson, is why," said Holmes. "What is

Baxter hoping to achieve? There has to be more to this than a simple matter of encouraging a Member of Parliament to throw himself in the river. Why are there pictures Professor Angelchrist and others on this table? What information is Baxter trying to get at?"

I was about to urge Holmes to continue, when I heard the scuff of a footstep behind me, and whirled round to see a wiry young fellow charging towards me from the shadows, his lips curled back in a savage snarl, his fists raised.

"Look out, Holmes!" I cried, as I brought my cane up in one swift motion, in the manner of swinging a cricket bat, as the man launched himself at me. The stick collided squarely with his jaw, sending a painful shudder up my arms, and without a sound, the man collapsed unconscious to the floor.

There was little time to congratulate myself, however, as I heard Holmes grunt and cry out, and I turned to see him grappling with a second assailant, as a third charged in from behind him, intending to join the fray. I was not, of course, about to stand for that, and with a war cry that would have made the ancients proud, I charged headlong at the man, once again wielding my walking stick as a club.

He turned, wild-eyed, at the sound of my howling approach, bringing both fists up to his face to form a defensive shield as I swung my club hard at his head. It rebounded off his forearms, and the man grunted something in German before swaying, first left, then right, then lashing out with his fist before I'd had a chance to recover from my swing.

He caught me hard in the jaw and I staggered back, reeling from the blow. I felt warm blood streaming down my chin from a split lip. A second blow, this time in the gut, doubled me over. I was old and out of practice, no longer used to trading blows, particularly with a man less than half my age.

I heard Holmes issue a cry of pain and my resolve hardened.

I gripped my cane firmly, still bent double, and as the man came close, preparing to strike me upon the back of the neck to put me down, I lurched upwards, thrusting the cane up as hard as I could and catching him under the chin.

He was caught off guard, and dropped to the floor, choking. A second blow across the temple laid him out upon the floor, suddenly limp.

Holmes and the third man were standing, but Holmes had the upper hand, pinning the attacker's arms behind his back. As he struggled to get free I came around to stand before him. He grinned inanely, lurching forward in Holmes's grip so that his face was close to mine, and spat.

Disgusted, I wiped the spittle from my cheek with the sleeve of my jacket. "Hold him still, Holmes," I said.

"I am trying, Watson," said Holmes.

I flexed my fingers, formed a fist, and then put the remaining man down with a swift right hook.

Holmes staggered back, looking relieved. I could see his cheek was swelling where he'd taken a blow to the face. I dabbed at my own bloody lip with my handkerchief.

"Not bad for a couple of old-timers," I muttered.

"Not bad at all, Watson," agreed Holmes, with a chuckle. He fished in his coat pocket for a moment, before producing a coiled length of twine. "Now quickly, help me to bind them before they wake."

I had long ago learned not to be surprised by the oddities that Holmes carried in his capacious pockets, and I set about assisting him, binding the feet and hands of the three unconscious men.

"Do you think these are the three Germans who were questioned by Grange?" I asked, as I finished tightening my final knot. "Baxter's employees?"

Holmes straightened his back, dusting off his hands. He'd just dragged two of the men a little further apart, so that if and when they did wake, they wouldn't be able to easily assist one another. "Quite possibly," he said, "although I'd wager there are many more associated with his organisation, German and British alike."

I shook my head in disgust. I could barely conceive of how a man could betray his own country in such a manner. I wondered what Baxter hoped to gain.

"What now?" I said. "Wait until they come around and put them to the question?"

"No," replied Holmes. "Men like this – they're unswerving in their loyalty to their cause. Extracting anything worthwhile from them will take days, if, indeed, we're able to get anything out of them at all. Neither is it safe for us to remain down here too long. It's likely there are other access points elsewhere in the street." He looked rueful, rubbing at his bruised cheek. "I'm not sure how many more of them I could comfortably take on."

I didn't point out that it had been my trusty walking cane that had done most of the work for us.

Holmes took a step back as the man at his feet began to stir, emitting a low groan. "Be a good fellow, Watson, and hurry on up to the bank. You should be able to locate a telephone in one of the offices, from which you can put a call through to Inspector Foulkes, requesting his urgent assistance. These men need to be taken into immediate custody. Also impress upon him the importance of sending yet more men to arrest both Henry Baxter and Seaton Underwood. We mustn't allow them to flee, which they surely shall once they realise that we have discovered their lair. I shall remain here until you return with news."

"Very well," I said. "Be mindful, Holmes." I hurried for the tunnel that led back up to the bank.

I stumbled up the gloomy passage, emerging a few moments later into the vault. Everything appeared to be as we had left it. Cautiously, I rounded the trunk and crept out into the small room on the other side. I was still clutching my cane like a club, and its weight was reassuring in my palm. I was half expecting someone to jump out at me as I came through the door, but the place appeared to be deserted.

I dashed on, up the next passage, through the loading area at the rear of the bank, and out into the dimly lit foyer. There was a telephone on one of the desks, and I made for it, snatching up the receiver and waiting for the operator to come on the line.

"Scotland Yard," I said.

"Yes, sir," said the woman on the other end.

The line burred for a moment, before a man answered. "Scotland Yard," he said, wearily. "Sergeant Hawley speaking."

"I need to speak to Inspector Foulkes as a matter of urgency," I said. "My name is Dr. John Watson—"

"Ah, Dr. Watson," interrupted the man on the other end. "So you received the Inspector's message?"

"His message? What?" I snapped, confused. "No, I've not received any message."

"The Inspector's been trying to reach you and Mr. Holmes. It seems there's been an incident. Sir Maurice Newbury called about an hour ago. He's at the home of Professor Angelchrist and he says the Professor is in danger. He said it was paramount that we reached you."

"Good Lord," I said. "You'd better put me through to Foulkes immediately."

"I can't, sir. He's already left," replied Hawley. "I can give you the address…"

"Yes, yes, in a minute," I said. "But I'm calling for assistance. I need help, man, as a matter of urgency. Holmes and I are at Tidwell Bank, where we've apprehended and detained three German agents. You need to send men right away to take them into custody and secure the bank."

"Tidwell Bank?"

"Yes," I said, impatiently. "Additionally, you should send someone to arrest Mr. Henry Baxter, the owner of the bank, as well as Mr. Seaton Underwood of Ravensthorpe House."

"On what grounds?"

"Conspiracy to murder, and treason," I said.

I heard Hawley swallow. "Those are serious charges, Dr. Watson."

"And there'll be serious consequences if they're allowed to go free," I countered. "Consider this – which is the bigger risk? To trust me, a well-respected figure with a history of assisting Scotland Yard with their investigations, and hope that I haven't accused the wrong men, or potentially to allow two murderous traitors to escape?"

"I'll despatch the men now," said Hawley. "An officer will be with you shortly."

"Excellent," I said. "Right, you'd better give me that address. We'll remain here until your men arrive, then Holmes and I will head directly to the Professor's house."

"Very good, sir. I'll try to reach the Inspector on the Professor's number in the meantime. Here's the address." He read it out, and I scratched it down on the back of an envelope I found on the desk.

"Thank you, Sergeant," I said, before hanging up the phone.

I hurried back to Holmes, my mind reeling at the news of Professor Angelchrist's perilous situation. What the devil was going on? Had Angelchrist been targeted by this bizarre German cult? His spectrograph *had* been amongst those on the altar in the undercroft.

I found Holmes standing by the altar, studying the objects on the table. One of the Germans had come round and was struggling ineffectually in his bonds, grunting and twitching as he tried to wrestle free. The others – the two I had hit with my walking stick – were still out cold.

"What news?" said Holmes, turning to look at me as I approached.

"The police are on their way," I said. "We're to meet them by the front door in a few minutes."

"Excellent," said Holmes.

"There's more," I said. "Foulkes wasn't there. A sergeant told me that he'd been trying to reach us for an hour. Something's wrong. He's with Newbury at Professor Angelchrist's house, where there's been some sort of incident. I have the address. We're needed there as soon as possible."

Holmes nodded thoughtfully, taking it in. "That makes sense," he said.

"It does?"

The German on the ground had stopped struggling, and was now peering up at us, laughing. "You're too late," he said, his accent thick and clipped. "The spirit box will be ours."

"The spirit box?" I exclaimed. I glanced at Holmes, whose expression remained impassive. I crossed to where the German was lying on the dirty floor, his hands bound behind his back. He grinned up at me defiantly. "Explain yourself," I demanded, but the man simply laughed again, turning his head away and spitting, as if to indicate his disgust.

"You damnable muck snipe," I said, gritting my teeth.

"Come, Watson," said Holmes, putting a hand on my shoulder. "Leave him. Let us wait for the police in the foyer, and from there, make haste to the Professor's house. Soon, everything will become clear." He started off toward the tunnel.

Reluctantly I followed on behind, feeling as if the answer to all that had been occurring was only just out of my reach.

CHAPTER THIRTEEN

Within ten minutes of my telephone call, a veritable army of uniformed constables arrived at the bank, along with an inspector by the name of Cuthbertson – a dour, po-faced fellow who was barely out of his twenties, and wore a long, scruffy moustache, which perched upon his top lip like a hairy caterpillar.

Like many policemen of his age, Cuthbertson seemed somewhat in awe of Holmes, and hung intently on his every word as Holmes slowly and deliberately outlined the situation. Nevertheless, he proved most efficient, and his men, armed with electric torches, had soon scoured the undercroft and taken our three German prisoners into custody.

It appeared there was, indeed, another entrance to the subterranean system, this time leading from the basement of a nearby insurance brokerage firm. Cuthbertson stationed some of his men there while he despatched one of his sergeants to investigate the name of the property's owner.

Sergeant Hawley had briefed Cuthbertson regarding Foulkes's instruction for us to meet him at the home of Professor Angelchrist, and consequently Cuthbertson offered us the loan of a police carriage to expedite our journey. I had no doubt that the following day Holmes and I would be called to the station for a more robust round of questioning regarding our evening's little adventure, but for now, Foulkes's word seemed good enough to ensure we did not find ourselves encumbered with unnecessary bureaucracy.

Outside, I gave the driver the address provided to me by Sergeant Hawley – a residential street close to Berkeley Square – and Holmes and I hopped up into the carriage. A rainstorm had started up while we'd been occupied inside the bank, and the water droplets drummed noisily on the roof of the passenger box as we charged through the streets, the driver whipping the horse up into a lather.

I wondered what could have happened to the Professor, whether the Germans had made an attempt on his life, and if so, for what purpose. I found it difficult to imagine what ends they were working towards. Angelchrist was well connected amongst men of a political persuasion, that much was clear, but surely his years of active service were now long behind him? I couldn't see what they hoped to achieve by threatening the man. Whatever the case, it had to be connected to our ongoing investigation. Why else would both Foulkes and Newbury request our urgent presence?

Holmes remained silent as we thundered on, slouching back in his seat. His hands were folded neatly upon his lap, his head bowed so that his chin rested upon his chest. His eyes were closed in quiet contemplation. I imagined he was pondering many of the same questions as I, but I knew better than to disturb his train of thought. Down in the undercroft he had intimated that he was close to a solution, suggesting that everything would soon become clear. I hoped that was true. Presently, it felt as if I was wading through thick fog, unable to discern anything clearly.

I was still somewhat taken aback by the revelation that both

Baxter and Underwood were working for the Germans, but aside from that, I was yet to fully grasp their motives, let alone the esoteric nature of their methods. Additionally, of course, there was the question of the spirit box, whatever that might turn out to be.

I was so lost in my thoughts that I failed to realise the carriage had come to a stop. I peered out of the rain-beaded window to realise, with a start, that we had arrived at our destination.

Holmes had already roused himself and was getting to his feet. Following suit, I opened the carriage door and hopped down into the street. Above, the night sky was leaden and smeared with rainclouds.

"That's the one, sir," said the driver, pointing toward a large, three-storey house at the end of a terrace.

"Thank you," I said, as Holmes came around to the other side of the carriage.

"Let us hurry, Watson," he said. "Professor Angelchrist could be in grave danger."

Anxious to assist in any way that I could – and also to get out of the rain – I half ran, half walked across to the house in question, noticing as I did so that Foulkes's automobile was parked just a little further down the street.

The door was pillar-box red and recently painted. I rapped loudly with the gargoyle-headed knocker.

Hurried footsteps sounded in the hallway, and a moment later the door opened to reveal an ashen-faced Inspector Foulkes. "Ah, Mr. Holmes, Dr. Watson – you are most welcome," he said. "Hawley called to say he'd managed to get hold of you. Come in, come in." He stood aside as he ushered us into the house.

It was a little like entering a time capsule. The hallway was dressed in the style of twenty years previous, although the place certainly felt well lived in: a jacket had been tossed haphazardly over the end of the banister; an empty glass stood discarded beside a comb on the hall table; opened envelopes had been screwed up and dropped in a small wastepaper bin.

I could hear the muffled sound of voices coming from a room a little further down the hallway. I glanced at Foulkes. His eyes met mine. I could see he was troubled. "What is it?" I said. "What's happened to him? Does he need medical attention?"

Foulkes shook his head. "No. At least… I don't think so. The thing is, Dr. Watson, he's out of his mind, raving incoherently. Newbury thinks he might represent a real danger to himself."

I looked at Holmes, who was quietly assimilating this information.

"What's more," continued Foulkes, "his behaviour matches the description Miss Brown gave of how Herbert Grange was acting on the day of his death. It's almost identical. He just keeps going over the same things, about how he has to stop 'them' from getting to the spirit box." He knitted his brows in a deep, concerned furrow. "I have no idea what he's going on about, to be honest, but it was this that prompted Newbury to send for you. He said it was connected to your case."

"Indeed," said Holmes. "You'd better show us through."

Foulkes nodded. "They're in the Professor's study, just down there."

Holmes made haste toward the sound of voices.

"Did Sergeant Hawley fill you in on what transpired at Tidwell Bank?" I said to Foulkes, as we followed behind.

"Yes," replied Foulkes. "He said you'd apprehended some German agents, operating from a cellar beneath the bank. What exactly were they up to?"

"A church undercroft in fact," I said. "And Holmes will explain it better than I. But it's a damnable business, Inspector. It seems Henry Baxter is a traitor who has been leading some sort of devilish cult. They've been selecting high-profile victims, such as Grange and Professor Angelchrist, as the objects of their unholy attentions."

"So you believe the Professor's current situation to be related to Baxter?" asked Foulkes.

"Undoubtedly," I confirmed. "Although as to what *exactly* is going on, I fear I'm still as much in the dark as you."

"But surely, as a medical man, you don't put any stock in talk of witchcraft and sorcery?"

He held open the door for me. "Honestly, Inspector," I said, stepping through into the study, "I no longer know *what* to believe."

We found Holmes standing with Newbury, and both men were observing Professor Angelchrist, who was pacing back and forth behind a large desk, drumming his fingertips against the sides of his head.

The room – Angelchrist's study – was something really quite exceptional. If Holmes's old sitting room at Baker Street had existed in a perpetual state of disarray, then this room represented utter, unadulterated chaos. It was more like the storage room of an eclectic, disorganised museum, than any place a person might actually inhabit.

Maps plastered the walls, stuck with colourful pins and marked with lines of string, showing routes across the city and beyond. Bookcases burst with frayed leather-bound tomes, and other, unusual knick-knacks – the fossilised hand of a bear, a roman brooch, a quill pen with a vibrant orange feather, a wax seal, an unsheathed sabre. The life-sized model of a Neanderthal man was propped in one corner, staring at us forlornly from beneath his heavy brow and holding his hand aloft, where clearly it had once held a club. A grandfather clock ticked ominously from where it stood against the far wall, almost hidden behind a pile of crates. The contents were hidden, save for the crate on top, in which I could see the bleached skull of a large mammal, surrounded by packing paper. Most peculiarly, a clockwork owl sat on a perch that hung from the ceiling, preening its brass feathers and turning its head to regard us as we entered the room.

"I must stop them! I must!" called Angelchrist suddenly, causing me to start. He turned and looked at me, wild-eyed, still holding his fingers to his temples as if warding off an evil thought. "They can see it," he mumbled, his expression pained. "They know where to look."

Alarmed, I looked to Newbury for any explanation he might offer. He broke off from his conversation with Holmes and crossed the room to greet me, clapping me firmly on the shoulder. "It's good of you to come, Dr. Watson," he said. "I'd like to be able to wish you a good evening, but as you can see, I fear it is anything but. Archibald is in a bad way. He appears to have succumbed to some external influence. Either that, or something has caused his mind to entirely snap."

I frowned. "Whatever is he referring to?"

"I don't know," said Newbury, the frustration evident in his voice. "He keeps on talking about how 'they' can see into his head, how they'll discover all of the secrets of the spirit box if he doesn't stop them, but he gives no sense of who 'they' are."

"You've tried questioning him, of course?" I asked, aware of the likely redundancy of my enquiry.

"I've done nothing but," replied Newbury, "but so far I've been unable to get through. I'm not sure he's even hearing my questions." He sighed. "Would you examine him for me, Doctor?"

I glanced at Holmes, who nodded his assent. "Very well," I said, slipping my coat from my shoulders, and tossing it over the back of a chair. It was arranged beside another chair, opposite a sofa, with a low table between them. Upon the table sat the remains of a small parcel – brown paper and string – and beside it rested its former content: an amber, half-globe paperweight, engraved with a five-pointed star.

"Holmes!" I exclaimed, pointing to the offending object. "Have you seen?"

"Yes, Watson," said Holmes. He crossed to the table and picked up the paperweight, weighing it in his hand. "It's best we place this momentarily out of sight." He slipped it into his coat pocket. He turned to Foulkes. "When was the package delivered? I presume it was by hand. The devils wouldn't have wanted to risk their plans going awry by entrusting it to the postal service."

Foulkes – who seemed unperturbed by Holmes's pocketing of a vital piece of evidence – nodded in confirmation. "Yes, by hand, and not even that, according to the housekeeper. She answered a knock on the door at approximately four in the afternoon, but there was no one there, just the parcel on the step. The Professor was out at the time, so she placed it in his study. Presumably he opened it upon his return, which was around six. Sir Maurice had an appointment with the Professor at quarter past, and seems to have arrived just as the fit took hold."

Newbury shook his head regretfully. "I would that I had been there earlier. Angelchrist was firmly in the grip of the affliction when I arrived. I tried to reason with him, but soon realised I had no resources to break the spell. After half an hour I rang the Inspector. I gather that Scotland Yard tried you and Dr. Watson at the Doctor's home, but by that time you would have already been on your adventures at the bank."

I nodded. At a quarter to seven I was waiting for Holmes outside the Tidwell building, far away from the ringing telephone in Ealing. There was nothing to be done about it now, however, and as a medical man, I had a job to do.

"Right then, Professor," I said. "Let's take a look at you." I crossed to where Angelchrist was standing. He was staring at his shoes, apparently lost in thought. "Professor? Professor, can you hear me?"

He looked up suddenly, his eyes wide. He was staring right at me, but I could tell that his thoughts were far away.

"Professor Angelchrist?" I ventured again.

His eyes seemed to focus on me. "Oh, Dr. Watson," he replied, after a moment. "Thank goodness you're here." I was filled with a momentary sense of relief. Could it be that his lucidity was returning?

"How do you feel?" I asked. "Would you care to sit down?"

Angelchrist shook his head. I could already see that there was little I might be able to diagnose from a medical perspective – his pupils were not dilated, and although his cheeks were rather flushed, he appeared generally fit and well. There were none of the tell-tale signs that might suggest he'd been administered a mind-altering drug – aside from his rambling, of course – and his breath didn't smell of alcohol.

"You must keep your voice down," said Angelchrist, in a forced whisper. "They can hear everything."

"You're saying the house is bugged? A Dictograph or some such?"

"No," he said, tapping his index finger against the side of his head. "They're in here, watching."

My heart sank. His earlier appearance of lucidity had been a fallacy. Either he'd ingested something that was having an adverse effect on his sense of reason, or he was operating under some other, unknown influence.

I left the Professor and joined Newbury, Foulkes and Holmes on the other side of the room. "He's in some kind of trance, would be my best estimation," I said. "I can see no evidence that he's been subjected to any of the typical psychotropic drugs, although I cannot be certain, not without a blood test and a thorough medical examination. He's clearly disconnected with reality, however. He recognised me, but just as you explained, Sir Maurice, he believes that someone or something can see into his head."

Holmes nodded, taking it all in. "Just like Herbert Grange," he said. "Do you happen to have any tranquilisers about your person, Watson?" he asked.

"Tranquilisers?" I said. "Of course not, Holmes!" I realised with a flash of embarrassment that to even ask such a question, he must have discovered that I had been administering mild sedatives to myself of a night to help me sleep.

"Then be a good chap and go and check the cupboards, would you, Watson, for anything you might use to induce the Professor to sleep?"

I felt decidedly uncomfortable poking around uninvited in Angelchrist's cupboards, but Holmes was right – the man was distraught, and we needed to do something to help calm him and allow him to sleep for a while. At least that way we'd be able to keep a watchful eye on him.

There was, however, nothing in his cupboards or drawers that came close to being the sort of sedative we needed. I returned to the study a few minutes later, empty-handed. "Nothing but a tot of rum," I said, in answer to Holmes's inquisitive look.

"Very well," said Holmes. "We shall simply have to settle for more direct means."

He walked over to Angelchrist, put his left hand on the man's shoulder, and then drew back his right hand and delivered a sharp, brisk slap to Angelchrist's face.

Angelchrist yelped, raising a hand to his smarting cheek.

"Holmes!" I exclaimed. "What on earth are you doing? Was there really any need for that?"

"Every need," replied Holmes, firmly, as he lowered his head, trying to catch Angelchrist's eye. "Professor?" he said.

Angelchrist looked stricken and confused. Clearly, Holmes's brisk slap had done nothing to rouse him from his fugue state.

"I'm sorry, Professor," said Holmes. He drew back his hand again, this time forming a tight fist, and with a sudden, sweeping movement, delivered a perfect right hook to Angelchrist's lower jaw.

Angelchrist's face relaxed, and he slouched forward into Holmes's waiting arms. Holmes staggered slightly beneath the weight.

"Good Lord!" said Foulkes, utterly flabbergasted.

"Help me here," said Holmes, rather urgently. Newbury rushed over and grabbed Angelchrist's feet, and together they manhandled him onto the sofa, where he lay, slack-jawed, amongst the cushions.

"I hope you know what you're doing, Mr. Holmes," said Foulkes, clearly unsure about my companion's methods.

"He needs to sleep," said Holmes. "It's the only way we'll get any sense out of him and prevent him from putting himself at risk. I believe he'll have recovered his senses again upon waking."

"Well, I…" muttered Foulkes, clearly unsure.

It did, I conceded, seem a most extreme measure, but in that studied, decisive blow, I had seen the echo of Holmes's former boxing prowess, and knew very well the precision of which he was capable. Angelchrist would feel it, of course, but Holmes had been dutiful, and had administered his prescription with due care. Angelchrist would sleep for only a short while.

"Right," said Holmes, dusting his hands and regarding us each in turn. "Time for a pot of tea while he sleeps it off."

"Really, Holmes," I said, shaking my head.

Newbury made tea in an ancient clay pot, which he carried through on a tray from the kitchen, teacups rattling noisily in their saucers. We perched on chairs or crates around the low table, while Angelchrist remained unconscious on the sofa.

In truth, I felt most uncomfortable sitting there in the man's study while he lay prone and vulnerable before us. I could see that Foulkes felt the same, for he kept eyeing the sleeping figure, as if willing him to wake and dispel any sense of discomfort.

Newbury passed me a teacup and I sipped at the hot liquid

gratefully, only now realising how weary I was following the day's exertions. The tea was revitalising. I was anxious to understand what had happened to Angelchrist, and was full of questions, which I put to the group.

"So tell me," I said. "We've established that the Professor is, or was, under some malign influence. Given the nature of our recent investigations and what Holmes and I discovered beneath the bank, I must ask the question – is there any chance that what Baxter and Underwood have been doing down there, whatever unconscionable rituals they've been performing – are responsible? Could Professor Angelchrist's sudden alteration have come about following the application of an occult ritual?"

Newbury ran a hand through his hair. "Anything is possible, Dr. Watson. As I've said before, I keep an open mind, although I find it difficult to believe that someone could have such a profound influence on another's state of mind, simply due to his or her possession of a photograph." He paused, glancing at Holmes. "However, I find myself at an impasse. I can see no alternative explanation."

"Inspector?" said Holmes, looking to Foulkes for an opinion. "What do you make of all this?"

Foulkes looked even more uncomfortable to be under such a spotlight. "I've seen many strange things in my time, Mr. Holmes. Sir Maurice might attest to that. Men forged of iron; parasitic fungus that invades a person's nervous system; plague revenants; engines built to prolong life – but this? It appears to me to be nothing but the onset of sudden madness. If it weren't for the fact that Grange suffered from near-identical symptoms, I'd have written it off as a sorry case of dementia. I cannot bring myself to believe in witchcraft or sorcery."

Holmes nodded, a wry smile curling on his lips.

"Well, Holmes," I said. "Isn't it time you gave up your own opinion on the matter?"

Holmes laughed. "This, gentlemen, is a clear case of hypnotic suggestion."

"Hypnotic suggestion?" echoed Foulkes.

"Quite so," said Holmes. He took a sip from his teacup, drawing out the suspense. Over the years I had learned to indulge Holmes these small moments, the theatre of his explanatory flourish. "There is no sorcery involved. I believe we shall find, upon questioning him, that Professor Angelchrist is in possession of information regarding the true nature of this mysterious 'spirit box', information which I believe Henry Baxter and his German masters to be very intent on getting their hands on."

"But how?" said Foulkes. "How could they affect the Professor in such a profound way without him realising it?"

"The spectrograph!" said Newbury, excitedly, sitting forward in his chair. "Seaton Underwood."

"Precisely," said Holmes. "Underwood is their instrument. Their means of getting to the right men."

"I'm sorry, Holmes," I said. "But you've lost me."

"It's really quite simple, Watson," said Holmes, dismissively. "Henry Baxter, as we have already established, is a traitor, working for the German cause to attempt to destabilise British politics – and thus the war effort – by seeding sedition and undermining high-profile targets. He has forged a relationship with Seaton Underwood in order to use him to get to the men in Lord Foxton's inner circle."

"Men with tremendous political influence," I said. "Yes, I see that. But you're saying Underwood's spectrograph generator is actually a machine for effecting hypnosis?"

"No," said Holmes. "Not at all. I believe that Seaton Underwood truly thinks the machine is capable of photographing a person's soul. He's allowed it to become considered a parlour game, however, as we saw when we visited Ravensthorpe House

– the means by which he's able to entice Foxton's guests to participate. To them, it is nothing but a light-hearted diversion, but to Underwood it is both an opportunity to test his equipment, and to carry out the work he's been charged with by Baxter. What was it Foxton told you about Underwood, Watson?"

"That he'd become obsessed with his quest to prove that the soul exists independently of the body, driven by his unwillingness to truly accept the death of his parents," I said.

"Baxter will be using that," said Holmes. "Clearly, he has his own unhealthy interest in matters of the occult." I glanced at Newbury, who was smiling indulgently, and clearly hadn't taken offence at Holmes's derogatory remark. "He's involved Underwood in his little cult. Manipulated him. No doubt he's promised Underwood access to all manner of arcane knowledge to continue his work, in exchange for his assistance extracting information from certain individuals. Perhaps he's tempted him with resources that can only be provided by his German masters. There is a deep seam of Teutonic folklore and mysticism, supposedly dating back a thousand years. What wouldn't a man like Underwood do to gain access to such treasure? Watson and I have seen the altar Baxter set up beneath Tidwell Bank; it was clearly no more than a piece of scene dressing for Underwood, to help convince him that his master had access to mystic knowledge of real power. Seaton is a disturbed and credulous individual, who is obsessed with proving that his parents' spirits are truly tangible. Just the sort of man to fall in with a cult that seems to offer him everything he desires."

"Foxton said that Baxter had fanned Underwood's obsession," I said. "Now it begins to make sense. He hoped to gain something in return."

"A true deal with the Devil," said Newbury.

"Yes, but you still haven't explained the hypnosis," said Foulkes. "How Underwood is actually doing it."

"Well we know the 'how'," said Holmes. "The technique of placing a individual under hypnosis is not a difficult one. I have mastered it myself with little difficulty, and Watson and I saw several volumes on the subject when we visited Underwood's rooms. As for the 'when', I'd wager the targets are selected by Baxter, and it's a relatively simple matter for Underwood to engineer a situation where he's left alone with each guest and his machine during one of Foxton's gatherings. In fact, he said as much to Watson, I believe?"

I nodded. "Indeed, he mentioned that he preferred to be alone with a new subject."

"No wonder he didn't press the matter in Watson's case," Holmes smiled wryly. "Watson was of no use to Baxter, having no political importance, if you'll forgive me, my friend." I could not deny it, and at that moment was very glad of the fact. Holmes continued. "He generates a spectrograph, so that the visitor leaves with exactly what they expected, but he takes the opportunity to hypnotise and question them while they're there. The questions are given to him by Baxter, which he may not even truly know the significance of. He then feeds that information to Baxter, who uses it for whatever nefarious purposes he's planned."

"Yes," I said. "But it doesn't explain why Herbert Grange threw himself in the river, or why we found Professor Angelchrist in such a sorry state. And then there are the paperweights, of course. Surely they point to a deeper connection between Baxter, Underwood and their victims?"

"Ah-ha!" exclaimed Holmes, suddenly animated. "Excellent, Watson. You've hit on it exactly. I believe that Underwood has planted a hypnotic suggestion in the minds of those men he put to the question, triggered by the sight of an amber paperweight bearing the symbol of Baxter's cult. We saw Seaton's own example of the object at Ravensthorpe, clearly on hand as a prop during the sessions. Rather careless of him." He reached into his pocket and produced the half globe that had been sent to Angelchrist, which he held out for us to see. "Once the information had been gained, the subjects were just loose ends that could lead the authorities to the plotters. By implanting a hypnotic suggestion that could be triggered at a later date, the subject could be 'removed' at a time of Baxter's choosing. Clearly our sniffing around forced their hand, and the Professor is paying the price. Otherwise I imagine they would have preferred to wait a little longer to truly let the trail go cold."

I frowned. "You know as well as I do, Holmes, that a hypnotic suggestion breaks if the recipient is forced to place themselves in danger. Their survival instincts are too strong, and override any impulse to harm themselves. It cannot be the answer. Grange could not have been hypnotised to throw himself into the river."

"No," said Holmes. "But if the belief was sufficiently powerful that he felt he had no choice…"

"So the trigger itself didn't inspire the impulse to commit suicide," said Newbury, "but he made the choice to do it because of something he believed."

"Exactly," confirmed Holmes. "Remember what Miss Brown said to us, Watson. That Grange, when overcome, put his hand to his head and uttered 'My God, they're here. They're in here.' At first I took that to mean that he thought there were traitors in the War Office, but I soon realised he meant something else entirely. He thought they were in his head. That the enemy could see his thoughts."

"Good Lord," said Foulkes. "Just like Professor Angelchrist."

"Of course, truthfully, they can do nothing of the sort," continued Holmes. "It was simply an implanted fear, a belief, triggered by the sight of the paperweight. The hypnotic suggestion was the certain knowledge that the enemy knew the subject's thoughts, including those of utmost importance to the security of the nation."

"So Grange killed himself in an attempt to protect whatever secrets he held in his head, specifically regarding this 'spirit box'?" said Newbury.

Holmes nodded.

"But why hadn't it happened before?" I asked. "The paperweight was on the bookcase in full view. If that was the trigger, surely it would have done its work long before that fateful lunchtime?"

"It was precisely that fact, Watson, which convinced me of Baxter's involvement. Grange had interviewed three German men that morning at the War Office," said Holmes.

"Employees of Baxter's," I said, recalling our earlier line of questioning.

"One of whom delivered the paperweight in question. I imagine that the man distracted Grange, or made an excuse to step to the window. An untied shoelace or some such would give the perfect opportunity to kneel down, extract the paperweight from an inner pocket, and place it on the bookcase, in view but not prominently, allowing the man time to be far away before any scene transpired. After that, it was only a matter of time before Grange saw the object, and the trigger was pulled. In fact, we know the exact moment. Remember, Miss Brown told us that Grange went to the window to see if there was rain on the way, at which point he suggested postponing their outing. He then immediately went into the same state as the Professor here. He saw the paperweight as he approached the window, triggering the hypnotic suggestion." Holmes took one last look at the paperweight in his hand, and then slipped it back into his pocket. "I can only fault myself for not confirming with Miss Baxter that the paperweight was a new addition to the office. But one cannot retain all the brilliance of youth, and I'm sure such a small matter could be dealt with by one of Foulkes's men."

"It all makes sense," said Newbury. "A terrible, disturbing

sense. Clearly, Archibald is another of their victims. He told us he'd undergone the spectrograph a couple of weeks ago, during one of Foxton's gatherings. Underwood must have nobbled him then."

"And we discovered pictures of the Professor in the undercroft beneath Tidwell Bank," I said. "Where Baxter and his cronies were carrying out their rituals." I turned to Holmes. "That's a point. What was the purpose of the altar? You spoke of 'scene dressing'. Were there truly rituals carried out? If Underwood was getting the information from Angelchrist and the others at Foxton's house, surely the targets never went to the undercroft themselves?"

Holmes nodded. "Very perspicacious, Watson. I believe that the altar and all that window dressing was created by Baxter for Seaton Underwood's benefit, a location where they would meet at night – with Baxter's employees as extra gilt to the proceedings – and Seaton would pass on the information he had gleaned in an occult setting, perhaps with some hocus-pocus ritual focused on the spectrographs. The fact that when we arrived the candles had been lit, and our German friends were present, suggests that a gathering was planned for this very night."

Foulkes shook his head in disgust. "So perhaps the Professor's usefulness to him was at an end, and with Mr. Holmes and Dr. Watson taking an interest, Baxter arranged to have a paperweight sent to trigger the implanted suggestion, hoping that he'd follow Grange's example, no doubt, taking his own life for the good of the country."

"Which means," went on Newbury, "that they must have already extracted all of the information they needed from him. I wonder what it was, and what they're planning."

"For that, we're going to need to talk with the Professor," said Holmes.

Newbury glanced at Angelchrist. "Do you think he's going to be alright?"

"I believe so," said Holmes. "Provided he doesn't come into contact with one of these paperweights again, of course." He patted his pocket. "One usually finds hypnosis wears off after a good sleep." He delivered this with the confident air of a man who had previous experience of such matters.

"I hope you're right," said Newbury. "He's a proud man, and I'd hate to see him reduced to... well, to lose his mind like that."

It was obvious that Newbury was deeply concerned. I knew he'd been a friend of Angelchrist's for well over a decade, and he was clearly feeling a deep responsibility for ensuring the man – a confirmed bachelor, with no family that I knew of – made it through this harrowing episode unscathed.

"There's only one thing to do in a situation such as this," I said, getting to my feet. "Make more tea." I set about collecting the cups and saucers and loading them onto the tray.

Newbury gave me a grateful smile in acknowledgement.

"Might I suggest, Inspector," said Holmes, "that while Watson is busying himself in the kitchen, you might put a telephone call through to your Sergeant Hawley to enquire whether he's been successful in apprehending both Henry Baxter and Seaton Underwood? The successful conclusion of our investigation rather hinges on it."

Foulkes tugged at his beard. "A most sensible thought, Mr. Holmes," he said. "I'll see to it right away." He stood and went out into the hall to find the telephone. I followed him out, leaving Holmes and Newbury to keep watch over Angelchrist.

When I returned a few moments later bearing the tea tray, Foulkes was still on the telephone to the Yard, deep in muffled conversation. I kicked the door to the study open with the edge of my boot to find – to my surprise – Angelchrist sitting up on the sofa, being fussed over by Newbury. The Professor was rubbing his jaw ruefully.

I hurriedly put the tray down on the table and went over to him, sitting next to him on the sofa. "How do you feel, Professor?" I said, taking his wrist and measuring his pulse.

"Oh, hello, Dr. Watson," he said, his voice tremulous. "A little shaken, if truth be told, but well enough. Newbury and Mr. Holmes were just explaining to me what occurred. I must say, I'm able to recall very little of it, which is decidedly worrisome."

I examined his eyes and had him follow my finger back and forth. He didn't appear to be suffering from any ill effects. "I'm pleased to see you've regained your senses," I said.

"Indeed," replied Angelchrist. "Although I fear my greatest trial might be yet to come, if what Mr. Holmes has told me is correct. I can hardly warrant it – Seaton Underwood, falling in with traitors. It troubles me to consider what they might have learned from me whilst I was under their influence."

"That's what we must discover, Professor," said Holmes. "I understand my questions might place you in a difficult position, but it's imperative we're able to assess the nature of the risk. Can you tell us – what was the nature of your relationship with Herbert Grange?"

I sat back, allowing Angelchrist some room. Newbury did the same, perching on the edge of his chair.

Angelchrist looked decidedly unsure. He glanced at Newbury.

"I believe these gentlemen are to be trusted, Archibald," said Newbury. "You should tell them what it is they need to know."

Angelchrist swallowed. He appeared to make a decision. "Pour me a cup of tea first, would you, Dr. Watson, and then I'll explain."

I did as he asked, handing it to him on a saucer. His hand trembled as he took it from me. "I tell you this, Mr. Holmes, because of my faith in the work of your brother, and because of the danger that I fear I may have inadvertently placed him in."

Holmes leaned back in his chair, resting his head against

the seat back. He closed his eyes. He steepled his hands beneath his chin. "Please proceed," he said.

"Four years ago, Herbert Grange was one of a small group of men selected by your brother, Mycroft Holmes, to form a secretive bureau within the British government." He glanced from Newbury to me, judging our reactions. "I was another of those men, along with four more who, for now, shall remain nameless. We were charged with the task of protecting the 'spirit of the nation', as Mycroft liked to put it – with steering policies within the House, ensuring the right men were elected to key positions in all of the important organisations, and generally upholding British interests wherever we saw cause to intervene. We would do so free from the asinine politicking that plagues the usual democratic processes or the careers of party members." He looked over at my companion. "Your brother is an extraordinary man, Mr. Holmes. He foresaw this present conflict years before even the most perspicacious of other men. He thought it vital to make sure that if war came, only the worthy and truly patriotic would hold the reins. Too often politics can lead to unnecessary deaths on the field of battle."

He sighed, as if he were finally getting something off his chest that he had held onto, silently, for years. "It has been a great burden, a stewardship that has dominated all of our lives, and every fortnight we have met clandestinely in Whitehall to discuss our progress and concerns."

"You old dog," said Newbury, clearly impressed. "I knew you were up to something, but I'd imagined it to be advisory work back at the Service, never something like this."

Angelchrist laughed, but it was a sad, uncomfortable laugh. "I do not suspect that you, Mr. Holmes, are quite as surprised as my old friend. Although I am aware that your brother has kept this from you, I also know that he has a long history of such endeavours, of which I am sure you are more than aware."

"Indeed," said Holmes, without opening his eyes.

"So these men, these traitors, they're aware of all of this, and they've been using you and Grange to extract information," I said, "regarding the activities of this secret cabal?"

"I'm afraid it seems so," replied Angelchrist, hanging his head in shame. "If those secrets were to get out, they could cause untold damage. Some of them are quite incendiary. The methods required to engineer our ends have not always been… democratic."

"And the spirit box," said Holmes. He opened his eyes and sat forward, observing Angelchrist. "I take it, then, that this is a repository of all such secrets; records, documents, minutes of your meetings and such like?"

"Precisely so," confirmed Angelchrist.

I looked at Holmes, astounded. "The 'spirit of the nation', Watson," he said. "How terribly like Mycroft."

"So all this time, we've been assuming the spirit box was something related to Underwood's occult practices, when in fact, it's a repository of state secrets," I said. I could barely believe it.

"This, of course, will be what they're after," said Newbury.

Angelchrist nodded. "The contents of that box could alter the outcome of the war," he said. "It would incite political uproar, not to mention seriously undermine the situation in France. The government could collapse, and take any coherent leadership with it. That must be why Grange threw himself in the river. If he thought they could see into his head, uncover its location, then he must have believed it was his only course of action."

"The poor man," I said. "What a waste."

"Particularly as it was clearly too late," said Holmes. "I'd wager they've already ascertained its location, and now, by sending you the paperweight, they're tying up loose ends."

"That's what the German said, Holmes!" I exclaimed, suddenly recalling our earlier encounter beneath the bank. "He said it was too late, that they would soon have the spirit box!"

I heard the door open as Foulkes returned from the hall, having finished his telephone call.

"Where is it, Professor?" said Holmes, with some urgency. "Where is the spirit box?"

"Your brother has it, Mr. Holmes," said Angelchrist. "He keeps it at the Diogenes Club. We have our meetings in the Stranger's Room, and there is a hidden cavity in the wall, which holds the safe, which in turn contains a large, plain box. I have seen him put papers in it at the conclusion of our gatherings." Angelchrist looked suddenly frantic. "I fear Mycroft might be in grave danger."

I looked to Foulkes, whose face was ashen. "What news, Inspector? Have your men successfully apprehended Baxter and Underwood?"

"I fear not," replied Foulkes, his voice level. "Lord Foxton has not seen Underwood since yesterday afternoon, and his whereabouts are currently unknown. Worse, when my men arrived at Baxter's house, they found the place had been cleaned out. It was utterly abandoned, and all of Baxter's belongings had gone."

"Then the German was right. We're already too late," I said, bitterly.

"Not necessarily," said Holmes, jumping to his feet. "We'd have heard from Mycroft if they'd already made their move. We must make haste to the Diogenes Club, and hope that there is still time."

"I hope, for all our sakes, there is," said Angelchrist.

I got to my feet.

"We'll take my motorcar," said Foulkes.

Newbury remained seated. "Forgive me, gentlemen, but I feel

I should stay here with Archibald. He is not yet fully recovered from his ordeal."

"Most wise," I said. Holmes and Foulkes were already at the door. "Until later," I said.

"Good luck," replied Newbury.

As I hurried after the others, I couldn't help thinking that we'd need it.

CHAPTER FOURTEEN

"I have no idea where this 'Diogenes Club' of yours is, Holmes," shouted Foulkes over the sound of the engine, as we barrelled through the streets in his motorcar. "In fact, I can't say I've ever heard of the place." He was hunkered down over the steering wheel, peering out through the windscreen at the dark road ahead. The beam of his headlamp trembled as we bounced over the bumpy road.

"Fear not, Inspector," replied Holmes. "I shall direct you. For now, simply head toward Westminster with all due haste."

"I'm going as fast as I can," muttered Foulkes.

He followed Holmes's instructions to the letter, and a short time later the motorcar pulled to a halt on a quiet Pall Mall. Hurriedly, we bundled out of the vehicle onto the street. At this time the place was deserted, with most people already retired for the night, or else still ensconced in their pubs and clubs to while away the remaining hours until bed. Immediately, however, I saw that we were not entirely alone – another, familiar motorcar was parked just a little further along the street. It was green with white

trim around the windows – the same vehicle we had seen during
our evening vigil outside Henry Baxter's house.

"Hold on," said Holmes. He walked the thirty yards toward the
parked motorcar. The hood was up over the passenger compartment,
so I was unable to see whether there was anyone inside. Holmes
approached the vehicle cautiously, bending low by the driver's
window. He cupped his hands to the glass and peered inside.

He straightened up a moment later and shook his head.
Evidently there was no driver awaiting Baxter's return. Holmes
hurried back to us.

Foulkes looked impatient. "Where to now?" he said.

"Just behind you," replied Holmes.

Foulkes turned on the spot and regarded the row of tall, white
buildings. There was nothing but an unmarked door and a bay
window anywhere in the vicinity. The curtains in the window
were drawn. "In *there*? It's like no gentleman's club I've ever seen,"
he said sceptically.

"It's like no gentleman's club you will ever see again," I
remarked. "In my experience, the Diogenes is quite unique."

"Be on your guard," said Holmes, approaching the door. "If
Baxter's inside, we may already be too late."

He rapped five times in quick succession, tapping out a short
rhythm. There was a momentary pause, and then the door opened
just a sliver, and the face of an elderly man peered out through the
crack. "Yes?" he said.

"Open up," said Foulkes, from behind Holmes. "Police. We're
from Scotland Yard."

The door opened a fraction wider, allowing us a small glimpse
of the hallway beyond. "Indeed, sir?" said the doorman. "How
may we be of assistance?"

Holmes stepped forward and, in a rather heavy-handed
fashion, pushed the door open, causing the doorman to take a

step back in surprise. "Out of the way, man!" he snapped. "We must see Mycroft immediately."

"Mr. Holmes!" exclaimed the doorman in sudden, startled recognition. "Is it really you, sir?"

"Of course it's me!" said Holmes. "Now tell me, where's Mycroft? It might well be a matter of life and death."

"He's... he's..." the man stammered. "He's in the Stranger's Room. But he has visitors, sir."

Holmes glanced over his shoulder at us. "Do you have your service revolver, Watson?"

"Revolver!" said the doorman.

"No," I said, shaking my head. "I gave up carrying it a long time ago."

Foulkes slipped his hand into his coat pocket and retrieved a small handgun, which he clasped in his fist.

"Really," said the doorman. "I *cannot* allow such a weapon into the Diogenes."

"Stand aside," said Foulkes. "This is a police matter."

Holmes was already over the threshold in the hallway. Foulkes pushed past the doorman to follow him. With an apologetic shrug, I did the same.

Inside, it was just as I remembered it. A long, narrow corridor was flanked on one side by a wall comprised of a mahogany frame inset with panels of thick plate glass, behind which the member's area was visible. The décor was austere and old-fashioned, and didn't appear to have altered since my last visit, around a decade earlier. Three men sat inside in solitude, studying the latest periodicals. They did not look up at the sound of our entrance.

The members of the Diogenes Club came here in search of peace and respite from the pressures of the external world. They each professed their desire for isolation and silence, and the opportunity to spend their time at the club uninterrupted by others. The rules of the club were such that speech was permitted only in the Stranger's Room, and that once in the member's area, even the slightest utterance would earn a warning. Three strikes, and the offending patron would be ejected from the club. I had my suspicions that, many years ago, this was a fate that had befallen Holmes himself.

We followed the corridor to its full extent, the doorman trailing a few yards behind us, clearly unsure how to react to this sudden, overbearing invasion.

At the end of the passage was the door to the Stranger's Room, and dismissing all formality or etiquette, Holmes turned the handle, threw the door open and barged in with a dramatic flourish. "Mycroft?" he called.

Inside the sparsely furnished room were three men. Mycroft Holmes was standing by the far wall. His hair was now thinning, but he remained as corpulent and red-faced as I remembered. Behind him one of the wall's wooden panels stood open to reveal a hidden alcove holding a safe. Within it I could just see the shape of a large wooden box. My breath caught in my throat. We were only just in time.

Across the room from Mycroft stood Seaton Underwood, looking decidedly uncomfortable. Beside him was Henry Baxter, brandishing a pistol and wearing a furious expression.

"Sherlock!" exclaimed Mycroft, with a frown. "You're late."

"Stand down, Baxter," said Foulkes, raising his own gun. "The game's up."

Baxter grimaced. "I haven't come this far to fail now," he said. There was a sudden percussive bang as he squeezed the trigger of his pistol. The muzzle flashed, and Foulkes stumbled backwards, dropping his weapon on the floor. Blood sprayed from a wound in his right shoulder. He grabbed at it, clearly in terrible pain, clamping his left hand over the entry wound, blood seeping between his fingers. He fell to his knees, groaning.

I gripped my cane, preparing to charge at Baxter before he recovered enough to take a second shot, but before I had the chance, Underwood was upon me, pummelling me with his fists. He was a thin and wiry fellow, and a third of my age, and I barely had time to bring my arms up in defence before he struck me hard across the side of the head, and then again in the gut. I crumpled to the floor, gasping for breath.

I heard Baxter laughing triumphantly. "Now, Mr. Holmes. The spirit box."

Mycroft smiled. "There is no spirit box," he said.

"Enough of your lies!" bellowed Baxter, waving his gun. I was still attempting to regain my breath as I watched the scene unfolding before me. He pointed at the box, which we could all clearly see in the safe. "Take it out!"

Mycroft went to the alcove and withdrew the wooden box from its hiding place. The ease with which he lifted it immediately sent my mind racing. My suspicions were confirmed when he turned the key in the lock on its side, and with almost casual ease, flipped the box open and turned it upside down. Nothing fell to the floor, not a single sheet of paper. The box was empty.

My eyes were fixed on Mycroft, but I could hear Baxter's sharp intake of breath. "No lies," said Mycroft. "Only the truth." He stood with hands clasped behind his back, the box at his feet, for all the world like a schoolmaster giving Latin dictation. "You've been duped, Baxter. There never was a spirit box, just this," he prodded the empty box at his feet. "A mere prop. A method of drawing out traitors. Did you really think I'd document state secrets and keep them conveniently in a single box?"

I could barely believe what I was hearing. I had no idea if there was any truth to what Mycroft was saying, or whether it was simply an elaborate attempt at misdirection to throw Baxter's confidence. I glanced at Holmes, who remained silent, listening, watching.

"No!" said Baxter, but I could hear the doubt creeping into his voice. "Where is the real box?"

"Check for yourself," said Mycroft. "The safe is empty. There is no other box."

"You've moved it," said Baxter, with a hint of desperation.

Mycroft shook his head. "My associates saw me placing papers in a box during our meetings, this is true. But had they seen their subject matter, I imagine they would have been most confused. Memos concerning reforms in infant-school education are of very little interest to spies, though I'll admit they make for surprisingly diverting reading. And even those papers I would remove from the box when my associates left. It was simply play-acting. Not unlike your own endeavours really, Mr. Underwood, but a touch less melodramatic, and without the need for such elaborate stagecraft."

Baxter roared in anger.

"The game is, as the Inspector here so ably put it, well and truly up," continued Mycroft, his tone somewhat patronising. "You've played, and you've lost. Time to be a good sport now. There's nothing to be done."

I glanced at Foulkes. He was clutching his shoulder and gritting his teeth. I could see that the bullet had gone clean through, shredding the back of his jacket, and whilst he was clearly in terrible pain, he'd live if he received medical attention in good time.

"Put the gun down, Baxter," said Holmes. "It's over."

"No," bellowed Baxter, grabbing suddenly for Underwood, pulling him close like a shield. He wrapped his arm around the boy's throat and put the gun to his head.

"What are you doing?" cried Underwood, panicked. "Henry!"

"Shut it, you whelp!" said Baxter. "Your usefulness has reached an end, anyway."

Underwood's face creased in horror at the realisation of the betrayal. "But I… I don't understand."

"He was using you," said Holmes. "All along. This was never about your spectrographs, Seaton, or any of your work. It was simply about how useful you were to him, and how easy to manipulate. You gave him access to Lord Foxton's inner circle, those people with connections in the government or military. The men who met in this very room."

Baxter sneered. "Fools, every one of them," he spat.

"Yes, but useful fools," said Holmes. He looked at Baxter with utter contempt. "You needed the information they gave Seaton to pass on to your German masters. How large *are* your gambling debts, Baxter? They must be sizeable indeed to betray your country."

Baxter sneered. "This has never been about creed or idealism. I care for the Germans as little as I care for the English. But the Kaiser has paid me well for what I have already given him, and would have paid extremely handsomely for this further intelligence. More capital than any of you would have seen in a lifetime."

"Then you're as foolish as Underwood," said Mycroft, "and twice as blind. Did you really think the Germans wouldn't put a bullet in your skull the moment you gave them what they wanted? Your usefulness was also coming to an end. That's the thing about traitors, Baxter – they can't be trusted."

"Enough!" said Baxter. "You're going to let me go. You're going to allow me to walk out of here, otherwise I'll put a bullet in the boy's head."

"We can't allow you to do that," said Holmes.

I was starting to get my breath back. I glanced at Foulkes. His revolver was only about two feet away from where he was kneeling. He saw me looking and nodded to show that he understood my meaning. He looked up to check that Baxter was preoccupied, and then, with a grimace, he released his grip on his shoulder, reached out and silently slid the weapon across the floor to me.

Still clutching Underwood, Baxter shifted position, looking to the door. I saw my chance – the clearest shot I'd get before he made a dash for it. There was a risk I'd miss and hit Underwood, but I couldn't see any other choice.

With a gargantuan effort I lunged forward, snatched up the gun and swung my arms up in a wide arc, locking my shoulders into position and bracing myself. Hoping beyond hope that my aim was true, I squeezed the trigger.

The gun bucked in my hand as the round left the barrel.

For a moment, everything was still and silent, as if it were happening in slow motion. Had I missed? I felt a sudden upwelling of panic. The sound of the shot was still ringing loudly in my ears.

Then I saw it – a bright flower of blood, blooming at Baxter's throat. It bubbled to the surface, streaming down his collar. He staggered back, incomprehension on his face, his weapon clattering to the floor.

Underwood took his chance to pull away, but Holmes made a run for him, tackling him by the door and pinning his arms behind his back. There was little fight left in the boy, and he didn't struggle.

Baxter's hands were scrabbling at his throat. He raised them, staring at the blood on his fingers in disbelief, then gave a strangled cry and collapsed to the ground in a heap.

I dropped the gun and got to my feet, rushing over to Foulkes, who looked as pale as a sheet. He was barely conscious. I wrenched his coat off and hurriedly tied the sleeve around the wound, forming a makeshift tourniquet. Then, seeing that Holmes and Mycroft were quite adequately dealing with Underwood, I rushed out into the corridor, where the doorman, obviously drawn by the sound of gunshots, was hurrying in our direction.

"Call an ambulance, now!" I bellowed. "And the police. Tell them Inspector Foulkes has been shot."

The doorman nodded and ran off in the other direction to find the telephone.

Exhausted, I slumped against the wall, expelling a long, tired sigh. Through the glass wall I could see the three men in the member's area were entirely unperturbed by all that had occurred, still sitting in silence with their newspapers. Not one of them had stirred since our arrival. Unable to control myself, I broke down into a fit of hysterical laughter.

CHAPTER FIFTEEN

A while later, after an ambulance crew had whisked Foulkes off to the hospital and the police had asked their interminable questions, I sat with Holmes and Mycroft in the Stranger's Room. Baxter's corpse had been removed, and Underwood had been dragged off to the cells. A strange peacefulness had descended upon the Diogenes Club, and although it was a most welcome reprieve, it was also a little disconcerting following the day's exertions.

It was late now, close to midnight, and weariness weighed heavily upon me. Nevertheless, I was anxious to hear what Mycroft had to say by way of explanation for all that had transpired. I was gladdened when he fetched a decanter of whisky, and we sat for a while in silence, sipping at our drinks.

"You understand, then, what has occurred here today?" said Mycroft, finally breaking the tension. The question was directed at Holmes. "You see the gravity of our actions?"

"I do," said Holmes, raising his glass to his lips. Mycroft nodded sagely in appreciation.

I looked from one man to the other. Was that really all that was going to pass between them, after all of this?

"Well, I'm afraid, gentlemen, that I lack the mental acuity of my friend, and should be well served by a full and frank explanation," I said, attempting to keep the indignation from my voice.

Mycroft grinned. "Forgive me, Dr. Watson. Allow me to lay it out for you." He placed his glass upon the side table and folded his hands upon his lap. I could see from the gleam in his eye that, in truth, he relished the opportunity to tell his tale.

"It began some months ago," he said. "As Angelchrist no doubt informed you, for many years I have worked within the British government with the intention of steering matters – policies, elections, the Secret Service Bureau – down particular paths, always working toward the most beneficial outcome for the nation. At times, too, this has brought me into conflict with certain agencies, both internal and external, and those in the House who see my input as unwelcome interference. But the seeds of the current war have been sprouting for many years, and I consider my actions to have materially aided our nation in the current fight." I discerned a slight puffing out of his already distended chest. Like his brother, Mycroft had absolute faith in his own judgement.

"So it was that, some time ago, I decided to form a group, a bureau, if you will, to assist me in my endeavours." He smiled. "None of us are growing any younger, Dr. Watson, and I thought to ensure the continuation of my work in the event of my... absence." He glanced at Holmes, who remained silent.

"Five months ago, however, I became aware – through means I shall refrain from outlining here – that the details of conversations which had taken place during gatherings of this secretive group had fallen into the hands of those who might use them against us."

"Baxter?" I said.

"Indeed," replied Mycroft. "Although I was unaware of his identity. It seems clear now that the Germans guessed that he had debts, and managed to make contact during his investment dealings on the continent. He clearly needed little persuading to betray his country. But at the time I knew only that there were traitors operating in London, those dedicated to furthering the enemy cause, or at least willing to do so in exchange for money. Somehow, these people had gained information that could only have come from a member of my small society."

He sighed. "As you can imagine, I was deeply troubled by this development, and devised a means by which I could flush the traitor out. As I explained to Baxter, I put papers in a wooden box during our meetings held in this very room, and made great play of securing it in the safe; after all, these were highly sensitive dossiers, memorandums and minutes pertaining to our work – I dubbed the vessel the 'spirit box', of which you have heard. None of the men in my inner circle, Grange and Angelchrist included, had any reason to doubt that it really contained important documents. I made it clear to them that should it fall into the hands of those who would use it for nefarious ends, the nature of its contents meant that the war itself might be lost."

"Months went by. For a time, I thought nothing more of the matter, wondering if perhaps the earlier transgression had been a simple aberration. Around six weeks ago, however, I received word through my network that questions were being asked in certain quarters about the existence of the spirit box. I knew then that my worst fears had been confirmed. That someone was leaking information to the traitors.

"From your investigation it is now clear that Baxter, using Underwood as his proxy, targeted likely men in Foxton's political circle. Eventually the questions put to them under hypnosis yielded fruit. We do not know for sure which of the members of my group gave up the existence of the spirit box, but given that only Grange and Angelchrist manifested signs of the hypnotism, and Angelchrist was only subjected to it a few weeks ago, we must assume it was Grange. What other information – that not related to the spirit box but likely of great significance – Baxter gleaned from the other men of Foxton's acquaintance we may never know."

This gave me pause. Of course, if Seaton Underwood had questioned only a fraction of the men who visited his patron, he could still have gleaned a great deal of sensitive information, information that would already be in enemy hands. My blood ran cold at the thought of how many British soldiers now lay dead because of Baxter's treachery. Mycroft paused for a moment while he took a swig of his drink. "After discounting the idea of disbanding my bureau, I made the decision to bide my time. It was paramount that the traitors were caught before they put any more of the information they had gleaned to nefarious use. I knew that these men, in due course, would make a play for the box. The prize I had laid out for them was simply too great, too tempting. And so I continued my charade, placing important-looking documents in the box, and tabling agenda items that I knew would prove incendiary and help to bring matters to a head.

"Of course, they did just that, but not in the way I had expected. The death of poor Herbert was a deeply felt blow, and a reminder of the dangerous game I was playing." He looked genuinely affected at the thought of Grange's death.

"It was at this point," he went on, "that I called in Sherlock to assist in my investigation."

I glanced at Holmes. "Then you knew of this?" I said. "All along, you've been aware of the truth."

Holmes shook his head. "Quite the opposite, Watson. At the beginning of the affair I was as much in the dark as you."

"I have no doubt that Sherlock had his suspicions, but he was never apprised of the details of the case. Rather, it was essential that he was *not*," said Mycroft.

"As I explained to you, Watson, when you encouraged me to contact Mycroft for more information, I could see that Mycroft had involved us in a scheme where the stakes were exceedingly high, and that everything was balanced most delicately," said Holmes. "Any perturbation, any *hint* that we were part of a trap, and the game would be up."

"It was paramount that you were both free to go about your investigation unencumbered by knowledge of what was at stake," said Mycroft. "Well-placed questions, asked at the right time, would help to bring things to a head – and besides, I was still not sure of the identity of the traitors, but knew that Sherlock would help to flush them out."

"It's a dangerous game you were playing," I said, feeling a trifle perturbed myself at the manner in which I'd been manipulated. "Two men are dead, and another came damnably close."

Mycroft nodded. "A most regrettable business," he said. "Yet I console myself in the knowledge that neither Herbert nor Archibald were new to such things. They were aware of the dangers associated with their positions, and both would have gladly given their lives for the British cause. Thankfully, Archibald made it out in one piece, and I am grateful to you for your intervention."

"The work we have done here, disbanding this group of traitors, is critical to the war effort. Had they been allowed to continue to operate in possession of state secrets, gaining access to the upper echelons of government, the situation would have become very grave indeed."

I nodded, finally beginning to appreciate the gravity of the matter. "You put a great deal of faith in the notion that Holmes and I would turn up in a timely fashion this evening," I said. "What if we'd been half an hour later? If Baxter had discovered the truth about the spirit box before we'd intervened?"

"Then I imagine I would not be here now, having this

conversation with you, Dr. Watson," replied Mycroft levelly. "I assure you, however, that it was not *faith* in Sherlock, but rather the meticulously planned outcome of a series of events. I know well my brother's methods, and, watching how events have unfolded over the last twenty-four hours, anticipated his every move."

I smiled. "That sounds a lot like faith to me."

Holmes laughed – that joyous, raucous laugh, that I had missed so much over the last few years. I couldn't help but smile.

I downed the last of my whisky, enjoying the warmth of it hitting my palate. "Well, I don't know about you, gentlemen, but it's well past time I retired for the evening. All this adventure is a little much for an old man such as I."

"Nonsense!" said Mycroft. "You played your part admirably, Dr. Watson, and I thank you, both on my own behalf, and that of the British government."

"In that case," I said, getting to my feet, "might the British government see to arranging a cab home?"

Mycroft chuckled, levering his considerable bulk from his chair. "Of course," he said.

CHAPTER SIXTEEN

'Well, Holmes," I said, as we tucked into a hearty breakfast of poached eggs and bacon the following morning, "another case successfully concluded. I don't know how long it's been since we've been in a position to say that."

"Indeed, Watson. I had thought my days as a consulting detective were long behind me, but I must admit – the whole experience has proved most invigorating." As Holmes speared a forkful of bacon, I could see there was something else behind his eyes, some emotion that he was battling and did not wish to give voice to. I wondered if perhaps he was suffering a modicum of regret. Was he now, after all this time, beginning to have second thoughts about his retirement? I dared not think that he might be persuaded to return to the city and his old life as a sleuth.

My own mood had lightened considerably following the conclusion of our adventure, even if I remained a trifle unsure of Mycroft's manipulative methods. The man had hardly covered himself in glory, and in truth, I couldn't help feeling that Grange's death might have been avoided if only Mycroft hadn't chosen to use him as bait.

Regardless, it was over now, and the outcome had been most satisfactory. Holmes and I had proved – to me, if to no one else – that even two old men could find a role to play in the war effort. It felt good to know that I had done my bit, albeit a small one, in seeing off the enemy and stalling their underhand schemes.

That I'd been forced to end a man's life in pursuit of this goal was an unhappy addendum to the matter. I could never be proud of it, even if the dead man was a traitor whose actions had left me with no other choice.

I knew, however, that I'd done only what was necessary to protect my friends, and more, the interests of the nation. It is the duty of soldiers, both young and old, to carry such burdens so that others do not have to. I have long ago reconciled myself to such things.

More than any of that, though, I felt that I'd done right by Joseph's memory. I had stood in solidarity with him against the march of the enemy, and from the bitterness of our previous defeat – his death upon the fields of France – we had snatched a victory. It was a small consolation, but a consolation nonetheless. There was hope yet that this dreadful business would be over soon, and that the Kaiser would be pushed back within his own borders, his tail between his legs.

"What do you think will become of Seaton Underwood?" I said.

"That is for the jury to decide. I'd imagine he's for the noose, or perhaps the lunatic asylum."

"And his work?" I said. "What do you think those spectrographs really represented?"

"I don't suppose we shall ever know," replied Holmes. "It's a question more suited to Sir Maurice, I think." He took a sip from his coffee cup. "I take it, Watson, that your brief exchange on the telephone this morning was with Sir Maurice?" said Holmes.

"Indeed," I replied. I'd spoken to Newbury a short while earlier, laying out the details of what had occurred after we'd left him at Professor Angelchrist's house the previous evening. "I was gladdened to hear that the Professor is recovering well from his traumatic episode, and that Newbury is hopeful there'll be no lasting effects."

"Other than, perhaps, a little damaged pride," said Holmes.

"Yes, well, there is that," I agreed.

Holmes had finished eating, and placed his knife and fork carefully upon his plate. "Your hospitality these past few days has been most appreciated, Watson," he said. There was a sense of finality to his tone that stirred old regrets.

"You know, Holmes, that you are always welcome. In truth, I wish you'd stay a little longer. We've barely had time to catch up."

"And reminisce about old times?" he said. "Surely the past is past, Watson. Far better, I'd argue, that we spend our time in the present, or looking to the future. Better the search for new adventure, than the constant re-treading of the old."

"Wise words, Holmes," I said.

I'd noticed, as I'd come down to start breakfast, that Holmes's bags were already packed and waiting in the hallway. He intended to leave that morning.

"What time is your train?" I asked, before taking another gulp of my coffee.

"I'm taking the nine minutes past twelve to Brighton," he replied, "and from there I'll catch the local train the rest of the way home."

Home. The word struck a discordant note. It seemed alien to me that Holmes should consider his home to be somewhere else, anywhere that wasn't here, in London, in the thick of things.

I realised then that, to my mind, the city and the man were inextricably linked, and having him back here these last few days had served as a reminder of what I had missed. Home, for me, was London, and it was incomplete without Holmes.

I'd been holding onto the notion that Holmes's retreat to Sussex was, in truth, nothing but a sabbatical, an extended period of recuperation away from his true home. I suppose I'd always assumed that the draw of the city would prove too strong, and that one day he would return. Perhaps I'd even hoped that this brief excursion, this new mystery, might have represented the opening chapter of that new story.

Things had changed, however. I could see that, whilst there remained a hunger in him for more adventure, more mystery, it was balanced by another hunger, too – for his quiet cottage and his bees. Here was a man who was torn between the two halves of his existence, and it would be unfair of me to press him any further to remain.

"Then we've time for another coffee," I said, "before we send for a cab. I'll come with you to the station, of course."

"There's really no need—" began Holmes, but I cut him off with a wave of my hand.

"I'll see you off safely," I said, "and that'll be the end of it."

"Very well," said Holmes, with a brief, characteristic smile. "But I assure you, Watson, it will certainly *not* be the end of it."

It was with a heavy heart that I stood on the platform at Victoria Station with Holmes, just before midday. We'd taken a hansom from Ealing, the same route I had taken with the unfortunate Carter a few days earlier.

The train was already waiting at the station, the engine hissing steam, which gushed along the platform, threatening to lift hats from heads as passengers scrambled for seats, dragging their luggage behind them.

"You'll miss out on all the good seats," I said to Holmes, as he regarded me with a sad smile.

"I booked a private compartment," he said. "Some solitude will be just the thing after the activity of the last few days."

"You always did enjoy spending time with your own thoughts, Holmes," I said. "I suppose that's why life in the Sussex Downs rather suits you."

He shrugged. "I do occasionally find myself craving company, Watson. You know that. If you had the inclination to see out the rest of the war somewhere a little quieter, you could always take the spare room, finish that novel you've been working on."

I felt a lump in my throat. "My novel?" I said, for want of a better response.

"Well, you know I find fiction a rather trivial form of expression," he said, "but what I've read of your manuscript is tolerable. I find the protagonist, the detective, a most intriguing creation."

I laughed. "You read it, then."

"I did."

The train conductor peeped his whistle in warning.

"Well, then," I said, clasping Holmes firmly on the shoulder. "I might just take you up on that offer, Holmes. For a short while, at least."

"Do so, Watson. The tranquillity of the Downs is quite sublime. Soothing, even. And besides," he said, with an impish grin, "London does not have the monopoly on crime and disorder. There's a grave need for someone to inject a little sense into the local constabulary. The newspapers were talking of a blackmail ring when I left. I've been wondering whether they've had any success in getting to the bottom of it while I've been away."

"You old devil!" I said, chuckling. "I knew it!"

"I shall expect to hear from you next Thursday, then, Watson," he said, turning toward the train.

"Next Thursday?" I asked, perplexed.

"You'll see," called Holmes, without turning back. I watched as he hurried across the platform, hopping up into the carriage and disappearing from view.

Grinning, I turned and walked away slowly. As I did, it struck me that at no point had Holmes explained how Underwood had managed to create his colourful spectrographs, and what those unusual auras had represented. It seemed unlike him – so much so, in fact, that I almost turned about and hurried back to the train to try to catch him. Then, on second thought, I decided to let the matter rest. Perhaps there were some things it was better not to question, and after all, I had a trip to prepare for. I had no idea what Holmes had planned, but for the first time in months, I had a spring in my step, and a new adventure to look forward to.

ACKNOWLEDGEMENTS

My thanks to all of the usual suspects:

Miranda Jewess, Cath Trechman, Nick Landau, Vivian Cheung and all at Titan for their stunning work and support. It makes a huge difference.

Paul, Stuart and Cav for chivvying me on when I needed it.

Fiona, James and Emily for putting up with an absent husband and father.

ABOUT THE AUTHOR

George Mann was born in Darlington and has written numerous books, short stories, novellas and original audio scripts. *The Affinity Bridge*, the first novel in his Newbury and Hobbes Victorian fantasy series, was published in 2008. Other titles in the series include *The Osiris Ritual*, *The Immorality Engine*, *The Casebook of Newbury & Hobbes* and the forthcoming *The Revenant Express*.

His other novels include *Ghosts of Manhattan*, *Ghosts of War*, and the forthcoming *Gods of Karnak* and *Ghosts of Empire*, mystery novels about a vigilante set against the backdrop of a post-steampunk 1920s New York, as well as an original Doctor Who novel, *Paradox Lost*, featuring the Eleventh Doctor alongside his companions, Amy and Rory.

He has edited a number of anthologies, including *Encounters of Sherlock Holmes*, *Further Encounters of Sherlock Holmes*, *The Solaris Book of New Science Fiction* and *The Solaris Book of New Fantasy*, and has written a previous Sherlock Holmes title for Titan Books, *Sherlock Homes: The Will of the Dead*.

READ ON FOR A SHORT STORY FROM

THE CASEBOOK OF NEWBURY & HOBBES

FEATURING SIR MAURICE NEWBURY

THE LADY KILLER

I

Ringing, deafening explosions. Bright lights. Chaos. Screaming. Then silence. Utter, absolute silence.

II

Sir Maurice Newbury came to with a start.

There was a hand on his cheek, soft and cool. Veronica? He opened his eyes, feeling groggy. The world was spinning.

The hand belonged to a woman. She was pretty, in her late twenties, with tousled auburn hair, full, pink lips and a concerned expression on her face. Not Veronica, then.

Newbury opened his mouth to speak but his tongue felt thick and dry, and all that escaped was a rough croak.

The woman smiled. "Good. You're coming round." She glanced over her shoulder. Behind her, the world looked as if it had been turned upside down. Newbury couldn't make sense of what he was seeing. He tried to focus on the woman's face instead. She was watching him again. "There's been an accident," she said. "My name's Clarissa."

Newbury nodded. An accident? He tried to recall what had happened, where he was. He couldn't think, couldn't seem to focus. Everything felt sluggish, as if he were under water. How long had he been unconscious? He studied the woman's face. "Clarissa?"

She still had her hand on his cheek. "Yes. That's right." Her voice was soft and steady. Calm. "Do you remember what happened?"

Newbury shook his head, and then winced, as the motion seemed to set off another explosion in his head. *Explosion?* A memory bubbled to the surface. *There had been an explosion.* He shifted, pulling himself into a sitting position. His legs were trapped beneath something hard and immovable.

Clarissa withdrew her hand and sat back on her haunches, still watching him intently. For the first time since waking he became aware of other people in the small space, huddled in little groups, their voices audible only as a low, undulating murmur. Someone was crying.

Newbury blinked. *Was it some sort of prison cell? No. That didn't make any sense. The explosion. An accident.*

Newbury swallowed, wishing he had a drink of water. He was hot and uncomfortable. The air inside the small space was stifling. He felt behind him and found there was something solid he could lean against. He blinked, trying to clear the fogginess. Clarissa looked concerned. "What happened?" he managed to ask, eventually. He was still groggy and his voice sounded slurred.

"I'm not sure. The ground train must have hit something. There was an explosion, and then the carriage overturned. I think I must have blacked out for a minute. When I came round, you were unconscious beside me."

The ground train. Yes, that was right. He'd been on a ground train.

He strained to see over her shoulder again. They were still in the carriage. It was lying on its side.

The vehicle had clearly overturned. How long had they been there? Minutes? Hours? He had no way of knowing. His head was thumping and the world was making no sense. What had he been doing on a ground train?

He rubbed a hand over his face, tried to take in his situation. His legs were trapped beneath the seat in front and his body was twisted at an awkward angle, so that the floor of the carriage was actually supporting his back. He didn't seem to have broken any limbs, but he wasn't quite sure if he was capable of extracting himself without help. He looked up at Clarissa, who was still regarding him with a steady gaze. "Are you a nurse?"

She didn't even attempt to repress her laughter, which was warm and heartfelt and made Newbury smile. "No. I'm afraid you're out of luck. I'm a typist. Just a typist."

Newbury shook his head. "No. I'm sure you're much more than that."

She gave a wry smile, as if he'd touched a nerve. "Are you hurt?"

"What? No. At least, I don't think so."

"It's just you asked if I was a nurse."

Newbury closed his eyes, sucking ragged breath into his lungs. He must have bashed his head in the aftermath of the explosion. Nothing else could explain the fuzziness he was feeling, his inability to think straight. "I was wondering why you were helping me. If you'd come with the rescue crew."

Clarissa shifted from her crouching position onto her knees. She rubbed her arms. "They're not here yet. I don't think they can get to us. The explosion..." She looked over her shoulder, tossed her hair with a nervous gesture that suggested she was more concerned about their situation than she was trying to let on.

"They'll come. I'm sure of it. It's just a matter of time."

Clarissa shrugged. "I hope you're right. It's just I—" She pitched forward suddenly, grabbing for Newbury as the carriage gave a violent shudder. There was a bang like a thunderclap. Newbury felt himself thrown backwards, and then Clarissa was on top of him, clutching at him, trying to prevent herself from sliding away, across the juddering vehicle. He wrapped his arms around her, desperately holding on. Somewhere else in the confined space a woman started screaming: a long, terrified wail, like that of a keening animal.

Newbury gasped for breath. The engine must have gone up. They were lucky they weren't already dead.

The carriage slid across the road with the grating whine of rending metal, windows shattering as the frames buckled, showering Newbury and Clarissa with glittering diamonds of glass. Newbury's face stung with scores of tiny wounds. He squeezed his eyes shut and clung to the slight figure of the woman until, a few moments later, the world finally stopped spinning and the carriage came to rest.

For a moment, Clarissa didn't move. He could feel her breath fluttering in her chest, the rapid beating of her heart. Her hands were grasping the front of his jacket, hanging on as if he were the only still point in the universe. Her face was close to his. She smelled of lavender. She raised her head, and he saw the terrified expression on her face.

"Are you alright?" No answer. "Clarissa? Are you alright?"

She seemed suddenly to see him; the vacant look passed out of her eyes. "Yes. Yes, I'm alright." Her voice wavered, as if she didn't really believe her own words. She still hadn't moved. She looked down at him, saw the lapels of his jacket bunched in her

fists, realised she was crushing him against another seat. "I'm sorry… I…"

Newbury shook his head. "No need."

She released her grip and eased herself free. As she pulled herself up into a sitting position, she glanced momentarily at her hands, a confused expression clouding her face. Then realisation dawned. She turned her palms out towards Newbury, brandishing them before her, eyes wide. "Blood…" Her voice was barely above a whisper. "Oh God, you're bleeding!"

Newbury stared at her bloodied hands, unable to associate what he was seeing with the words she was saying. He didn't know how to react, what to do next; since waking, everything had taken on a dreamlike quality, as if he were watching scenes from someone else's life unfold around him rather than his own. He stared blankly at Clarissa, waiting to see what she would do next.

She didn't hesitate. Pawing at his jacket, she leaned over him, searching for any signs of a wound. There was blood everywhere. "Where does it hurt?" And then: "You said you weren't injured!"

Newbury pinched the bridge of his nose, tried to concentrate. "I didn't think I was. I—"

"Stay still! You don't want to make matters worse!" She'd finished fiddling with the buttons on the front of his jacket and she yanked it open, exposing the clean white cotton of the shirt beneath. They both looked at it for a moment, dumbfounded.

"If it's not your blood, whose is it?" Clarissa glanced down at herself in surprise, her hands automatically going to her midriff. There was blood there, a dark Mandelbrot of it on her pale blouse, but it was only the impression she had picked up from Newbury's jacket while she'd been lying on top of him.

Newbury reached up and grasped the back of a nearby seat, using it for leverage as he extracted his legs from where they were entangled beneath the seat in front. He called out in pain – a broken metal spar had gouged a long scratch in his calf as he dragged it free. He righted himself, still groggy, then turned to face Clarissa. "Someone is obviously injured. We have to help them."

Clarissa looked at him, incredulous. "You're in no fit state… Look, I don't even know your name."

"Newbury. Sir Maurice Newbury."

She smiled. "Well, you might have a knighthood but it doesn't mean you're impervious to injury."

"I'm quite well. A little groggy, perhaps. But I'll be fine. I can't say the same about whoever has lost so much blood." Tentatively, he pulled himself to his feet, wobbling a little as he attempted to orientate himself in the overturned carriage. His head was swimming and he still felt dreadfully woozy, but he had no choice. He had to press on. "We need to find them and see if they're still alive."

Clarissa laughed. "You're a stubborn fool, Sir Maurice Newbury."

Newbury beamed. "Come on. Let's check on the other passengers."

Clarissa offered him a supporting arm, and together they stumbled the length of the overturned carriage, clambering over the ruins of broken seats and baggage that had exploded in a mess of brightly coloured cardigans and coats.

The roof of the carriage had crumpled during the second explosion, shattering any remaining windows and comprehensively trapping them inside. The openings where the windows had been were now nothing but small, ragged-edged holes, too small for even a child to fit through. They were going to have to wait for assistance.

"Ow!" Clarissa winced as she vaulted over a broken table.

"What is it?" asked Newbury. "Are you alright?"

"It's nothing," she replied, dismissively. "It's just… I bashed my leg in the explosion, is all. I'm fine. There are people here who are really hurt. We should focus on them."

Newbury nodded, climbing unsteadily over the obstruction behind her.

Their fellow passengers had formed into little clusters, huddling around the wounded and trying to calm those who would otherwise have given in to their rising panic. Newbury and Clarissa moved between them, ensuring none of them were seriously hurt. There appeared to be a raft of minor injuries – even a number of broken limbs – but nothing that could have conceivably resulted in so much blood. Not until, that was, they found the passenger at the back of the carriage.

It was Clarissa who spotted her first. "Oh God," she murmured, putting her hand to her mouth. "She's dead." She grabbed Newbury's arm, pointing to the rear of the carriage.

The woman was still slumped in her seat, her lilac hat pulled down over her brow. Her shoulders were hunched forward, and she was unmoving. There was a dark, crimson stain down the front of her white blouse, and as they drew closer, they could see that the bloodstain had spread to her lap, soaking into her grey woollen skirt. Her arms were flopped uselessly by her sides.

The sight of her caused a cascade of memories to bubble up into Newbury's still-sluggish mind. "Oh, no," he said, trailing off as he staggered towards her. He recognised her immediately, from the hat, the clothes. This was the woman he'd been following when he boarded the ground train. He remembered it now. She was the mysterious agent for whom he'd been searching.

The dead woman was Lady Arkwell.

III

The Queen, Newbury reflected, was looking even more decrepit than usual.

Her flesh had taken on a pale, sickly pallor, and the bellows of her breathing apparatus sounded strained, as if even they had begun to protest under the labour of keeping the woman alive. Her now useless legs were bound around the ankles and calves, and as she rolled forward in her life-preserving wheelchair, he saw that even more chemical drips had been added to the metal rack above her head: little, bulging bags of coloured fluid, feeding her body with nutrients, stimulants and preservatives.

She came to rest before him, folding her arms beneath the bundle of fat tubes that coiled out of her chest and away into the darkness. In the near-silence, he mused he could almost hear the ticking of her empty, clockwork heart.

He stood over her, both of them caught in a globe of orange lantern light in the gloomy emptiness of the audience chamber. She looked up at him from her chair, a wicked smile on her lips. "You do enjoy testing our patience, Newbury."

He nodded, but didn't reply. Following the events at the Grayling Institute, during which he'd uncovered the truth about her patronage of Dr Fabian and his diabolical experiments on Veronica's sister, Amelia, he'd taken to ignoring her summons – preferring, instead, to lose himself to the vagaries of London's many opium dens. It was only out of protest and a sense of duty to the Empire – not the monarch – that he was here now.

Victoria laughed at his uncomfortable silence. "Know that we are watching you, Newbury. We tolerate your insolence only because you remain useful to us. Do not forget that."

Newbury swallowed. "You wished to speak with me, Your Majesty?" he prompted, attempting to change the subject. He'd long ago grown tired of the woman's threats, although he understood all too well that they were far from hollow.

"There is a woman, Newbury," said Victoria, her tone suddenly shifting from one of amused scorn to one of stately

authority, "who is proving to be something of a thorn in our side." She emitted a wet, spluttering cough, and Newbury saw a trickle of blood ooze from the corner of her mouth. She dabbed it away. Her bellows sighed noisily as they laboured to inflate her diseased lungs.

So, she had a job for him. "A foreign agent?" he prompted, intrigued.

"Perhaps," murmured the Queen. "Perhaps not. She operates under the alias 'Lady Arkwell'. It is imperative that you locate her and bring her to us."

"What has she done?" enquired Newbury.

"Ignored our invitation," replied Victoria, darkly. She grinned. Newbury nodded slowly and waited for her to continue.

"She is a slippery one, this woman. A trickster, a mistress of sleight of hand. A thief. She has many aliases and she always works alone. She has been linked to a number of incidents throughout the Empire, from thefts to sabotage to political assassinations. Her motives are obscure. Some believe she sells her services as a mercenary, working for the highest bidder, others that she is a foreign agent, working for the Russians or Americans. Perhaps she works alone. We, as yet, are undecided."

Newbury shifted slightly, drawing his hand thoughtfully across his stubble-encrusted chin. He'd never come across the name before. "Do we have any notion of her actual nationality?"

Victoria shook her head. "Unclear. Her various guises have at times suggested Russian, Italian and, indeed, English." She gave a wheezing sigh. "It may be, Newbury, that we are dealing with a traitor." She spat the last word as if it stuck in her throat.

Newbury had dealt with "traitors" before – people like William Ashford, the agent Victoria had mechanically rebuilt after his near-death, a man who was declared rogue because he'd come out of cover in Russia to seek revenge on the man who had tried to kill him. Newbury wondered if he was being handed something similar here. It wasn't only *Lady Arkwell's* motives that were obscure.

"Her age?" he asked, trying to ignore the sinking feeling in the pit of his stomach. The Queen wasn't giving him much to go on.

"Indeterminate."

Newbury tried not to sound exasperated. "But we have reason to believe she is active in London? Do we know what she is planning?"

Victoria laughed, detecting his frustration. "We have heard reports that she is operating in the capital, yes. We do not yet know why. You are charged, Newbury, with uncovering her motives and bringing her in. Preferably alive."

Newbury sighed inwardly. Where to even start with such an endeavour? "With respect, Your Majesty, you're describing a needle in a proverbial haystack. Amongst all the teeming multitudes in this city…" He trailed off, his point made.

Victoria watched him for a moment, a curious expression on her face. When she spoke, her voice had a hard edge. "You are resourceful, Newbury. You will find her." Newbury was in no doubt: this was an order. Victoria's will *would* be done.

She reached for the wooden wheel rims that would allow her to roll her chair back into the darkness, drawing Newbury's audience to a close. Then, pausing, she looked up, catching his eye. "Be warned, Newbury. She is utterly ruthless. Do not be fooled. Do not let your guard down for a moment. And what is more," she drew a sharp intake of breath, reaching for her wheels, "do not fail us."

Newbury watched the seated monarch as she was slowly enveloped by the gloom, until, a moment later, she was swallowed utterly, and he was left standing alone in a sea of black. The only sounds in the enormous audience chamber were the creak of the

turning wheels against the marble floor and the incessant wheeze of the Queen's breathing apparatus.

IV

"Oh God. This wasn't an accident, was it?"

Clarissa was standing aghast over the corpse of the dead passenger, her hands to her mouth, her eyes wide with shock. Newbury wanted to put his arm around her; she looked so young and vulnerable. Propriety, however, dictated he did not.

"No. Someone has very purposefully slit her throat," he replied, keeping his voice low to avoid any of the other passengers overhearing. He released his hold on the corpse and the head lolled forward again, the body slumping to one side. He straightened the hat on the dead woman's head, arranging it carefully to cover her blood-smeared face in shadow. He straightened his back.

"Oh God," Clarissa repeated. She remained staring at the body for a moment longer, before tearing her eyes away to look at Newbury. "Whoever did this… do you think they caused the accident?"

Newbury blinked, still trying to shake the grogginess. He must have struck his head badly to be so concussed. It was strange there was no pain. "No," he said, "I don't think so. I imagine it was more opportunistic than that. Whoever did this must have remained conscious during the explosion and the ensuing chaos, and acted swiftly while the rest of us were still blacked out."

Clarissa looked wide-eyed at the dark bloodstains on the front of his jacket. "Why is her blood all over you? You were sitting up there at the front of the carriage near me. How do I know it wasn't you who killed her while I was unconscious?" She looked startled and terrified, and she was backing away from him.

"Don't be ridiculous! Of course I didn't do it!" Newbury didn't know what else to say.

"So you can explain the blood?"

"Well, not exactly," he said, with a shrug. "There's nothing to say whoever did it didn't move the body afterwards. I don't know. But I didn't do it. You need to believe me." He reached out a hand and leaned heavily on the back of a nearby seat. His legs felt like jelly. "And remember, my legs were trapped beneath that seat. How could I have done it?"

Something about the conviction in his voice must have reassured Clarissa, as she gave a weak smile and stepped forward again. Nevertheless, he could see that she was still wary. Perhaps she could sense that he was holding something back, keeping from her the fact that he knew who this dead woman actually was.

"Alright. Assuming I believe you, that means there's a murderer somewhere on this carriage." Her voice was a whisper. "No one could have got out. We're trapped in here until the firemen arrive to cut us free. So whoever did it is still here." She glanced around as if sizing up the other passengers, looking for a likely suspect.

Newbury could see the sense in her words. The killer still had to be on board the train.

"And why would they do it? This poor, innocent woman? What could have possibly inspired them to cut her throat?" She shuddered as she spoke, as if considering how different things might have been – how it could have been her, slumped there in the seat with her throat opened up.

Newbury knew the answer to that but chose not to elaborate. It wouldn't do to go involving this girl in the affairs of the Crown, and if he did tell her why, it would only give support to her fears that he was somehow involved in the woman's death. Aside from all that, he didn't want her raising the alarm. The other passengers were scared enough as it was, wondering when – and if – they

were going to be free from the buckled remains of the carriage, or whether they were only moments away from another explosion. The last thing these people needed to know was that there was also a murderer on board.

Besides, from everything he knew of her, "Lady Arkwell" was far from innocent. Rumour had it that she was involved in everything from political assassinations to high-profile thefts. No doubt she had scores of enemies, with as many different motives for ending her life.

That suggested the killer had to be another agent. But which nation or organisation they were representing was another question entirely. It wouldn't surprise him to discover the Queen had organised a back-up, a second agent on the trail of Lady Arkwell, just in case Newbury failed. Or perhaps the intention had been for Newbury to lead an assassin to their target all along. Whatever the case, this wasn't a motiveless murder. The killer knew what they were doing, and whom they were targeting.

That in itself begged another question: did the killer also know who he was? Was he also at risk? In his current state, with his head still spinning, he knew he wouldn't be able to handle himself in a scuffle. He had to be on guard.

"What are we going to do?" asked Clarissa, tugging insistently on his sleeve. He looked down at her pretty, upturned face, framed by her shock of red hair, and realised that he hadn't answered her questions.

"I don't know," he replied, shaking his head. "You're right. The killer must still be on board. But we have no way of telling who he might be. I suggest we tread very cautiously, and stick together. We should cover up the body and try not to panic anyone. When they finally cut us free, the killer is going to try to slip away. We need to be alert, watching for anything that might give him away. That way we can alert the authorities when the time is right."

"That's it?" she said, with a frown. "That's all we're going to do?"

"I'm not sure we have any other choice," said Newbury, in a placatory fashion. "If we alert the killer that we're on to him, things could turn very bad, very quickly. We're trapped in an overturned train carriage with no exits. A killer loose in a confined space, desperate and wielding a weapon…" He trailed off, his point made.

Clarissa gave a short, conciliatory nod. "Very well." She stooped and collected up a handful of discarded items of clothing – a man's tweed jacket, a woman's shawl, a tartan blanket – and proceeded to set about covering the dead woman.

Newbury leaned against the wall – which had once been the floor – his head drooping. His memories of the events leading up to the accident were hazy at best, but they were slowly returning. It was surely just a matter of time before he could piece together what had occurred. Yet everything felt like such an effort. All he wanted to do was go to sleep. He lifted his hands to rub at his eyes, but realised they were smeared with the dead woman's blood. Grimacing, he put his right hand into his jacket pocket to search out his handkerchief.

His fingers encountered something cold and hard. Frowning, he peered down as he gingerly closed his hand around the object and slid it out of his pocket. His eyes widened in shock, and he quickly stuffed the thing back, glancing around to make sure no one else had seen.

Clarissa was still busying herself covering the corpse.

Newbury took a deep breath, trying to steady himself. What the Hell was going on? His heart was racing, his head pounding, and he couldn't remember what had happened, what he might have done.

He wasn't a killer. He *had* killed, yes, but he'd been a soldier out in India, and latterly an agent of the Crown. He'd killed in self-defence, in the course of duty, but never in cold blood.

So why, then, was the object in his pocket a sticky, bloodied knife?

V

"So, how are you, Charles?" said Newbury, swallowing a slug of brandy and regarding his old friend, Chief Inspector Charles Bainbridge of Scotland Yard, from across the table. The older man looked tired, careworn, out of sorts. As if he had the weight of the world resting on his shoulders, and was beginning to buckle beneath it.

The two men were sitting in a private booth in the drawing room of Newbury's club, the White Friar's. Over the years Newbury had come to consider the place a second home, enjoying the general ambience and the intelligent banter he often overheard in the bar. The clientele was mostly composed of artists, poets and writers, and although he knew Bainbridge didn't approve of this more bohemian of crowds, Newbury often insisted on meeting him there. It was good, he assured himself, for the older man's soul. And besides, Bainbridge's club was generally full of policemen; useful, perhaps, when one needed such things, but hardly a haven away from the busy matters of everyday life.

Bainbridge gave a heavy sigh. "Darn near exhausted, Newbury, if truth be told. That's how I am. This Moyer case is taking everything I've got."

Newbury gave a resigned smile. Bainbridge had been tracking a killer for weeks, a surgeon by the name of Algernon Moyer, who had – for reasons that appeared to be politically motivated – taken to abducting politicians and minor royals, chaining them up in abandoned houses and infecting them with the Revenant plague. He would then move on, disappearing into the great wash of the

city, leaving his victims to slowly starve to death as the plague took
hold and they degenerated into slavering, half-dead monsters.

Three days following each of the abductions, a letter had
turned up at the Yard, addressed to Bainbridge, teasing him with
the location of the most recent crime. By the time Bainbridge
got there, of course, it was already too late. The victims would
be beyond saving, reduced to nothing but chattering, snarling
animals, straining at their chains as they tried desperately to get at
the soft, pink flesh of their rescuers. Every one of them had been
put down, electrocuted, their corpses burned in the immense
plague furnaces at Battersea or dumped far out at sea along with
the mounting heaps of bodies from the slums. Bainbridge hadn't
even been able to let the victims' families identify the bodies.

There had been four victims to date, and the police expected
another to turn up any day. And, as Bainbridge had continued
to bemoan, they were no closer to finding Moyer or uncovering
the criteria by which he selected his victims. He struck without
warning, abducting them in broad daylight, no obvious
connections between them. It was a campaign of terror, and
politicians and councillors were increasingly growing wary of
leaving the relative safety of their homes.

Newbury echoed his friend's sigh. "I wish I could help you,
Charles. I really do. But this Arkwell thing – the Queen…" He
trailed off. Bainbridge knew all too well what the Queen was like
when she had a bit between her teeth.

Bainbridge looked up from the bottom of his glass. A faint
smile tugged at the corners of his mouth. "Ah. Well. That's where I
might just be able to help *you*, Newbury."

Newbury leaned forward, pushing his empty glass to one
side. "Go on."

"One of our informants, a delightful little man named Smythe…"
Bainbridge pronounced the man's name as if he were describing a

particularly venomous breed of snake "…Paterson Smythe. He's a burglar and a fence, and not a very successful example of either. But he has a secondary trade in information, and that's what makes him valuable to us." He waved his hand in a dismissive gesture. "Times, places, names. You know the sort of thing."

Newbury nodded. "He doesn't sound the type to be involved with a woman of Lady Arkwell's calibre."

Bainbridge laughed. "Well, precisely. It looks like he might have gone and gotten himself in over his head. He turned up at the Yard this morning claiming he had something big for us, but that he needed our protection."

Newbury raised an eyebrow. "And?"

Bainbridge shrugged. "And it sounds as if it could be your Lady Arkwell. Smythe said he'd been doing some work for a woman, 'a right smart 'un', as he described her, sitting in Bloomsbury Square all night and reporting back to her the next morning to describe everything he'd seen."

Newbury frowned. "Interesting. Anything else?"

"He said it had been going on for a week. No specific target or brief. Simply that she'd told him to note all the comings and goings in the area."

"A scoping job?"

"Precisely that. Descriptions of everyone he saw, when they came in and out of their properties, what time the postman or milkman called. But nothing that might give away the actual target. It could be any one of those grand houses she's interested in, for any reason." Bainbridge frowned, tugging unconsciously at his moustache. "She's clearly a clever one, Newbury. She hasn't left us with much to go on, even after her hired help tried his best to sell her up the river."

"It's already more than I've been able to ascertain so far," replied Newbury. "Where do they meet? That would be a start."

Bainbridge shook his head. "As I said, she's a clever one. They always meet in the back of a brougham. She picks him up at Bloomsbury Square and they drive around the city while he hands over all the information he's gleaned. They always take a different route, and she always deposits him in a different street when they're finished, leaving him with the cab fare home."

"Fascinating," said Newbury, impressed. "Does he have a description of the woman?"

"Only that she wears a black veil beneath a wide-brimmed, lilac hat, along with black lace gloves, so as not to be recognised. He says she dresses smartly in the current fashions, and is well spoken, with an educated, English accent. He does most of the talking, and she issues payment and instructions." Bainbridge shrugged. "That's it. That's all we could get out of him."

Newbury sipped at his brandy while he mulled over his friend's story. Was this the mysterious woman he'd been looking for? And if so, what was she up to? It seemed like an extraordinary effort to go to for a simple robbery. But then, perhaps there was more to it than that. Perhaps this was an invitation to dance.

Bainbridge was looking at him expectantly. "Well? What would you have me do?"

Newbury smiled. "Nothing."

"Nothing?" echoed Bainbridge, confounded. His moustache bristled as he tried to form his response. "Nothing!" he said again.

"Precisely," said Newbury. "Tell Smythe to continue just as he is. Tell him to keep reporting back to this woman on all of the comings and goings to the square, and to make a particular effort to ensure he offers accurate descriptions of all the people he sees."

"Is that all?" asked Bainbridge, clearly unimpressed. "I fail to see how that constitutes an effective plan."

"Not at all," said Newbury. "I believe it's time I offered to play Lady Arkwell at her own game."

"Stop being so bloody cryptic, would you, and spit it out."

Newbury laughed. "If she's as clever as I believe her to be, Charles, she won't have chosen a mealy-mouthed snitch like Smythe without reason. She has no intention of effecting a burglary in Bloomsbury Square. She's doing all of this to announce herself to us – to *me*. She knew full well that Smythe would go running to the Yard. It's an invitation."

"An invitation?" asked Bainbridge. He looked utterly perplexed.

"Indeed. An invitation to respond."

Bainbridge shook his head. "If you're right – and I am not yet convinced that you are – what will you do?"

"Show myself in Bloomsbury Square. Smythe will do the rest," replied Newbury, with a grin. "And then we shall see what move she makes next."

"Good Lord," said Bainbridge, draining the last of his brandy. "You're enjoying this, aren't you?"

"Oh yes," said Newbury, laughing. "Absolutely."

VI

Was it possible? Could he have somehow been driven to kill the woman?

Newbury considered the facts. He'd boarded the ground train while trailing the female agent known as Lady Arkwell, the woman who was now dead from a knife wound to the throat. She'd taken a seat at the rear of the carriage, and so, trying to at least make the pretence of conspicuousness, he'd gone to the front on the opposite side, where he'd been able to keep an eye on her reflection in the window glass. The train had started off, rumbling down Oxford Street, and he'd settled back into his seat, content that he had until at least the next stop before he'd have to make a move.

Despite the fuzziness still clouding his thoughts, he was able to recall at least that much.

The next thing he remembered was waking up with a thick head, Clarissa's hand on his cheek, his jacket covered in blood. Now, additionally, he'd discovered he had a bloodied knife in his pocket. He had no notion of what might have occurred in the intervening time.

He supposed there were two possibilities. Firstly, that he'd been forced to end the woman's life during the aftermath of the accident, before he received the blow to his head that had rendered him unconscious and affected his recollection. Secondly, that the killer had taken advantage of his dazed state to plant the weapon on him, thereby making an attempt to implicate him in the murder.

Despite the apparent outlandishness of the notion, he decided the latter was the most likely option. He was, after all, dealing with assassins and spies, people who might have recognised him and decided he'd make a viable scapegoat to cover their tracks.

Newbury searched the faces of the other people in the carriage. There were at least twenty of them, still huddled in little groups on the floor. None of them seemed familiar. A dark-haired young man with a beard was slumped to one side by himself. His black suit was torn and he was bleeding from a wound in his left forearm. He was watching Newbury intently. Could it be him? Or perhaps the middle-aged man at the other end of the carriage, squatting close to where Newbury had been sitting. He was whispering now to two young women, but his eyes were tracing every one of Newbury's movements, his rugged features fixed in a grim expression.

It was useless to speculate. It could have been any one of the other passengers. He'd have to wait to see if they'd give themselves away. There was nothing else for it.

Newbury rubbed his palm over the back of his neck, wishing the fuzziness in his head would clear. He could feel no lump, no tender spot where he had bashed it during the accident. Why, then, did he still feel so sluggish, so groggy? *It was almost as if...*

A thought struck him. Perhaps he hadn't banged his head at all. If someone really was attempting to frame him for Lady Arkwell's murder, he might have been drugged. A quick prick with a needle while he was down, a dose of sedative to keep him under, to keep him slow. That had to be it. It was the only explanation for why he was feeling like this. Perhaps the killer had been carrying it in his pocket, intending to use it to incapacitate Lady Arkwell when she alighted from the train. The crash had provided him with a different opportunity, and he'd discharged the syringe into Newbury instead, while everyone else on board was still distracted in the midst of the initial panic and confusion.

It all seemed to make a terrible kind of sense to Newbury, but even so, it brought him no closer to identifying the killer, and at present, he had no way of proving any of it. All he knew for sure was that someone on the train was out to get him, or at the very least, was using him to protect their secret.

"Do you think anyone will notice?" whispered Clarissa from beside him.

He glanced round. She'd done an admirable job. The body might have been a heap of clothes, spilt from a burst case. "Not until we draw their attention to it," he replied, "or one of them comes looking for their coat."

Clarissa gave a wry smile. "I'm scared, Sir Maurice. I keep thinking that no one's going to come and find us and we'll remain trapped in here, with someone capable of... *that*." She put her hand on his chest, and, throwing propriety to the wind, he put his arm around her shoulders and drew her in. They stood there for a moment, holding on to one another as if they were the only still point in the universe.

"It'll be alright," he said, with as reassuring a tone as he could muster. But what he really meant to say was: "I'm scared too."

VII

"Sir Maurice Newbury, I presume?"

The voice was cultured and luxurious, like the purr of a well-mannered cat.

Newbury peeled open his eyes, but for a moment saw nothing but darkness. Then, slowly, shapes began to resolve out of the gloom, as if the shadows themselves were somehow coalescing, taking on physical form.

Around him, figures lay supine on low couches, draped across the daybeds as if they had given themselves up to the deepest of sleeps. Their pale faces might have belonged to spirits or wraiths rather than men; ghostly and lost, these waifs, like Newbury, were adrift on the murky oceans of their own minds.

Gas lamps, turned down low, cast everything in a dim, orange glow.

Newbury turned his head marginally in order to take in the appearance of the man who had spoken. It wasn't a face he recognised. The man was Chinese, in the later years of his life – judging by his wizened, careworn appearance – and was standing politely to one side, his hands clasped behind his back. He was dressed in a fine silk robe and wore an elaborate moustache that curled immaculately around his thin lips, draping solemnly from his chin. His eyes were narrowed as he regarded Newbury through the haze of opium smoke.

Newbury blinked and tried to stir himself, but the drug

continued to exert its influence. He couldn't even find the motivation to move. "You presume correctly, sir," he replied, his voice a deep slur. "Of whom do I have the pleasure?"

The other man smiled for the briefest of moments, before swiftly regaining his composure. "My name, sir, is Meng Li."

"Meng Li?" echoed Newbury, unable to contain his surprise. He'd heard the name a hundred times before, always spoken in whispered tones, even amongst the upper echelons of Scotland Yard.

Meng Li was perhaps the most significant of the Chinese gang lords to exert his influence on the British Empire. His network stretched from Hong Kong to Vancouver, from Burma to London itself, and was considered to take in everything from the opium trade to people trafficking, and most other illicit trades besides.

That he should be there in the capital was barely conceivable, let alone consorting openly with a British agent in such insalubrious surroundings. This was, after all, a filthy opium den in Soho – about as far from the Ritz as one could imagine. Clearly, Newbury decided, whatever reason Meng Li had for being there, it must have been of grave importance. The Chinaman was putting himself at great risk.

He mustn't have been alone. Newbury craned his neck. He couldn't see any bodyguards, but that didn't mean they weren't there. For all he knew, half of the patrons of the house might be in Meng Li's employ, ready to leap up from their apparent stupors if Newbury tried anything.

Not, he supposed, that there was any risk of that. Meng Li had timed his appearance to perfection, approaching Newbury while he was still incapacitated from the drug, but cognisant enough to hold a meaningful conversation.

The Queen would be furious if she discovered Newbury had been face to face with the crime lord and hadn't killed him on sight, but he was presently far from capable of that, and besides, he was curious to see what the man wanted, why Meng Li would risk his life in such a manner to speak with one of Victoria's agents.

"You do me a great honour," said Newbury, without a hint of irony.

Again, that subtle smile. "I hope that we may – temporarily, at least – speak as friends, Sir Maurice?"

"Friends?" echoed Newbury. Was this to be a proposition? He would have to tread carefully.

Meng Li gave a slight bow of his head, as if conceding some unspoken point. "If not as friends, then perhaps at least as men of a common purpose, who share a common enemy?"

Newbury raised an eyebrow. "Go on," he said, intrigued.

"The operative known as 'Lady Arkwell'. You seek her, do you not, for your English Queen?" The words were wrapped in amusement, not scorn.

Newbury considered his response. Meng Li was obviously well connected, and dangerous, too. Any denial would be seen for the blatant lie that it was, and he didn't wish to anger the man, particularly given his present situation. "Indeed I do," he said, levelly. "I take it, then, that you also have an interest in finding this mysterious woman."

"In a manner of speaking," said Meng Li. "She has taken something that belongs to me, and for that, I owe her a response."

"Ah," said Newbury, "and so you're proposing an alliance in order to find her?"

Meng Li shook his head. The gesture was almost imperceptible in the dim light. "I wish only to impart to you some information," he replied.

Newbury frowned. More games. "I'm listening."

"It is said that Lady Arkwell is an expert at covering her tracks. She passes like a leaf, blown on the wind, and is soon lost amongst the many others that have fallen from the tree. She never repeats herself, and she never returns to the same place twice."

He folded his hands together inside the sleeves of his *cheongsam*. "She has, however, one weakness – her fondness for a particular blend of tea. It is a Yunnan leaf, grown in China, and is found in only one establishment in this great city of London. A tearoom on New Bond Street known as the 'Ladies' Own Tea Association.'" He withdrew his hands from his sleeves. In one of them he held a small, white card, which he handed to Newbury.

"And you believe she will be found there?" asked Newbury, surprised.

Meng Li inclined his head. "What is more, you may identify her by means of an old injury. Two years ago, a bullet was lodged in her right knee during an incident in Singapore. The bullet was removed, but the knee was damaged. The affliction is barely noticeable, but alters her gait: every third step she takes is uneven."

"Then why tell me?" asked Newbury. "If you know all of this, why not send a handful of your own men after her?"

"Because it amuses me," replied Meng Li, although this time, his smile did not reach his eyes. Newbury had heard others call this man inscrutable, but to his mind, that was simple ignorance. Meng Li was not so hard to read, and although he hid it well, Newbury could see the truth in the man's expression: he was scared. When Meng Li spoke of Lady Arkwell, he had the look about him of a man who knew he was outclassed. He was aiding Newbury because he did not wish to engage the woman in her own games, for fear he might lose. The crime lord, it seemed, was nothing if not a pragmatist.

Newbury nodded. "Tell me – what did she steal from you?"

"An object that has been in my family for many hundreds of years," replied Meng Li. "The Jade Nightingale."

Newbury almost baulked. He'd heard talk of this precious stone before: an enormous, flawless emerald mounted in a gold ring, and dating back to the ancient, early dynasties of the Far

East. Many had tried to steal it, but none had ever succeeded. How it had come into Meng Li's possession, Newbury did not know, but now the crime lord had lost it again, to Lady Arkwell.

"And you do not wish to retrieve it?"

"It is merely a bauble. She may keep it." Meng Li shrugged. "My revenge is simply to assist my good friends of the British Crown to locate her."

Merely a bauble. The Jade Nightingale was priceless. It would sell for thousands of pounds, even on the black market. Newbury could hardly believe how easily Meng Li had dismissed the matter. It had clearly pained him that the gem had been stolen – enough to reveal himself to an agent of the British government and assist them in locating the thief – but to Newbury it seemed that Meng Li was more concerned with revenge, with the embarrassment of the whole matter, than the actual recovery of the stone.

"It is a matter of honour," said Meng Li, as if reading his thoughts. "Do you understand *honour*, Sir Maurice?"

"I believe I do," replied Newbury, meeting Meng Li's unwavering gaze.

"Then I believe we have an understanding," said Meng Li. "You may leave this house unmolested, and you go with my blessings behind you. When we meet again, we will not be friends."

Newbury nodded, slowly.

Meng Li bowed gracefully, and then seemed to melt away into the darkness, leaving Newbury alone on the divan. His head was still swimming with the after-effects of the Chinese poppy, and for a moment he wondered if he might not have dreamed the entire encounter. But then he remembered the card Meng Li had handed him, and turned it over in his palm, casting his bleary gaze over the legend printed there in neat, black ink: *LADIES' OWN TEA ASSOCIATION, 90 NEW BOND STREET.*

Newbury smiled. Tomorrow, he would finally close the net on the elusive Lady Arkwell.

VIII

"Something's wrong. I don't think anyone is coming." Clarissa was perched on an upended seat across the gangway from Newbury, a frown on her pretty face. Her foot was drumming nervously on the floor, and she was clenching and unclenching her hands on her lap. She kept glancing at the other passengers, and then at the heap of clothes she'd piled over the corpse in the corner. Newbury wondered if perhaps she was showing the early signs of claustrophobia, or whether it was simply the proximity of the corpse, and what it represented, that was troubling her. It was certainly troubling him.

He was slouched against the crumpled ceiling of the overturned carriage, fighting a wave of lethargy and nausea. Whatever was in his system – for he was now convinced that he had been drugged – was threatening to send him spiralling back into unconsciousness. He couldn't allow that to happen. Too much was at stake.

When he saw Clarissa was watching him, a pleading look in her eyes, he took a deep breath, forcing himself to stay alert. "You know what London traffic is like these days," he said. "The roads are awash with people, carriages, carts and trains. The fire engines are probably stuck somewhere, trying to get through to us."

Clarissa shook her head. "No. They should be here by now. It's been too long." She dropped down from her perch, crossing the makeshift gangway to stand over him. She offered him her hands, as if to haul him up. "Come on. I think we're going to have to find our own way out of this mess."

Newbury shook his head. "No. I can't. I'm so tired."

Clarissa folded her arms and glared down at him in a matronly fashion. "You need to keep moving. You know I can't let you fall asleep. Not after a blow to the head." She dropped into a crouch, bringing her face close to his. She smelled of roses. "I'm not sure how much longer I can stand being stuck in this tin can, to be honest," she said, in a whisper. Her lips were close to his ear and he could feel her warm breath playing on his cheek. "I've never been comfortable in confined spaces, and the thought that one of those men is a heartless killer is too much to bear. Please, Sir Maurice. Help me to get free."

She pulled back, her eyes searching his face. He could feel himself relenting. "Very well," he said. "What are you planning?"

She grinned, taking his hands in hers. "If we can bash a panel of this crushed roof away from where a window frame has buckled, perhaps we can make enough of a space to crawl free."

Newbury frowned. "It's perfectly mangled. We'd need cutters to even begin making a hole."

"At least help me give it a try," she said, standing and hauling him to his feet, reluctant though he was. His head spun wildly for a moment, and then seemed to settle. "What have we got to lose?"

Our lives, thought Newbury, *if we turn our backs on the wrong person for too long*, but he couldn't muster the will to fight – not least because she had a point.

"Over here," she said, leading him a little further away from the others, towards the body at the rear of the carriage. "This looks like the weakest point." She indicated a spot where the space between the top of the window frame and the side of the vehicle had been reduced to around two inches.

"The frame is completely buckled," said Newbury. He placed both of his palms against the metal panel and pushed with all of his remaining strength. It didn't budge. "We're going to need something heavy to hit it with."

"Like this?" asked Clarissa, and he turned to see her grappling with a wooden seat that had broken free from the floor during the crash. She swung it back like a golf club, gritting her teeth.

"Clarissa…" said Newbury, ducking out the way just in time to watch her slam the seat into the roof panel with all of her might. There was a terrific reverberation throughout the carriage, followed by the clatter of broken wood as the now demolished seat tumbled in a heap to the floor. The window frame hadn't shifted.

A woman started screaming somewhere at the other end of the carriage, and Newbury turned to see three men getting to their feet. "Now you've done it," he said.

"Shhh," hissed Clarissa. She scrabbled for a foothold and pressed her ear to the opening. "Yes! That's it!"

"What is it?"

"Listen!" said Clarissa, with palpable relief. "I can hear ringing bells. They're coming."

Newbury tried to focus, to suppress the dull roar inside his head. Clarissa was right – he could hear the distant jangle of fire carts, brass bells clanging wildly as they raced through the streets towards the site of the accident. He turned to see the rest of the passengers getting to their feet as they, too, heard the signals, awareness of their impending rescue spreading swiftly amongst them.

Newbury put his hand in his jacket pocket, reminding himself of the incriminating knife that was hidden there, of the difficulties still to come. Whatever happened next, he had to be ready. There was still a killer on board the train. While they were all trapped in there, the killer was, too. As soon as they got free, the man would make a break for it, and all chance of apprehending him would be lost.

He turned to Clarissa. "Whatever happens, you and I have to be the first ones out of this carriage," he said. "Remember that, at all costs. Once we're free we need to get the attention of the police, and make sure no one else gets out behind us."

She looked at him quizzically for a moment, before his intention suddenly dawned on her. "Oh," she said, "because that way, the killer will still be on the train."

"Precisely," said Newbury. "Can you do that?"

Clarissa beamed. "I can do anything if I put my mind to it."

Newbury laughed for the first time that day. "When this is over, I'd very much like to take you to dinner," he said.

"Would you, indeed?" she replied, with a crooked smile.

IX

The Ladies' Own Tea Association on New Bond Street was exactly as Newbury had imagined: overstuffed with dainty decorations such as lace doilies, sparkling chandeliers, pastel-coloured upholstery and overbearing floral displays. Young maids darted about between tables, dressed in formal black uniforms with white trim.

As he peered through the window from across the street, Newbury was filled with a dawning sense of astonishment. It all seemed so unnecessarily... *feminine*, as if the proprietors had never considered that the women who took tea in their establishment might have been perfectly comfortable in less exuberant surroundings. Veronica, he knew, would have found the place decidedly over the top. He could imagine the look on her face now, appalled at the very idea of spending time in such a garish environment.

He sighed heavily, leaning against the doorjamb. Perhaps, he reflected, they were simply trying to scare away the men.

Newbury had taken up temporary residence in the doorway of a nearby auction house, sheltering from the persistent, mizzly rain. Mercifully, the auctioneer's was closed for the afternoon, and he'd loitered there for two hours unchallenged, attentively watching the comings and goings of the tearoom's clientele.

So far, he'd seen no one matching his – admittedly limited – description of Lady Arkwell, but he decided to wait it out for a short while longer. It wasn't as if he had any other significant leads, after all.

He'd considered enquiring after Lady Arkwell with the staff, posing as a friend, but in the end decided it would be too conspicuous. He didn't wish to show his hand too soon, and if she *had* become a regular patron and the staff alerted her to his questions, he'd have given away his only advantage.

So, with little else in the way of options, he turned his collar up against the spattering rain, hunkered down in the doorway and endeavoured to remain vigilant, despite the gnawing chill.

It was almost half an hour later when the woman in the lilac hat emerged from the tearoom, unfurling her umbrella and stepping out into the street. At first, Newbury dismissed her as simply another of the tearoom's typically middle-class customers, heading home after a late lunch with her friends. She was young and pretty and not at all the sort of woman he was looking for, and he hardly paid attention to her appearance. Except that, as he watched her stroll casually away down the street, she seemed to stumble slightly, as if from a sudden weakness in her right knee.

Frowning, Newbury stepped out from the doorway, ignoring the patter of raindrops on the brim of his hat. He squinted as he studied the dwindling form of the woman. One step, two steps – there it was again, the slightest of stumbles, before she caught herself and corrected her gait.

Newbury's heart thudded in his chest. Was this, then, the woman he was searching for, the woman with whom he was engaged in such an elaborate game? He hesitated, unsure whether to give chase. Given what he knew of Lady Arkwell, it wouldn't have surprised him to discover she had paid someone to affect a limp, simply to throw him off her trail.

He decided he had little to lose. If this woman in the lilac hat proved to be a red herring, then either Lady Arkwell had set up a decoy and was never going to be found at the tearooms, or else it would prove to be a case of mistaken identity, and Newbury could return the following day to continue his observations.

He set out, pulling the brim of his hat down low and hurrying after the young woman, his feet sloshing in the puddles that had formed between the uneven paving stones.

He followed her along New Bond Street, remaining at a reasonable distance so as not to arouse her suspicions. All the while the little stumbles continued, like clockwork, with every third step. Such an injury, he reflected, would be difficult to affect successfully, and the woman had evidentially grown accustomed to it; it did not appear to have a detrimental impact on her speed or confidence.

After a minute or two, the woman turned into Brook Street, which she followed as far as Hanover Square. She halted at an omnibus stop and lowered her umbrella, ducking under the shelter to await the next bus. A small crowd of five or six people were already gathered beneath the shelter, and so Newbury hung back, keeping out of view.

It was no more than five minutes' wait before the rumble of immense wheels announced the arrival of a passenger ground train. The machine was a hulking mass of iron and steam – a traction engine fitted with fat road wheels – and it came surging around the corner into Hanover Square, belching ribbons of black smoke from its broad funnel. It was painted in the green and black livery of the *Thompson & Childs Engineering Company*, and was hauling two long carriages full of people.

The ground train trundled to a rest beside the omnibus stop. Immediately, a number of carriage doors were flung open and a flurry of passengers disembarked. Newbury watched the woman in the lilac hat step up into the second carriage, and quickly dashed forward, hopping up onto the step and into the same carriage, just as the driver's whistle tooted and the engine began to roll forward again, ponderously building up a head of steam.

The woman had already taken a seat at the rear of the carriage, and so Newbury, still wary of drawing her attention, decided to take one of the empty seats on the opposite side, close to the front, from where, if he turned his head, he could just make out her reflection in the window glass.

The carriage was around half full, following the mass disembarkation at Hanover Square, with a mix of people from all walks of life: office workers, shoppers returning home with stuffed bags, a mother with her little girl, socialites returning home from their clubs. Nothing appeared to be out of the ordinary.

Newbury eased himself back into his rather uncomfortable seat, certain that he could relax until at least the next stop, where he would have to make sure he didn't lose the woman if she chose to alight.

He was about to glance out of the window when there was a sudden, jarring jolt, followed by a thunderclap as loud as any he had ever heard.

Everything went black.

X

"We'll have you free in just a minute, miss. Remain calm." The man's gruff voice was accompanied by the sound of bolt cutters snapping into the iron plating of the carriage roof, as the firemen worked to create a makeshift exit.

Clarissa's relief was palpable. She'd followed Newbury's instructions, doing everything possible to ensure they were the first to be freed from the wreckage. She'd rushed to the small opening in the buckled window frame as soon as she heard voices outside, pushing her arm through and waving for attention. Consequently, the firemen had focused their attention on widening the existing gap and forcing their way in.

Despite their imminent rescue, however, Newbury couldn't shake the feeling of dread that had settled like a weight in the pit of his stomach.

Aside from the injured, the other passengers were all up on their feet, clamouring at whatever openings they could find, calling out to the firemen for help. Soon, someone was going to discover Lady Arkwell's dead body, and Newbury still didn't have sufficient evidence to exonerate himself. He was covered in the dead woman's blood and was carrying a knife that was sticky with his own fingerprints. Discarding it at this point would be a pointless exercise.

Worse still, the real killer had a chance of getting away scot-free in the chaos, or perhaps even implicating Newbury further. After all, they were the only other person on the train who knew that Newbury was carrying the planted murder weapon. All it would take was a quiet word in the ear of the police, and Newbury would likely be restrained and carted away to a cell. Bainbridge and the Queen would, of course, ensure his eventual release, but by then the real murderer would be long gone, and with him, any hope of discovering the truth of what had really happened.

And, just to make matters worse, Newbury was still feeling decidedly woozy.

There was a terrific *clang* of metal striking stone, and he turned to see daylight streaming into the gloomy carriage through a small, ragged hole in the roof. He squinted against the sudden brightness, and rushed forward to Clarissa's side. "Go!" he said, urgently, putting his hand on her back and urging her forward.

She did as he said, ducking low and wriggling out through the hole.

Newbury felt a press of people at his back, heard bickering over his shoulder, but paid them no heed. He had to get free and speak to the police before it was too late.

He followed Clarissa out through the hatch, dropping to his belly and worming his way out on to the wet street. The fresh air hit him like a slap to the face, and he dragged it desperately into his lungs. He felt hands on his shoulders and, a moment later, two firemen had hauled him up to his feet.

"Thank you," he murmured, as he turned on the spot, taking in the scene of utter devastation. The wreckage of the ground train littered the entire street.

The remains of the engine itself were at least a hundred yards further down the road, steam still curling from the hot, spilt coals as they fizzed in the drizzling rain. The engine casing had burst apart, shredding the metal and spewing shrapnel and detritus over the cobbles and surrounding buildings. Nearby windows were shattered, and the front of one building – a hotel – was smeared with streaks of soot.

The first carriage was jackknifed across the road, and appeared to have suffered more damage than the second, bearing the brunt of the explosion. The whole front of it was missing, leaving a jagged, gaping hole where it had once been tethered to the engine. The rest of the carriage was twisted and crushed and, inside, Newbury could see the bodies of passengers, flung around like dolls by the force of the explosion. He'd been lucky – the carriage he'd been travelling in was relatively unscathed in comparison, on its side, its roof crushed flat as it had rolled across the street.

Crowds of onlookers had gathered at either end of the street, and fire carts were parked in a row, their doors still hanging open where their drivers had abandoned them to get to the injured or trapped.

Newbury caught sight of a lone bobby in the midst of it all and staggered over, grabbing the young man by his cuff. The policeman shook him off irritably, looking him up and down.

"You must send for Sir Charles Bainbridge of Scotland Yard immediately," said Newbury. "There's a dead woman in that carriage." He pointed back the way he had come.

The bobby looked at him as if he'd cracked a particularly bad joke. "Yes, sir," he replied, sarcastically. "There's been an accident."

"No, no!" Newbury shook his head in frustration. "You don't understand. She's been murdered."

The bobby raised a skeptical eyebrow. "Indeed, sir?"

"Listen to me!" barked Newbury. "My name is Sir Maurice Newbury, and I'm a good friend of your chief inspector. I'm telling you, a woman has been murdered on that train. The killer is still on board. My friend here can confirm it." He turned to beckon Clarissa over.

She was nowhere to be seen.

"Clarissa?" called Newbury, perplexed. Had she gone back to help free the others from the wreckage? "Clarissa?"

Concerned, he turned his back on the policeman, scanning the scene for any sign of her.

For a moment he stood there, utterly baffled, while the storm of activity raged on around him. She seemed to have disappeared. One moment she'd been standing there beside him, the next she had gone.

He searched the faces in the crowd. It was then that he saw her, about two hundred yards up the street, walking away from the devastation. Where was she going? "Clarissa?" he called again.

She ignored him and continued walking, her back to him. Confused, he watched as she gave a little stumble, as if suffering from a slight weakness in her right knee. Newbury's heart thudded. *No! It couldn't be…*

There it was again, on the third step – another little stumble.

His head was swimming. He started after her, but stumbled, still woozy from whatever sedative had been administered to him. He'd never catch her now, not in this state.

He watched for a moment longer as she receded into the distance. Then, at the last moment, she stopped, turned, and blew him a kiss, before disappearing out of sight around the corner.

Newbury stumbled back towards the carriage, ignoring the protests of the bobby behind him. "Get out of my way!" he bellowed, pushing past the firemen and dropping to his knees before the makeshift hatch in the roof.

The other passengers had all been helped from the wreckage now, and as Newbury wriggled back into the gloomy carriage, he realised he was alone. He clambered shakily to his feet and crossed immediately to the heap of clothes at the rear of the carriage, beneath which the dead woman was buried. He began to peel the layers off, flinging coats, cardigans and jackets indiscriminately to the floor.

Moments later he uncovered the head of the bloodied corpse. He wrenched the hat from the head and saw instantly that the woman's hair, pinned up, was in fact a deep, chestnut brown. Blood had been smeared expertly on her face to obscure her features, but it was clear almost immediately that this was a different woman from the one he had followed from the tearooms.

How could he have been so stupid? Clarissa had kept his attentions away from the body, had even taken great pains to cover it up so he wouldn't realise that this dead woman was not, in fact, Lady Arkwell at all. He'd missed all of the signs.

Clarissa – the real Lady Arkwell – must have killed the woman and switched clothes with her while Newbury was out cold from the crash. She'd then drugged him and planted the evidence before bringing him round.

Newbury let the lilac hat fall from his grip and slumped back against the roof of the carriage, sliding to the ground. No wonder Meng Li had been so apprehensive when he'd spoken of the woman. No wonder the Queen had warned him of her ruthlessness. Newbury had been totally outclassed.

"Well played, Clarissa," he mumbled, his face in his hands. "Well played indeed."

XI

"We find it interesting, Newbury, that she deigned to allow you to live. Perhaps she has a weakness for pretty men?"

"With respect, Your Majesty, she is a cold-blooded killer," replied Newbury. "She took that innocent woman's life purely to evade capture. I suspect she allowed me to live only because she considered me useful. I was her intended scapegoat, and she was relying on me to help her to escape from the wreckage."

Victoria gave a disturbing, throaty cackle. "Don't be so naive, Newbury. Do you think for a moment she didn't know what she was doing? That 'innocent woman' you refer to was a German agent, most likely sent to assassinate Lady Arkwell following her alleged involvement in a theft from the Kaiser's court. She probably killed her in self-defence."

Newbury frowned. Perhaps things weren't as black and white as he'd at first imagined. Could she really have killed that woman in self-defence? If so, that put an entirely different complexion on the matter. Perhaps she was more the woman he'd taken her to be, after all. He sighed. "I fear it is a moot point, Your Majesty. She's probably halfway to Paris by now, or some other such destination where she might go to ground to evade capture."

"Perhaps so," the Queen conceded.

"Then that is an end to the matter?"

Victoria laughed. "No. You shall remain focused on the

woman, Newbury. You shall track her down and bring her here, to the bosom of the Empire, where we may question her and discover her true motives." Victoria grinned wickedly, baring the blackened stumps of her teeth. "We think she might yet prove useful."

"Of course, Your Majesty," said Newbury. He stifled a smile. He knew that what he'd just been handed was a punishment for allowing the woman – Clarissa – to slip out of his grasp, but in truth, he couldn't help feeling buoyed by the notion that, some day soon, he might see her again.

"Go to it, Newbury. Do not disappoint us again."

"Very good, Your Majesty," he replied, with a short bow, then quit the audience chamber to the sound of the Queen's hacking, tortuous laughter.

XII

"I was played, Charles. There's no other way to look at it."

Newbury crossed the room to where Bainbridge was sitting by the fire and handed him a snifter of brandy. Then, with a heavy sigh, he dropped into his battered old Chesterfield and propped his feet up on a tottering pile of books.

"Don't look so dejected, Newbury," said Bainbridge, unable to hide his amusement. "It's no reflection on you that you were beaten by a pretty young woman."

Newbury offered his best withering glare, but couldn't help but smile at the gentle provocation.

The two of them had met at Newbury's Chelsea home for dinner, and now it was growing late, and the mood more contemplative.

"It's just… I was completely taken in by the woman, Charles," replied Newbury. "As if she'd somehow bewitched me. I can't believe I missed all the signs."

"I refer you to my previous sentiment," said Bainbridge, grinning. "You're not the first man to be distracted by a feisty, intelligent – and beautiful – young woman, and you won't be the last." He took a long slug of brandy. "And let's not forget, your brain was somewhat addled by the sedative. You shouldn't be so hard on yourself."

He knew that Bainbridge was right, but couldn't shake the feeling that, in losing this first round of the little game he had entered into with Lady Arkwell, he was now on the back foot. He wasn't used to being the one running to catch up.

Newbury shrugged and took a sip of his drink. "What of you, Charles? Are you faring any better? Tell me about Algernon Moyer."

"All over and done with," said Bainbridge, merrily. "It turned out he'd pushed his luck just a little too far. He got careless."

"And you managed to find him?" asked Newbury.

"In a manner of speaking. It looks as if one of his victims might have bitten him after he'd administered the Revenant plague. We found him climbing the walls in a hotel room in Hampstead, utterly degenerated. The hotel called us in because of the noise and the smell."

Newbury wrinkled his nose in disgust. "You had to put him down?"

Bainbridge nodded. "The blighter got what was coming to him. His corpse was incinerated yesterday."

"It brings a whole new complexion to that old adage, 'treat others as you mean to be treated yourself,'" said Newbury.

Bainbridge laughed. "It does that."

There was a polite knock at the drawing room door. Newbury glanced round to see his valet, Scarbright, silhouetted in the doorway. He was still dressed in his immaculate black suit and collar, despite the lateness of the hour.

"I'm sorry to disturb you, gentlemen, but I have a message for

Sir Maurice," he said, holding up an envelope.

"Come in, Scarbright," said Newbury, intrigued.

"A message? At this time of night?" exclaimed Bainbridge, with a frown. He sat forward in his chair, glancing at Newbury with a quizzical expression.

Newbury shrugged. He hadn't been expecting anything.

"It arrived just a moment ago," explained Scarbright, "brought to the door by an urchin, who insisted the message it contained was quite urgent." He passed the envelope to Newbury and waited for a moment while Newbury examined it. "If there's anything else you need…"

"What? Oh, no," said Newbury, distracted. "We're fine, Scarbright. Thank you."

The valet retreated, closing the door behind him.

Newbury turned the envelope over in his hands. There was no addressee. He lifted it to his nose and sniffed the seal. It smelled of roses.

"What the devil are you doing?" asked Bainbridge. "Just open the ruddy thing, will you?"

Newbury chuckled. "It's advisable when one receives anonymous post, Charles, to first ensure it's not going to kill you."

Bainbridge's eyes widened. "You don't think it's poisoned, do you?"

Newbury shook his head. "Thankfully not." He ran his finger along the seam, tearing it open.

Inside, there was a small, white notecard. He withdrew it. Printed on one side in neat, flowing script were the words: *Still on for dinner?*

Newbury dropped the card on his lap and threw his head back, laughing.

"What is it?" said Bainbridge. "What does it say?"

"It's from her," said Newbury.

"Who? The Queen?"

"No. Lady Arkwell. Clarissa."

Bainbridge looked utterly confused. "And?"

"She's letting me know that the game is still on," replied Newbury. "That there's more still to come." He handed Bainbridge the note.

Bainbridge glanced at it almost cursorily. "The gall of the woman! You should toss this in the fire and forget about it."

"That would hardly be following orders, Charles," said Newbury. He drained the rest of his glass. "You know what Her Majesty had to say on the subject."

"So you'll do as she asks?" said Bainbridge, incredulous. "You'll keep up the search?"

Newbury grinned. He took the card back from Bainbridge and looked wistfully at the note. "Yes, Charles," he said. "I rather think I will."

SHERLOCK HOLMES

THE WILL OF THE DEAD
GEORGE MANN

A rich elderly man has fallen to his death, and his will is nowhere to be found. A tragic accident or something more sinister? The dead man's nephew comes to Baker Street to beg for Sherlock Holmes's help. Without the will he fears he will be left penniless, the entire inheritance passing to his cousin. But just as Holmes and Watson start their investigation, a mysterious new claimant to the estate appears. Does this prove that the old man was murdered? Meanwhile Inspector Charles Bainbridge is trying to solve the case of the "iron men", mechanical steam-powered giants carrying out daring jewellery robberies. But how do you stop a machine that feels no pain and needs no rest? He too may need to call on the expertise of Sherlock Holmes.

SHERLOCK HOLMES

THE THINKING ENGINE
JAMES LOVEGROVE

March 1895. Hilary Term at Oxford. Professor Quantock has put the finishing touches to a wondrous computational device which, he claims, is capable of analytical thought to rival that of the cleverest men alive. Indeed, his so-called Thinking Engine seems equal to Sherlock Holmes himself in its deductive powers. To prove his point, Quantock programmes his machine to solve a murder. Sherlock Holmes cannot ignore this challenge, so he and Watson travel to Oxford, where a battle of wits ensues between the great detective and his mechanical counterpart as they compete to see which of them can be first to solve a series of crimes. But as man and machine vie for supremacy, it becomes clear that the Thinking Engine has its own agenda. Holmes and Watson's lives are on the line as a ghost from the past catches up with them…

AVAILABLE AUGUST 2015

TITANBOOKS.COM